MADE SAFE

By
Francis Sparks

pandamoon
publishing

© 2017 by Francis Sparks

This book is a work of creative fiction that uses actual publicly known events, situations, and locations as background for the storyline with fictional embellishments as creative license allows. Although the publisher has made every effort to ensure the grammatical integrity of this book was correct at press time, the publisher does not assume and hereby disclaims any liability to any party for any loss, damage, or disruption caused by errors or omissions, whether such errors or omissions result from negligence, accident, or any other cause. At Pandamoon, we take great pride in producing quality works that accurately reflect the voice of the author. All the words are the author's alone.

All rights reserved. Published in the United States by Pandamoon Publishing. No part of this publication may be reproduced, stored in a retrieval system, or transmitted in any form or by any means—for example, electronic, photocopy, recording—without the prior written permission of the publisher. The only exception is brief quotations in printed reviews.

www.pandamoonpublishing.com

Jacket design and illustrations © Pandamoon Publishing

Art Direction by Don Kramer: Pandamoon Publishing
Editing by Zara Kramer, Rachel Schoenbauer, Jessica Reino, and Heather Stewart: Pandamoon Publishing

Pandamoon Publishing and the portrayal of a panda and a moon are registered trademarks of Pandamoon Publishing.

Library of Congress Cataloging-in-Publication Data is on file at the Library of Congress, Washington, D.C.

Edition: 1, Version 1.0,

ISBN-10:1-945502-23-1
ISBN-13:978-1-945502-23-1

DEDICATION

For my wife, Kelly. You let me chase my dreams.

To Kelly

MADE SAFE

Chapter 1

The man looked funny lying there on the bed naked with his mouth half open and his legs twisted in the bed sheets. It was his expression that nearly sent Moses Winter into a fit of laughter. It was a look of shock mixed with fear, like he had broken his mother's favorite vase and been caught in the act of cleaning it up.

Moses jerked his head to look at Sharon standing behind him. She was pressing a gun into Šejla's neck. Šejla was kneeling at her feet, naked except for her underwear. The gun was Moses'. She must have taken it from the glove box of his car when he wasn't looking.

The man on the bed was Fred Dunsmore. Moses had followed him for weeks and now he cowered on the bed, a breath away from begging for his life.

"Sharon, put the gun down," Moses said.

"Quiet," Sharon said. She drew back the gun and struck Šejla in the side of the face with the barrel of the pistol, knocking her to the floor. She lay motionless. Her skin glowed a dusky red from the flickering flames coming from the fireplace behind her.

"No!" Fred shouted.

In an instant, Moses was at the injured woman's side. "That's enough. This wasn't part of the plan!" Moses screamed, shielding the fallen woman with his body.

"I say when it's enough," Sharon said. She lowered the pistol, stepping around Moses and the injured woman as she moved toward her husband, Fred Dunsmore. Fred still hadn't budged an inch since they had burst into the room a minute before. Even when Sharon dragged Šejla off the bed at gunpoint, he'd just sat there with that dumb look on his face.

MADE SAFE

Moses watched Sharon with one eye as he rolled Šejla's limp body onto her back. An angry red mark had already formed on her cheek where the gun had struck her. He checked her neck for a pulse. It was strong. She was just out cold. Moses shrugged out of his coat and placed it over her naked chest. He turned his attention back to Sharon. She stood over Fred, her expression blank as she trained the gun on her husband. The crackling fire was the only sound in the room. The cold wind howled outside, rattling the window of the cabin, searching for a way inside.

"What is her name?" Sharon waved the gun at the other woman.

"You know her name," Fred said.

"I want to hear you say it."

"It's Šejla."

"Šejla what?"

"Šejla Tahirović."

"And what is she to you?"

Moses watched as Fred struggled to find the words. He wanted to jump in and say something to defend him, to stop this, but Sharon was too unpredictable. A few minutes ago, she had been an almost timid soccer mom. Now, she was a raging bundle of violence in yoga pants and fur-topped boots.

"She's my girlfriend," he said. Fred's shoulders squared slightly, his chin raising an inch.

"Your *girlfriend*," Sharon said, shifting her gaze to the other woman. Moses felt like a voyeur, his presence forgotten, as he watched the confrontation unfold between wife and husband.

Sharon pushed the barrel into her own cheek like it was a pen and pursed her lips, seeming to consider the girl. Then she turned back to Fred, leveling the gun at him.

"On your feet." She motioned with the pistol.

Fred pushed himself to a sitting position with his back resting against the wall and one hand out like a stop sign. "No. Not until you put the gun down," he said.

"Shut up. On your feet or I'll make it so you can never stand again," she said, pointing the gun toward his toes.

"Just don't shoot, please, Sharon. I'll do what you say." Fred hung his head as he got off the bed, leaving one hand for his modesty. Moses shifted on his knee, watching as Sharon used the gun to prod Fred up against the wall by the fireplace. Moses stood with one thought in his head. He needed to stop this, gun or no gun.

Sharon seemed to sense his movement. "Stay where you are, Moses," she said, turning her head his direction, still holding the gun on Fred.

Moses stared back at her, holding his ground, waiting for the opening he needed to act.

Sharon turned back to Fred, "Okay, Fred, give me a reason." Fred looked to Moses with eyes begging for help.

"Don't look at him, look at me. What do you have to say, Fred?" Sharon said, her voice rising.

Moses took a step toward them.

"Don't fucking move!" Sharon said, shaking the pistol at Moses.

Moses froze. Was there a round in the chamber? He couldn't remember. Sharon smoothed her hair and nodded at Moses like a teacher to a pleasing student.

"Thank you. Now, Fred, were you going to say something?"

Fred looked at the floor. "You know."

"What was that?" Sharon said, leaning forward, tilting her head lower and attempting to force Fred to look at her.

"You know," Fred said, his voice stronger now.

Moses heard a low groan behind him. He chanced a quick look and saw Šejla roll over, shaking her head as she got to all fours. The movement seemed to go unnoticed by Sharon, and Moses allowed himself a chance to breathe.

Fred was speaking now, drawing Moses' attention back to the unfolding confrontation. Moses was stunned by the transformation of the other man. Timid Fred was gone; in his place, a defiant man. His eyes were devoid of fear, replaced with something else, something like pain or the memory of pain.

"You know that we haven't been 'us' for a while now, Sharon. Your work and my work. The kids. It's just not what we set out to be. We were going to be better."

"Oh, this is, though?" Sharon said, pointing the gun in the direction of the bed. "You stupid, stupid man. If only you could have kept your dick in your pants or been more careful at least, for my sake. My mother saw you with her. Do you have any idea what it's like? Lying to someone you love for someone who is crushing your soul?"

Fred laughed. "You know what, Sharon, I do. I have done that. I've done it for you."

Moses glanced back. Šejla wasn't there. Moses craned his neck until he found her by the bed. She was bent down, digging in her purse. What was she after? Her phone? *Good, she'll call the cops*, Moses thought. He turned back to Sharon and Fred. Sharon's hand holding the gun quivered as she listened to Fred speak. Moses took a quick step forward.

"You lie," Sharon said, quietly.

"How many times have I had to tell the kids you will be home soon? That you'll make the next game or recital? That you love them more than anything else?" Fred continued.

"Shut up," Sharon said.

"And you know what? You don't. You love that business of yours more than anything. What is it? The control? The power? It's definitely not glamorous."

"Go to hell, Fred. You have no idea. You don't know what I want. You don't know me."

Sharon's eyes watered and her upper lip curled over her teeth.

"Sharon," Moses said. "This has gone far enough. Fred gets it. You guys are through. You scared him enough. Just put the gun down and we'll leave."

Sharon shook her head, focused on Fred. "We aren't quite done yet, Mr. Winter." She extended her arm, aiming the weapon into Fred's face. Fred shrank into the wall, closing his eyes, courage abandoning him in his final moment. But then Fred opened his eyes and focused on something behind Sharon.

"Don't do it!" Moses shouted. Sharon jerked her snarling face in Moses' direction. Fred saw his chance. He grabbed the gun and forced it above her head.

"No!" Sharon shrieked.

Francis Sparks

A burst of flame shot from the gun, splitting the air with the acrid smell of burnt gunfire as the bullet slammed into the wall next to the fireplace with a puff of plaster powder.

"Sharon!" Moses yelled, his voice sounding muffled with the report from the gun still ringing in his ears. The gun swung his direction and he ducked.

Sharon kneed Fred in the groin. He stumbled off balance and Sharon tripped him, sending them to the floor with Sharon on top of Fred. Fred showed his teeth as he fought for control of the gun. In a blur of blonde hair, Šejla appeared. She latched onto Sharon's neck with one arm, holding a long knife in the other, poised to strike. Moses dove at her.

His shoulder slammed into Šejla, tossing her and Sharon to the side. Moses found himself on top of Fred now. Next to him, Šejla and Sharon wrestled on the floor. The gun and knife were gone. Then Moses realized Fred wasn't moving. He looked down and saw Fred's eyes were fixed blankly on the ceiling. Moses leaned over his mouth and listened. He was still breathing. Then he saw the handle of the knife jutting out of Fred's side. He checked the wound. A small trickle of dark blood leaked around the edge of the blade.

"Stop it! Fred's hurt," Moses yelled at Sharon and Šejla. Then to Fred he spoke at a level just above a whisper. "Fred. Can you hear me, Fred?"

"Yeah," he said, putting his hand to the knife handle.

"Don't touch that. It's not that bad," Moses said. He patted Fred on the shoulder and then looked over at Sharon and Šejla. They were sitting together on the floor not more than a foot apart. Šejla held her hand to her mouth. Sharon's shoulders slumped forward against her heaving chest. Both pairs of eyes were trained on the knife handle jutting from Fred's gut.

"Sharon, get a blanket and cover Fred up. Šejla, call 911." Neither moved. "Now!"

* * *

Moses sat in the corner of the room, leaning his head on the wall. After they had watched the EMS crew load Fred into the ambulance, the cops had escorted them back inside the cabin. They separated them, putting Sharon on the bed and Šejla in a chair in the opposite corner closer to the fireplace.

MADE SAFE

Moses put his hand to his eyes and leaned forward, putting his elbows on his knees. What a terrible mistake. He pushed the baseball cap back on his head and looked at Sharon. This had been an easy case. A month ago, she had walked into his office and asked him to find out if her husband was cheating on her. It didn't take much to figure out that Fred Dunsmore was shacking up with Šejla at a swank downtown hotel on a regular basis.

He had done a little background, but he had half-assed it. It was a simple infidelity case anyway. Then, when he had shown Sharon the evidence, she asked to confront him. "Catch him in the act," she said. Moses shook his head. He still couldn't believe he had agreed to it. All it had taken was double his rate. Cheap. But he would have done it anyway. It was the way she looked at him. She needed this. She needed him.

It had gone wrong right away. Instead of going to the usual spot downtown, they had come here to this cabin on a frozen pond in the middle of nowhere. And now, Fred had a blade sticking out of his chest and it was Moses' fault. None of this would have happened if he had just refused Sharon, but he hadn't. Time to own up and face the music, as his grandfather had said. Only thing to do now was to make sure no one went to jail over this. It was an accident. Shit, for all he knew, he had stabbed Fred when he tackled Šejla.

Then he remembered. He tried to maintain his posture, but he couldn't prevent a slight stiffening of his spine. He scanned the room. He saw it, wedged in between the fire poker and the other tools for the fireplace.

Three uniformed state troopers stood next to the fireplace, looking like they had nothing better to do. He pulled his cap forward on his head, low to his eyes. Between first aid on Fred and keeping the women from killing each other, he had forgotten the gun and now the cops were here. He didn't know when Sharon had taken his gun, but he didn't want to have a conversation about it with the cops tonight.

* * *

Raif Rakić walked into the cabin and let his eyes adjust to the light. He removed his thick, insulated gloves as he surveyed the room. There were too many people standing around.

Francis Sparks

"Anyone that doesn't have a reason to be here, get out," he said.

People stopped talking and looked at him. A few grumbled, but within thirty seconds, the room had thinned out to half the number of people. Rakić's partner, Ken Wilson, was sitting on a wooden chair next to the bed, interviewing a woman in her thirties. There was a man in a dark baseball cap sitting in the corner with a county deputy guarding him. Then he saw Šejla by the fire. Anyone closely studying Rakić might have noticed a twitch in the muscle of his jaw, but other than that he gave no sign that he recognized Šejla. *What in the hell was she doing here?* Putting his thumb to his lips, Rakić walked over to Wilson and tapped him on the shoulder. Rakić motioned him away from the woman he was interviewing.

"So what happened?" Rakić asked.

Wilson was a big man compared to Rakić, under six foot, but thick with a hint of a beer gut. "Let's see," Wilson said, flipping through his notebook with his pencil. "She, Mrs. Sharon Dunsmore," he pointed his pen at the woman he was talking about, "came here to catch her husband cheating on her with," he paused and flipped back a page, "A Shee-lah Tah—Tah—you can say it better than I can. S-E-J-L-A. T-A-H-I-R-O-V-I-C. Who is sitting over there." He pointed her out. "Hey, you probably know her."

"Because I'm Bosnian? And you know every drunk in town too, right?"

Wilson smiled. "Most of 'em. We're thick as thieves."

Rakić managed a grin and glanced at Šejla. She clutched a blanket under her chin. Šejla seemed fine other than a slightly wild glint in her eyes. He fought the urge to run to her and turned back to Wilson.

"What's his story?" Rakić asked, nodding at the man in the baseball cap.

"He's some private eye Mrs. Dunsmore hired. Name is Moses Winter."

"So, what happened?" Rakić asked.

"Looks like one of them stabbed her husband, Fredrick or Fred Dunsmore, but no one is owning up to what exactly happened yet."

Rakić nodded. "Okay, I'm going talk to Ms. Tahirović." Rakić walked over to Šejla. She looked up at him and then glanced at the state trooper standing guard over her.

"I have this," Rakić said, waving the man away. He found a chair at a small table and pulled it over. "So, Ms. Tahirović, what happened tonight?" he asked, sitting down.

"It was an accident."

"Whose knife was it?" Rakić asked.

"Mine," she said. Rakić glanced back at Wilson, then leaned closer to Šejla.

"*What the fuck were you thinking? Why do you have a knife anyway?*" he asked quietly in Bosnian.

Šejla shrugged her shoulders, responding in Bosnian, "*I work late. I keep it in my purse and she had a gun. I thought it would be big enough to scare someone off if they messed with me. Besides, she tried to shoot Freddy. Have you heard anything else about Freddy?*" she asked.

Rakić shook his head. "*No word yet. Back to the gun. Where is it now?*" Šejla shrugged and slumped back in her chair. "*It got knocked out of her hand.*"

"*Okay, don't talk to anyone else. Ask for a lawyer if someone tries to talk to you. You're family. You're not going to jail tonight.*"

Rakić glanced around the room as he got up. The evidence team was working on a dark stain on the floor in the center of the room. One of them held a tape measure next to it as another took pictures. The man called Winter was still in the corner, and Wilson was talking to Sharon Dunsmore by the bed. He walked over to the small kitchenette on the back wall, looking for the gun. No sign of it. He walked back over to Ken and Sharon, looking in every corner. Maybe it was under the bed, he thought.

Rakić motioned Wilson over to him. "Anything new?" Rakić asked.

"Nope. She's saying that she didn't see where the knife came from or who stabbed her husband."

"Were there any other weapons involved?" Ken shook his head. "Okay, let me talk to the private eye and see what he knows. Maybe we can chalk this up to an accident."

Ken looked at him. "Really?" Rakić shrugged and walked over to the private eye.

"What's your name?" Rakić asked, pulling out a pack of cigarettes.

"Moses Winter."

"Okay, Winter. What the fuck happened tonight?" he asked, lighting up.

"Care if I smoke?" Moses asked.

"Tell me what you got and then we'll see."

"I've been tailing Mr. Dunsmore for a couple of weeks for Mrs. Dunsmore," Moses said.

"What for?"

"It was an infidelity case. Mrs. Dunsmore thought that he was cheating on her, and she was right. The first Thursday I followed him to the Mayan Hotel downtown and he met Šejla there." Moses pointed a finger at Šejla. "So, after I showed Mrs. Dunsmore the proof, she wanted to follow him again and catch him in the act."

"And this time they came here instead?" Rakić asked.

"Yeah."

"Who stabbed him?"

"I don't know. It was messy."

"Stabbing can be. Who pulled the knife?"

Winter shook his head.

"Alright, let me see your hands." Moses pulled his hands from his pockets and showed them to Rakić.

"They got bloody when I did first-aid."

Rakić nodded. "Who pulled the gun?"

"What gun?"

Rakić held the man's stare, looking into the dark pools of his eyes as they glittered back at him from below the bill of the cap. Something in those eyes made him want to be on his side. Rakić shook his head. "Nothing. Nothing. Okay, Winter, sit tight."

Winter was protecting his client; Rakić respected loyalty like that even if it did get in his way at the moment. He walked over to the fireplace and tossed his cigarette butt into the dying embers. As he turned, something caught his eye. In a stand next to the fireplace, wedged next to the poker and a small shovel, was an old-style pistol, nearly camouflaged next to the similarly-colored tools. He glanced around. Šejla was looking at him, but the rest of the team was preoccupied with the crime scene. The techs had finished with the floor and now were making a sweep of the cabin for anything else. He took the poker off the rack and played with the dying fire, causing a few sparks to pop onto the floor. He looked at his hand on the wooden handle of the tool. He had taken his winter gloves off but hadn't put on a pair of disposable latex gloves used for gathering evidence. If he put them on now someone would see and ask what he had found. He put the poker back in the rack and knelt down. His naked hand darted out, snatched the pistol and quickly tucked it into the side pocket of his Department of Criminal Investigation jacket. He stood up and turned back to the bed and Wilson. He heard a cough from Moses Winter's direction and glanced over. It was hard to tell if Moses Winter was looking at him from the shadows, but he thought he saw a slight shake of his head like a warning.

Rakić turned back to Wilson. "Let's cut 'em loose, Ken."

Wilson raised his eyebrows. "You serious, Rakić?"

"Why not? We got their info. This seems like it got out of hand but..."

Another DCI agent burst into the room. "Rakić!"

"Here."

The agent rushed over to him. "Update on the victim. Fred Dunsmore is in surgery. The doctors say it's fifty-fifty at best."

"Okay, thanks."

A buzz was coming from the area of the fireplace where a group of crime scene techs had congregated.

"What is it?" asked Rakić.

"We got a bullet hole!"

"If he dies, it's murder. You know that?" Wilson said.

Rakić looked around. He didn't have a choice. Šejla was mixed up in a potential murder and there was nothing he could do. "Okay, people, there is a gun here somewhere. Find it! Wilson, scratch my last thought. Let's take them back to Des Moines." Rakić glanced back at Šejla and then walked out of the cabin.

Chapter 2

Rakić sat alone in the office he shared with Wilson in the law enforcement building in downtown Des Moines. He was waiting for his cousin and the other suspects to be processed. Leaning back in his chair, he tapped absently at his computer keyboard. He still wore his navy DCI jacket and could feel the weight of the old pistol in his pocket as he shifted in his chair. He put his hand inside his jacket pocket and touched the solid wood handle of the old gun as he contemplated the night's events. *What was she thinking going around with a married man?* Šejla was the daughter of his mother's brother. Rakić was ten years older than her and had watched out for her when they were in Sarajevo during the bad times and now in Des Moines. The last few months they had grown apart. He tried to think of the last time he had talked to her. He couldn't remember. Damn her. Getting mixed up in this was bad. She was having an affair with a married man. A married man who was nearly killed. Damage had already been done to Šejla's reputation, but now he had to save her from the law. He didn't want to think about what his mother would say when she heard what had been going on.

The good news was he had just gotten word that Dunsmore had pulled through the surgery. He was still weak and not out of the woods, but there was good reason to believe he would survive. *So at least it wasn't a murder*, he thought. Even with a murder charge looking less likely, the three suspects could be facing serious time. The initial evidence wasn't good either. Sharon didn't have any blood on her hands, but both Moses and Šejla did. The forensic evidence was inconclusive so far. Rakić's gut told him that Winter was telling the truth about how his hands had gotten bloody, but he had lied about the gun.

He gripped the handle of the gun again. It was warm in his fingers now and the weight felt good in his hand. That gave him an idea. He had information that they didn't. If he could press Sharon Dunsmore or Winter, maybe he could get them to admit to what had happened. An attempted murder charge might scare them into giving him something he could use to keep Šejla out of jail. He checked his watch and picked up his phone.

"They out of booking yet?"

"Yeah, they are in the interrogation rooms," the night clerk said.

"Thanks," he said and dropped the receiver back into the cradle. Popping out of his seat, he was halfway out the door when he paused. He checked down the hall. It was empty. He moved back inside the office and closed the door. He removed the gun from his pocket and placed it in the top drawer of his filing cabinet. He turned the key in the lock and dropped it in his pocket on his way out of his office.

* * *

Rakić entered interrogation room three. Sharon Dunsmore sat at a small table in the center of the room. He closed the door behind him and threw a file down in front of her.

"Your husband isn't doing very well, Mrs. Dunsmore," Rakić said.

"Will he make it?" she asked.

"Maybe. He made it through surgery."

She lowered her head to her hands, pressing her long thin nose between her forefinger and thumb. He thought she looked relieved.

"Did you fire a gun tonight, Mrs. Dunsmore?" Rakić asked.

She didn't answer. Rakić sat down. He leaned back in the chair and studied the woman across from him. Sharon Dunsmore seemed easy to read. She portrayed the appropriate amount of concern and asked the right questions, while maintaining the sadness of a spurned wife. Rakić wanted to believe her, thought he believed her, but he knew prejudging the situation wouldn't help his cousin. So he pushed those thoughts aside. He would work the case.

"I know he's an asshole. Pardon the language. He was cheating on you, it looks like. But you must still care for him. He might die. If he dies, then it will be bad if you went there with intent. Do you understand?" Rakić asked.

"I didn't stab him," Sharon said.

"Did you want to? It's okay, if you did. I know what it's like to be cheated on," he said.

Her face changed. For the briefest moment, ugly anger flickered across her normally gentle face, but then it was gone again just as fast as it had appeared. She shook her head.

"No."

"You look tired, Sharon. You need a coffee or something?"

"A coffee would be good," she said.

Rakić nodded and went to the door. Pulling it open, he leaned out. "Coffee, interrogation three, please!" Rakić yelled.

Rakić paused outside the door, trying to gather his thoughts. He had seen something in her face for a brief instant before she regained control. He needed to press her, bring that emotion back to the front and maybe he could get her to tell him what happened.

"Coffee is on the way. Now, what other weapons were there tonight?" Rakić asked as he returned to his chair, his pen hovering over his notepad.

"I don't know what you mean."

"There was a bullet hole in the wall, Mrs. Dunsmore. Ballistics will return the details soon. You can't beat science. We can tell if you fired a gun. Now, was it your gun? Did you take a gun there tonight? Maybe just to scare Fred and his girl?"

"No. I don't own a gun."

"I believe you. Tell me what happened then."

"Well, I had a feeling a few weeks ago that Fred was…"

"Just what happened tonight please, Mrs. Dunsmore, at the cabin. Then we'll get to the other part."

"The cabin, right. Mr. Winter and I followed my husband to the cabin. We waited for a while. Mr. Winter tried to talk me out of it, but I insisted that we go in. We got inside and then, well, they were, you know." Her hands were waving as she talked now.

"Yes. Go on."

"Well, I sort of freaked out. I started screaming and Mr. Winter was screaming at me and then there was this knife. And then I think Šejla stabbed

Fred." She made a stabbing motion with her hand and then folded her arms together on the table.

"Hmm." He flipped through the notes that Wilson had taken. The same story more or less. "Ms. Tahirović stabbed Fred you say."

"I think so. It happened fast."

"Why would she stab Mr. Dunsmore? I thought they were together. Lovers." Rakić concentrated on Sharon, hoping to see a reaction to his casual framing of her husband's infidelity.

"I don't know. Ask her. Why would she wreck a family? Why would she ruin Fred's life?"

"Okay, okay. I get it," Rakić said, lowering his voice into a soothing tone. He busied himself with the file, watching her body language from the corner of his eye. It still seemed appropriate—tense, angry, scared; all the right notes were getting hit. He decided to press her a bit more. "When did the gun go off?"

"I didn't fire the gun."

"I know you didn't. Who did?"

"Šejla."

Rakić arched an eyebrow. "When did she fire the gun?"

"It was right before she stabbed him," Sharon said.

"Did she run out of bullets?" Rakić asked.

"What do you mean?"

"Why would she stab him if she could shoot him?"

"No, you don't understand. She was, well…"

"Well what?" he asked.

"Well, she wasn't trying to stab him. Well, maybe she wasn't. I don't know. She was crazed and you know I don't think she's the brightest girl."

Rakić smiled and scribbled on the file. "Ah. I see. So she didn't know what she was doing."

"No, I guess not."

"Do you think you can sign a statement saying that it was an accident?"

"Do you think it was? I don't know," she said.

"Let me check on that coffee." He got up and walked out of the room. He closed the door and paused, taking a breath. Then he walked down the hall to the main desk.

"Any word on the GSR tests?"

A bald man he didn't recognize appeared from behind a cubicle partition shaking his head and disappeared back into the cubicle. Rakić walked to the coffee pot sitting on the table next to the desk and poured a cup. He grabbed some packets of sugar and creamer. "How about anything from ballistics?" he asked.

The man popped out from his cubicle again, shaking his head.

Rakić brought the coffee back to number three and gave it to Mrs. Dunsmore. He watched as she prepared the coffee. One cream, one sugar. She stirred it and, holding the styrofoam cup with both hands, she dipped her tongue in, testing the temperature.

"Okay, Mrs. Dunsmore. Let's do this statement. I'll write." He wrote down a simple statement saying the night had been an accident and she was not holding anyone responsible. He pushed it over to Mrs. Dunsmore.

Sharon read through the statement. "But this doesn't say anything about the gun," she said.

"Yeah, we haven't found one. Let's keep this neat. We'll get you out of here and over to the hospital to check on your husband."

Sharon picked up the pen and pressed the tip to her cheek. She tilted her head to the side and a small crinkle of skin formed below her right eye. She shook her head and set the statement down. A knock sounded on the metal door.

"Think about it, Sharon," Rakić said on his way to the door.

It was the bald man from the cube. "Here are the GSRs."

"So this will tell me anyone that shot a gun tonight?"

"Absolutely," the bald man said.

Rakić glanced at Mrs. Dunsmore. No change in her demeanor; she didn't seem to care one bit about a GSR test. Rakić pulled the door shut, followed the man down the hallway, and took the report from him.

"Fred Dunsmore. Negative for hands and traces on clothes." He flipped the page. "Moses Winter. Negative for hands, traces on clothes." He flipped again. "Sharon Dunsmore. Negative for hands, traces on clothes. Šejla Tahirović. Negative for hands, traces on clothes."

"She was only wearing panties according to the reports anyway," the bald man said.

Rakić looked at him and realized he hadn't meant anything by the comment other than the fact of the matter so he ignored it. He pushed the report into the hands of the bald man. "So, no one shot a gun, but everyone was in a room where one was shot. Are we missing a person?"

The man shrugged. "You know it can get washed off. Or they could have been wearing gloves."

"Yeah, shit. They find the gun yet?" Rakić asked. The man shook his head. Rakić chewed on his lip. Šejla was closer to getting out of this.

"Thanks for this. You new?" Rakić asked.

The man shook his head. "Transferred from western district. I'm Johnson."

"We'll have to find you a nickname." The man snorted as Rakić disappeared back into interrogation three.

"Well, Sharon, you sign yet?" Rakić asked, standing in front of her holding the GSR report.

"No, I can't."

"Any reason why?"

"Šejla stabbed him, I'm sure of it."

Rakić tossed the GSR report onto the other files and placed his hands on either side of the documents. "We know there was a gun there tonight, Sharon. We already have your private eye, Moses Winter, saying you were the one shooting up the place."

"No, he wouldn't."

"No? Let me change the picture here. You go out to this cabin knowing that your husband has his mistress there. Why would you do that? A jury might ask. What was your intent? Then we find the cabin wall all shot up and your husband stabbed. Where did the gun come from? Why would someone bring a gun?"

Sharon had gone blank again, staring past him into space. Rakić couldn't tell if this was breaking her or if she was clamming up. He kept pressing.

"Fred didn't need a gun. He had his plans set for the night. Šejla, same story. Moses, he might have had a gun. But you hired him, didn't you? You hired the brute to take care of Fred, maybe. But I don't think so. I think the gun is yours. You took it there to frighten at first, and then you lost control and shot the place up. Either way, your private eye is looking for a way out now and he's dishing you up."

Now she was breathing deeply. Her eyes were closed, her arms folded together over her chest.

"It's okay. We all get emotional." Rakić sat down and reached his hand across the table. "No one would fault you for shooting the place up. You didn't shoot anybody anyway. But I think you know that Moses and Šejla didn't try to hurt anyone tonight. What say you sign this and let them out of this family problem you have."

Sighing deeply, Sharon finally opened her eyes. "I want to talk to my lawyer."

* * *

Moses sat in a small room with a table and three chairs. Video cameras watched him from high on the wall in two corners of the room. The DCI agent that had talked to him earlier in the cabin was sitting across from him, studying a file. The agent started speaking without looking up.

"Moses Winter, I'm DCI Special Agent Rakić." Rakić flipped a document over and sighed. "Stabbed husband. Cabin shot up and three people who can't tell me a thing. Help me out here, Winter. What the hell happened?"

Moses shook his head. "I don't know."

Rakić pushed back from the table and put his hands behind his head, looking at him now. "How much is Mrs. Dunsmore paying you?"

"Not enough."

Rakić smirked. "You didn't agree to go out to that cabin and kill Fred Dunsmore. I know that. Maybe scare him, but no one was supposed to get hurt. But what I can't figure out is who brought the gun?"

Moses shifted in his seat. How had his gun ended up in Sharon's hands? He had had it in the glove box of his car, but he hadn't brought it inside the cabin. How had she even known it was there? Not really a stretch to think that a guy like him might have a gun, he supposed. Not exactly the best place to hide it either.

"That's alright. We can start with the knife," Rakić continued. "Set the scene for me, Moses. How did the knife end up stuck in Fred Dunsmore's ribs?"

"I don't know. It just happened."

"Just happened. Okay. Did Sharon stab him? She had the right. He was cheating on her. Who knows with how many." Rakić waved his hands around as if to encompass the whole state.

"No, it was just her. I did my work. It was just Ms. Tahirović."

"Alright. So, no one knows how Fred got stabbed. How about you tell me how the girl got marked up." Rakić tossed a few pictures in front of Moses. The first was a profile showing a dark bruise on the cheekbone of Šejla's pale face. The next was a close-up of the laceration and bruise. The bruise was long and thin. At its darkest, it was maybe a few inches in width.

Moses sighed and pushed the pictures away. "It got out of hand."

"So you hit the girl with your gun?"

"No. Never."

"Then Mrs. Dunsmore did."

Moses held his tongue. Sharon deserved what she got for hitting the girl, but he bore responsibility for allowing the confrontation to happen at all.

"Looks like a…I don't know. What does it look like to you? Maybe a gun barrel?" Rakić folded his arms and leaned forward, looking at the pictures. "Yeah, maybe the sight caught her skin and tore it like that. What do you think, Moses?"

Moses needed to shift him off of Sharon. She had lost it. But she had kids to take care of and a life to put back together. Who could blame her for losing it after finding her husband in bed with a younger version of herself? Moses had let it get that far, and now he needed to take responsibility. She was his client and he never let a client down.

"I think I might have stabbed Dunsmore," Moses said.

"Why do you say that? It's not that easy to stab someone without meaning to, is it?" Rakić asked.

"There was a struggle. I ended up on top with the blade sticking out of him."

"Did you pull the knife?"

Moses shrugged.

"Bullshit, you don't shrug me off. Who pulled the knife?"

"I'm not going to rat anyone out. I'm to blame," Moses said.

"What about Šejla? She stab or shoot at anyone?"

"No."

"You're sure."

"Yeah, I suppose she is as innocent as they come in this."

Rakić seemed to relax. "Good. So, you'll sign saying you accidentally stabbed Fred Dunsmore?"

"Yeah, put it in front of me. I'll sign."

"Okay. Good." Rakić started writing on a yellow legal pad, then pushed it over to Moses.

It was a simple statement to the effect that they had discussed. Moses took the pen Rakić offered and started to sign his name. A thought occurred to him and he paused.

"I'm going to need my gun back," Moses said.

"What gun?"

"I saw you pick it up at the cabin."

Rakić's forehead bunched up above his nose. "You saw something?" Rakić stood up, glaring at Moses. He turned and disconnected the cable from the back of the camera in the corner behind him. Then he walked over to the other camera and did the same.

"Okay, Moses, here's the deal. You're going to shut up and sign this confession, and then you're going to hope and pray that the judge doesn't throw the book at you, and then we are going to put this all behind us. Forget the gun. There is no gun."

"I know you have the gun. I don't know your angle, but you don't want anyone knowing about it either. I just want you to know. Don't get rid of it. It's important." Moses watched for his reaction. Nothing changed in Rakić's expression other than a slight darkening of his eyes.

"I don't know what you're talking about."

"I'm going to need it back."

"Sign the fucking statement."

Moses pushed the statement at Rakić. "The gun is special."

Rakić leaned over the table until his face was so close to Moses that he could smell the coffee on his breath and the stale sweat from his body.

"You realize the shit you're in right now? You are a puff cake for a jury. Big tough guy stabs an upstanding citizen and roughs up a girl for a paycheck. That's the way they'll see it. If they get that impression." Rakić sat down, cocking his head to the side, hands on the table. Moses sensed the bluff. Rakić wanted this to go away more than he did. He could feel it. He just couldn't figure out his angle.

"I can't let this go. I know you have it. I'll get it back. But I'll sign." Moses picked up the pen. The gun was important to him, but he couldn't let his client hang for this. He signed his name and pushed it back to Rakić.

Rakić took the statement. "This is the right thing, Winter," he said on his way out the door.

Moses leaned back in his chair, staring at the closed door. He hoped so.

* * *

Rakić paused for a moment in the hallway, collecting his thoughts. He wanted to check on Šejla before he worked on dropping the charges against her.

"Rakić." He turned to the night commander's voice. He was a tall, thin man in his early fifties who always seemed to have part of his shirttail untucked. "We are sitting on these two women and the PI unless you find something different. That wife is homicidal and the girlfriend has half his blood on him."

"Maybe not. Got a confession out of the PI." Rakić smiled and entered the third interrogation room of the night, leaving the commander smirking.

"Hello, Ms. Tahirović," Rakić said.

"How is Freddy?"

"He is pulling through."

Šejla was younger than Rakić, but had never spoken English beyond the halting, utilitarian form of the language. She still thought in Bosnian. He didn't. He had gone away to school, but she had always stayed close to home, until now.

"Tell me about what happened. Who stabbed Mr. Dunsmore?" Rakić asked. Šejla looked down and wouldn't meet his gaze.

"I think I did," she said.

"Are you sure?" Rakić asked.

"No. It happened fast, that man jumped on me."

"Why did he do that?"

"Because I was trying to get that bitch off of Freddy."

"What was she doing?"

"She was trying to shoot him. They were struggling and—"

"Are you sure you stabbed him?"

"I think so," she said, nodding.

Rakić swore in Bosnian. "Listen, that other man is admitting it. Just keep your mouth shut until I get you out of this," Rakić whispered, glancing at the camera over his shoulder.

"My mouth *is* shut," she said.

Rakić put his hand out to her, but she ignored it. Standing up he gave her his most reproachful look, but she refused to look at him. He opened the door, glanced back, and then left. Rakić read the confession on his way to the night commander. Arriving at the commander's office, he knocked once and leaned inside.

"I think we cut the girl loose. Looks like a conspiracy on the part of Mr. Winter and Mrs. Dunsmore," Rakić said.

The commander interrupted, "No, we are keeping all three. Mrs. Dunsmore just gave a statement to Wilson saying that Ms. Tahirović did it. Are we even sure there was a gun there? Have we found a shell casing at least? No. We got no straight story here so we're going to sit on them until Mr. Dunsmore wakes up and we get his side."

"I thought she asked for a lawyer."

"She wanted to make a statement. We took it."

Rakić entered the office. He scrambled to come up with an argument to tell the commander, something that would let Šejla go free. He had gotten a confession from Moses and done well to minimize the gun angle. He had fooled himself. No one ever got out of an attempted murder without the DA taking a crack. *Attempted murder.* The thought gave him a numb feeling in his chest.

"Bail hearing in the morning," the commander said, arching his head back to read the text on his computer screen.

"Bail in the morning," Rakić replied, feeling the words echo around the small room. He put the confession on the desk. The commander picked it up and read it. The commander always read the reports. He read the statements, the logs, any piece of paper on a case. He read it.

"Good work, Rakić. We could use ten of you."

Rakić backed out of the office. He turned and stuck his hands in his pants pockets, staring at the floor as he went to the back staircase and down the two flights to street level. He opened the exit door and lowered his head as a blast of cold air met him on his way out. He stood in the deserted alley. He lit a smoke, rubbing his head. *Why had Sharon Dunsmore flipped her story?* The wind picked up. Fine-grained snow peppered his cheeks. He tossed his barely-smoked cigarette into the alley and went back inside.

Chapter 3

Moses had gotten a private room in lockup. Lying down with his back to the gray steel door of his cell, he stared at a small mark on the wall. He rolled over and buried his face in the thin, blue-striped pillow.

He needed a way to get them out of this. One of his childhood friends was a good lawyer. He might know a way to fix this. Moses rolled onto his back. His friend was a good guy, but he hadn't talked to him in a while and wasn't sure how he'd take the call. Moses had a few other lawyer acquaintances that he'd done work for, but no one that he could trust. He'd get his phone call soon. He needed a plan. Maybe he could call a bondsman and get them bailed out. The only problem with that was there were no charges and no bail so far. Fred was the key and he needed to convince him not to press charges, that it was an accident. It made the most sense even if it was a long shot. The door to the cell clanged and Moses rolled over and sat up. It was a pudgy, rosy-cheeked guard he hadn't seen yet.

"Winter. Time for your call." Moses rolled off the bed and followed the guard out of the cell.

* * *

"You got two minutes," the guard said. Moses nodded, listening to the ringing phone pressed to his ear.

"Hospital information. How can I direct your call?" a pleasant female voice asked on the other end.

"Can I be transferred to Fred Dunsmore's room, please?" Moses asked.

"Just a moment." The hold music played for a while and then the line rang as the call was transferred.

"Hello?" a matronly voice answered.

"Hello, is this Fred Dunsmore's room?" Moses asked.

"Yes. Who is this?"

"This is a friend of Fred's, can he talk?" Moses asked.

"Just a moment."

"This is Fred." Fred's voice was barely audible; his words seemed unfinished, almost slurred.

"Fred. This is Moses Winter from last night. The guy with Sharon."

"Oh, you."

"Yes. Listen, I don't have much time."

"What do you want?" Fred's tone was half annoyed, half sedated.

Moses looked at the guard as he spoke. "I want you to think about not pressing any charges against Sharon." The sound of Fred breathing filled the line as Moses waited for a response. None coming, he continued, "Listen, I know it's hard to think of it this way, but it was an accident. Sharon didn't mean to hurt you."

"I don't want to talk about it. She deserves to rot."

"One minute left, Winter," the guard said.

Moses nodded at him. "Hey Fred, honestly it was probably me that stabbed you. When I tried to pull Šejla off of you, I think the blade slipped. Blame me, not Sharon."

"She tried to shoot me."

Moses sighed. "She wouldn't have even been there if it wasn't for me. I drove her out there. Look, she lost it. You aren't exactly an angel in this either, Fred."

"Are you trying to blame me for getting stabbed?"

"No. Wait. That's not what I mean. Blame me. It was my gun. My fault for driving her out there and agreeing to follow you."

"Finish up, Winter," the guard said.

"Look, my time is up. Just let Sharon off the hook. It was my fault."

"I can't do it. I told the cops that you and Šejla had nothing to do with it. That you tried to help. But Šejla and I agree, I am pressing charges."

"What? When did you talk? What did Šejla say?"

"Time's up." The guard was leaning over him now.

"Fred, you have to drop those charges."

The guard grabbed the phone from Moses' hand and slammed the receiver down on the cradle.

"Time is up."

Moses slapped the concrete wall in frustration.

"Hey. Cut it out!" the guard yelled, grabbing Moses by the arm.

"Okay, don't touch me. I'm going," he said, jerking his arm free as the guard led him away.

* * *

Raif Rakić was on the third floor of the Hope Hospital in downtown Des Moines, waiting to see Fred Dunsmore. Having his cousin locked up overnight had been difficult for him. Worse was not being able to tell anyone that Šejla was his cousin. He was worried that if anyone found out, he would be shuffled from the case and not be in a position to help her. She was a good girl. She just wasn't thinking clearly. He wasn't sure why she was with this older man. Šejla was good-looking. Most of the boys from the neighborhood were deadbeats or taken, so he could see her wandering outside of the group, but not with someone old enough to be her father. Keeping his contempt for Fred Dunsmore hidden would be a priority while he interviewed him.

"Mr. Rakić?" a nurse in lavender scrubs called from down the hall.

"That's me."

She smiled at him and waved for him to follow her. Her dark, shoulder-length hair bobbed as she led him down the hall. They arrived at an open doorway to a large one-patient hospital room. Inside, Fred Dunsmore was sitting up in bed, spooning food into his mouth from a tray over his lap.

"He's doing pretty well, but try not to tire him out," the nurse said.

Rakić nodded to her and stepped into the room. "Mr. Dunsmore."

Fred stopped eating and looked up. "Yes."

"I'm Raif Rakić, DCI. I need to ask you about last night if you feel up to it."

Fred looked pale, and his face betrayed a hint of apprehension as he slowly set his spoon down. Pulling out a notebook, Rakić dragged a chair over to the bed and sat down, pausing to let the full effect of his *don't lie to me* scowl be absorbed by Fred Dunsmore. As Rakić studied Fred Dunsmore, he imagined that the other man had had an easy life up to this point. He was tan, had a lion's mane for a head of hair and a face out of a catalogue. Rakić figured most things probably went his way without much effort. Rakić hated him more for that. He began. "What were you doing at the cabin last night?"

"I was meeting a friend."

"Šejla Tahirović?" Rakić asked.

"Yes. You can say her name better than most people," Fred said.

Rakić smiled. "Lots of school, I suppose. I sound out words pretty good. Now you were meeting Ms. Tahirović at this cabin off Highway 6."

"Yes," Fred answered.

"And then your wife shows up with this private detective, Winter?"

"Yes. We were there," Fred's voice rose. "Then they stormed in and Sharon went crazy and started waving a gun around." Fred finished speaking with a grimace, lowering his shoulder toward his injured side.

"What kind of gun?"

"I don't know. It was an older looking gun. Šejla thinks that it was a Nazi gun like in a World War II movie."

"You've spoken to Ms. Tahirović?" Rakić coughed, choking on her last name. "That is unfortunate."

"She called me from jail."

"You must be close."

"Yes, we've built a good relationship." Rakić felt his stomach jump into his throat and his blood simmered up his neck, flushing his face. He coughed into his hand.

"All while you were married with kids?" Rakić asked.

Fred frowned for a moment and then seemed deep in thought, going so far as to put his hand to his chiseled chin, looking off into the distance.

Finally, he answered, "Sharon and I were done long before Šejla and I started out. At least from my perspective."

From his perspective. A very convenient thing, perspective. Almost anything can look right if you are at the appropriate distance. "I find a great deal depends on perspective. We'll deal with Ms. Tahirović in a minute. What happened to it?

The gun. Did Mrs. Dunsmore throw it outside into a snowdrift? Did she hide it in the cabin somewhere?" Rakić asked.

"I don't think so. Last I saw it was in the cabin. You haven't found it?" A note of exasperation had crept into Fred's voice, pushing perilously close to outrage. Rakić had dealt with this before. People expected a case to be wrapped up like an episode of *CSI*. Sometimes common sense dictated a lesser charge, sometimes guns weren't found. A gavel didn't fall every hour. Rakić would need to shape Fred's expectations to fit the favorable narrative he was creating for Šejla.

"No, not yet, but we will. If you tell me all you remember, it will help," Rakić said, offering a slight smile.

"I don't remember seeing it after she shot at me and we fell."

"She shot at you?"

"Yes, well, we struggled and then yeah, the gun went off very close to my head. It still feels like my ears are ringing."

"So the gun was fired, then what?"

"The gun went off and Sharon was on top of me and I was bleeding all over the place and that Winters guy was yelling and then I woke up here."

"It is actually Winter not Winters, no *s*, but that's it? Nothing else you can think of?"

Fred stared at him for a second, a touch of incredulity in his eyes. "No."

"Okay, tell me about Šejla Tahirović."

"What do you want to know?" Fred asked.

"Where did you two meet?"

"What does that have to do with anything?"

"Just bear with me, Mr. Dunsmore. Every detail could help."

"I don't see how. We met at a bar downtown."

"What were you doing there?"

"I was having drinks with a friend and Šejla came up to me and introduced herself."

"Šejla did? When was this?" Rakić asked.

"Yes, she did. It was a few months ago, in the summer. It was a nice day and the bar had a patio, so we sat outside and drank margaritas."

"Good memory." Rakić crossed his legs and scribbled on his pad. "How old is she?"

"Twenty-eight."

"And how old are you?"

"I'm forty-two."

"What do you do for a living?"

"I have real estate and I'm a supplier."

"What kind of supplies?"

"Bar supplies. Food supplies. All things in between."

"Booze?" Rakić asked.

"Everything up to it. Glasses, napkins, swizzles…"

"Got it. Do you think that Ms. Tahirović stabbed you?"

"Absolutely not."

"Are you sure?"

"Yes. Why not?"

"Well, you just said you don't remember much after the gun went off."

"I am certain Šejla didn't stab me," Fred said, his voice rising again.

"Okay. Then you won't press charges against her?"

"No. Never!" Fred shifted in bed, emitting a barely audible moan.

"Okay. And this Moses Winter?" Rakić asked.

"He tried to help me. Us."

It was 'us' now. Peace give me strength. "So, no charges?"

"No. I guess not."

"And your wife?" Rakić asked.

Fred looked Rakić straight in the eyes. "Šejla and I agree. She can rot."

"You agree, I understand. Why do you think your wife attacked you?"

"I don't know." Fred Dunsmore looked out the window.

"Well, we can certainly hold her for a while. We have her on assault and possibly more, but this gun." Rakić tapped his knee with the notebook. "Are you sure there was a gun?"

"Yes, I'm certain."

"Okay, we will keep looking. If we find a gun, it could be attempted murder. But until then, we have her with assault. Everyone seems to agree that she didn't stab you?"

Fred frowned, but nodded.

"Okay."

"Do you think you and Šejla have a future?"

"What do you mean?"

Rakić stood up and walked over to the bed. "I mean you got lucky this time. I'd make it count from now on. Only be with people that matter, you know. People you have a future with."

Rakić patted him on the shoulder, flashing a quick smile as he flipped his notebook shut. "I will get her and the PI released, and your wife will stay in jail. You feel better. Okay?"

Chapter 4

Less than two hours after his call with Fred, Moses had been processed out of the county lockup. After signing a few papers, he was led by a guard down a narrow hallway to a staircase. They went up two flights of stairs and down a short hall where they met another guard standing at an exit door. Moses put his coat and hat on, waiting as a guard opened the door to the alley between the courthouse and the jail. Moses found Raif Rakić waiting for him when he stepped outside.

"Walk with me, Winter," Rakić said.

Moses fell in with Rakić. They walked down the narrow, paved lane of the alley toward the street. Moses was still amazed that he had been let out so soon. It was less than twelve hours since the confrontation at the cabin. He needed to get his car out of impound and figure out what to do about Sharon.

"You have an office around here?" Rakić asked.

"35th and Rollins."

"I'll drive you."

"I need to get my car. You guys have it in impound."

"I'll take you there."

"Okay." Moses wasn't going to turn down a free ride.

"My car is over here," Rakić said, pointing to a black Dodge sports car on the far side of the one-way street they were approaching. They got in and headed toward the impound lot on the east side of the river.

"They are letting Šejla out," Rakić said, looking at Winter and then turning down another one-way.

"No kidding."

"Yep."

"What about Sharon? She getting out?"

"They are keeping her locked up," Rakić said.

"Because Fred is pressing charges."

Rakić nodded as the car rolled to a stop at a light. "Don't get mixed up with this, Winter," he said.

"I think it's too late for that."

"Don't get smart. Leave the rest of this alone."

"Why, what's it to you other than a case?"

Rakić shook his head. "Just stay out of it."

Moses paused for a second and then nodded. *Why was he involved?* He had tried to get Fred to drop charges, but now, with Šejla filing assault charges against Sharon, he didn't know what he could do. The car was silent except for the grinding of snow under the tires as they pulled up to the impound lot.

"Thanks," Moses said.

Rakić acted like he didn't hear him and Moses started to get out.

"Wait." Rakić reached into his coat and pulled out the Luger. "I never saw it," he said, holding out the gun.

Moses took the gun and stuffed it in his pocket. "Thanks."

"For what?"

"Yeah," Moses said. He waited a beat and, with nothing left to say, he got out of the car.

Why does a cop like Rakić seem to care so much about this case? Why hide evidence? The questions stuck in his head as he got his car out of impound and made his way to his office.

* * *

Later that afternoon, Moses sat in his car, waiting. The engine of his black Jeep Cherokee idled. Small crystals of ice covered the paved street, sparkling in the fading light. Moses put the Jeep in gear as a dark Dodge Charger zipped past. The plates were right. *Dumb idea, following a cop*, he thought as he pulled his vehicle onto the street behind Rakić's police cruiser. The back tires of the Jeep spun on the slick surface of the street, causing the back end to fishtail. Finally, he was tailing Rakić.

In minutes, they were off the downtown streets and onto the three-lane freeway. Rakić merged through the light traffic and over to the passing lane. Moses stayed in the middle lane, letting Rakić build a lead. Crossing two lanes of traffic, Rakić exited on 63rd street. Boxed in by a semi and a car, Moses slammed on the brakes to make the exit.

Rakić barely slowed down as he took the off-ramp. Making a right turn, he headed north into the old western suburbs. Moses ran a red light to make the turn, catching up with Rakić as he crossed University Avenue. The street narrowed to two lanes, the traffic heavier now, forcing Moses to tailgate Rakić.

A shadow moved in the back of Rakić's cruiser. Moses squinted against the glare of the setting sun, trying to see who it was. Was it a prisoner? Then they pulled off on a deserted residential side street and Moses had to back off. Rakić pulled ahead half a block, turning into a driveway a half-dozen houses down. Moses hit the gas and sped past. When he'd gone a block, he turned the car around in a driveway and eased the Jeep back down the street toward Rakić's car.

By that time, Rakić was pushing a shorter, slender person in front of him. The person was wearing a long coat and a stocking hat and was partially blocked by Rakić. Moses pulled to a stop a few houses short and watched. Rakić shielded his view of the other person's face as he opened the door and then nearly dragged the person inside with him. Moses cruised up to the house and jotted down the address on a notepad he kept in the car's console.

A buzzing in his pocket distracted him from his notepad. He pulled out his phone and looked at the number. Not recognizing it, he flipped the phone open and answered it.

"Hello?"

"Is this Moses Winters?"

"Yes," Moses answered.

"Moses, this is Fred Dunsmore."

"What can I do for you, Mr. Dunsmore?" Moses asked, wondering how he knew he was out of jail already.

"Can you meet me?" Fred sounded like he was walking outside. Moses could hear the wind howling through the line.

"Sure, what room are you in at the hospital?" Moses asked.

"No, I'm not in the hospital anymore."

"What? Why not? You were hurt pretty bad, Mr. Dunsmore."

"I know, I just can't let anyone know where I am right now."

"My question is the same. What can I do for you?"

"You want Sharon out of jail, right?" Fred said, his voice rising. "Well, I want her out of my life."

"I don't see how I can help you with that. I want Sharon out of jail, but I think you both might need good lawyers. I can't help you."

"It's not that easy, Mr. Winters. I think you can help us get what we want."

Moses paused. He was close to figuring out something important about Raif Rakić, but Fred Dunsmore's voice had an odd tone, strange, with barely contained energy, so he forced himself to listen.

"Okay. Where do you want to meet?"

Moses took down the address on his notepad. He seemed to be collecting addresses today. After agreeing to meet Fred, he ended the call. He glanced at Rakić's unmarked police car parked in front of him. Was it his house? He pulled the pack of smokes out of his pocket and stuck one in his mouth. Lighting the cigarette, he closed his eyes, exhaling the smoke as he rubbed his forehead with his hand. He hadn't slept much since the cabin, making it hard to think. Something strange was going on, but he couldn't figure it out. Who was Rakić hiding? That would have to wait. Dunsmore had been stabbed half-to-death twenty-four hours ago, yet something had motivated him enough to get out of his hospital bed to meet him. The only thing he could do was meet Dunsmore. Rakić's secret had to wait. Moses sucked at the cigarette in his mouth, glanced back at the house one more time, and drove off toward the interstate and his meeting with Fred Dunsmore.

Chapter 5

Fred Dunsmore was running. He coughed. Tasting blood, he spat in the snow. Chancing a glance over his shoulder, he slipped, falling to one knee in the snow next to an old oak. He pressed down on his side where he'd been stabbed the day before, the pressure relieving some of the pain. Pushing himself off the trunk of the tree, he was on the move again. He slalomed off the next tree a few feet away, moving faster now.

Then he heard a loud blast in front of him. Near enough that he saw the flash light up the bare branches of the trees. Lurching to the right, away from the blast, he slid down a shallow ravine. Looking back, he saw the trail he had left through the snow. He whispered a curse. Then he turned and, finding a small game trail, pushed himself that direction, deeper into the forest. It was darker here, but he could make out the snow-covered path glowing in the light of the half-moon hanging low in the clear night sky. A barely-audible shout reached his ears over the crunching of his shoes in the snow. He paused, listening for another sound, but hearing only silence, he pressed on. The trail wound between the trees, sometimes dead-ending into bushes, forcing him to find another way. Then the trail looped around a fallen tree and he could go no further; he was facing the river.

Fred leaned one hand against a large root of the tree, looking down at the river. It appeared to be frozen, but he couldn't be sure, even with the early and frigid start to winter, that it would hold his weight. Turning back the way he had come, he cocked his head to the side, straining to hear any indication of someone approaching. He glanced at his feet; the running shoes were a good choice for a drive across town, but not for a hike through calf-deep snow. Reluctant to stamp his feet and give away his position, he felt his toes go numb. A sound, he heard a sound. Or did he? Fred leaned back into the exposed root structure of the tree, listening. Forgetting for a moment, he stamped his feet to stimulate the blood and, losing his footing, he slipped. One hand pressed on his wounded side and his free hand grasped for a tree root. His hand closed on a gnarled offshoot, but he couldn't hold on. He fell down, sliding into a dark hole.

He was flat on his back, the roots of the tree he had been leaning on a moment before silhouetted above him, looking like a fearsome sea creature with twisted tentacles reaching for him. He couldn't remember if he had made a sound when he fell. He rolled over onto his side. The fall had opened his wound, judging by the way it felt, burning worse now.

He got to his knees and then managed to stand up. The hole was shallow enough to see over the edge. Looking back in the direction he had come, making sure he was still alone, he turned to the roots and began to pull himself up and out.

He was breathing heavily, the sound of it roaring in his ears. Finally, he reached the top. Pulling himself over the edge, he scooted his back up to the roots and the river behind it. The woods seemed darker now as he squinted, searching for any sign of movement.

Then he was sure he heard something, off to the right and not very far away. It was a steady sound. It was an intelligent sound, maybe a man-made sound. He swung his head in the other direction. Glowing eyes floated feet away, bouncing toward him, and he stifled a scream. The owner of the eyes was a large canine, loping gracefully toward him through the snow. A strange breed of dog, massive, coal black with gray streaks. With its teeth bared, tongue hanging, and head held low to the ground, it came at him. Then it was on him.

"Stop!" Fred yelled, shielding his face with his arm.

From behind the dog, a single short whistle echoed across the snow, halting the dog where he was. Lying on its belly, it crouched a few feet from Fred.

Fred heard the steady sound again, getting closer. He knew now that it was someone crunching through the snow in a pair of winter boots. But the whistle had come from the other direction. He pushed back into the tree roots, slowly rising to a crouch. The dog answered by baring its teeth and emitting a low growl, but it stayed where it was, obeying the unseen master.

Francis Sparks

The *crunch-crunch-crunch* of the person approaching grew steadily louder. Materializing behind the dog, a man stood, his hooded face obscured by shadows. He whistled and the dog circled around, sitting on his right side.

"Wait. This doesn't have to happen," Fred said, unable to control the pitch of his voice.

Crunch. Crunch. Crunch.

Fred still couldn't see the origin of the sound, but it was close now.

"We have to happen," the male voice responded in thickly accented English.

Then the man whistled twice and the dog was leaping at Fred and he couldn't stop screaming.

Chapter 6

Moses parked on the street behind Fred Dunsmore's black SUV. He got out of the car and walked up to the driver's side of Fred's vehicle. Cupping his hands together on the tinted glass, he looked inside and found the car empty. Fred's SUV was parked in front of a massive three-story brick and stone mansion from early in the last century. Several large windows were spaced evenly along the first and second stories, with scattered smaller windows above them. Two peaks formed the center of the house, illuminated by small lights hidden in the landscaped bushes. Two arches beneath the peaks crowned the entrance to the extravagant dwelling, casting the doorway into shadows. Moses made the long walk down the sidewalk to the entryway. Standing over twelve feet, the coffee-colored, solid wood door wouldn't be out of place blocking the entrance to an ancient medieval keep. Hanging from the center of the door, a miniature black iron ball and chain served as the knocker to the house.

Moses swung the ball into the door three times. Each time the impact of the ball on wood produced a satisfying boom. Shuffling to the side, Moses waited. Then he heard movement inside and the door cracked open, revealing a sliver of a person's eye, nose, and lip.

"Dunsmore?" the male voice whispered.

"No, sir. I'm a friend of his. Are you expecting him?"

The door glided open without a sound, revealing a dapper gentleman just a bit beyond middle age. "And who might be asking?" the man asked.

"I am Moses Winter," Moses said, sticking out his hand.

The man shook the offered hand vigorously, baring his teeth in a wide smile. "Well, you better come in," he said.

The man surprised Moses with his strength, pulling him over the threshold and into the cozy warmth of the great house. Moses followed him as they retreated down a hallway and through pocket doors to a study with a roaring fire. He motioned for Moses to take a chair as he leaned against the mantle.

"Sorry, sir, to the point. Do you know where Mr. Dunsmore might be?" Moses remained standing.

"Fred will be along. Now, tell me about yourself." The man motioned, indicating he should begin.

Moses felt sweat begin to bead on his forehead and he unbuttoned his coat. The man stepped forward, took it from Moses, tossed it on the chair, then returned to the mantle.

"I am Moses Winter."

"Yes, you've said that."

"Yes. Well, what do you want to know?"

"What you are doing at my house is a good place to start."

Moses felt his face flush. "I am here to meet with Fred Dunsmore."

"Yes."

"And he was to meet me, but he wasn't in his car and I don't actually know who you are, sir," Moses said.

"I am Henry Duncan. What do you have to do with Fred?"

"Well, his wife is a client of mine. He called me and wanted to meet and discuss some of their business."

"Really? What is it you do?"

Moses glanced at his shoes. "I am an investigator."

"What do you investigate? You aren't with the police?"

"No, no. I am private. I investigate whatever anyone wants me to."

"I see." Duncan stepped forward, smiling.

"Well, I haven't seen him, but if I do I will let you know," he said grabbing him by the arm and putting his coat in his hands. Then Moses was being pushed back the way he came and was out on the front step before he could get his coat on.

"Wait," he said, putting his foot in the door as Henry Duncan attempted to close it.

"What is it?"

"You were expecting him?" Moses said. The man pursed his lips and opened his mouth, then closed it.

"Did he call you?" Moses asked.

"I thought you were him when I saw your lights. I noticed his car there an hour ago and thought he was getting dropped off."

"Where is he?" Moses asked.

"I don't know."

Moses pulled his foot back, and Henry Duncan nodded once and closed the door. The bolt clanged as it slammed home on the other side. Moses put his coat on as he walked away. He pulled his cell phone from his pocket and dialed Fred Dunsmore as he went up the walkway. The call connected, ringing through the speaker of his phone. Once. Then again. A flash of light caught his eye. He turned towards it. It was faint like a lightening bug, but it couldn't be, it was December. He stepped off the path toward the light and sank up to mid-calf in the snow. A few laborious steps later and the light had grown to the size of a credit card. Then it went dark. He hit redial on his phone. The light flashed again directly below him. He knelt and brushed the snow away from the light, revealing a cell phone with Moses' number flashing across the display. He checked his position in relation to the house and the street. He was maybe fifteen feet to where Fred was parked, right in line with the western side of the house. He could make out tracks leading to the car, then passing near where the cell phone had been, and around the side of the house.

Moses inspected the tracks. It was hard to tell, but it looked like there was more than one pair. He stuck the phones into his pocket and followed the trail around the house. If Fred had gone this way, then Moses was going to find him and whoever was following him.

* * *

Raif Rakić pulled the door shut behind him as he left his mother's house. He jumped into his police cruiser, spinning the tires on a patch of ice as he backed out of the driveway. He was down the street, smoking a cigarette, and barely hearing the radio traffic on the police band as he thought about his cousin and, invariably, his sister.

There was a light rain on the day she died, he remembered. The morning was cool and the rain spit on their three faces as they held hands. Raif would have to journey further away from the apartment complex after he escorted his cousin, Šejla, and his sister, Lejla, to the elementary school two blocks away. Šejla and her father had moved in that summer after the war started. Her father was his mother's brother. There were hushed conversations about the location of Šejla's mother, but Raif had not pieced together where she was yet. It was before his father and uncle were conscripted. A terrible day.

He always held Šejla and Lejla's hands on the way to school. Šejla was nine and Lejla only seven. He remembered Šejla going on about a math assignment and how excited she was to show it on the board if she were called on. He remembered Lejla quiet and smiling, blonde hair thick and wavy under her wool hat. Swinging her slight weight on his arm as they waited in a crowd on the curb to see if the street was clear of snipers before they crossed.

Then the crowd moved forward and they followed. Šejla was speaking of how she would solve the problem in front of the class if she were called on and Raif was thinking only of the moving people and to keep moving, keep moving.

He remembered not comprehending what was happening as the street erupted, sending people tumbling through the air. The sound seemed to come a moment late. The blast sent him backwards. He was still holding Šejla's hand as they got to their feet.

The normalcy of the street was gone as those that could ran in all directions away from the inevitable next mortar. That was when he saw her blonde hair and her lying in the street, tendrils of blood already mingling with rainwater.

"Lejla!" he remembered Šejla shouted as she pulled away from him. He raced after her and caught Šejla just as she was turning Lejla over. Šejla screamed at the sight of Lejla. She was dead. Her wool hat was gone, replaced by the gaping absence of her skull, dull-red against her shining blonde hair. He let go of Šejla and threw Lejla over his shoulder, feeling her arms dangle down his back limply. Then he grabbed Šejla's hand and bolted for the opposite side of the street and the safety of the buildings there.

They made it to the opposite side and no mortar fell. One mortar had taken his sister from him. One soldier had picked that moment to scatter innocent people like ants by launching hundreds of pounds of explosives down upon them from afar.

Raif remembered running the two blocks to the school with tears running down his face, the small weight of his sister on his shoulder and his cousin Šejla sobbing next to him. He had stood just inside the entrance to the school and wouldn't let go of his sister until his mother arrived.

A hole began to spread through their family that day. A hole that would swallow his father and nearly ruin his mother. It wasn't much later that the men of his family were taken to the front to fight, leaving him, barely a teenager, and his mother alone with young Šejla to survive. Together he and his mother had kept Šejla alive, the family alive.

He had gotten a uniform at the jail to release her into the alley so he could take her home. He made up some bullshit about it being a sensitive matter and his friend had taken the hint and made the arrangement. Once in the car, he told her she could not see Fred Dunsmore again. His words were met with crossed arms and silence. Silence that dominated the drive to his mother's house, but once inside, Šejla had blown up on him. She told him that she didn't need help and that he was going to screw this up for her.

"You don't need my help when you are rotting in a jail cell? Have you been to county, Šejla? Are you going to take care of Fred when he is old and using a walker?" he had screamed at her.

"I love him."

That had made Rakić see red. This relationship was doomed and it was going to jeopardize her future. Falling in love with an older married man was not a luxury that Rakić could allow for his younger cousin. He hadn't kept her alive this long to let her waste her life on someone else's midlife crisis.

"You are a fool," he had said.

His mother had tried to calm them both, taking Šejla into her arms. Rakić hated what he had said and when his mother had mouthed the word "go" to him over Šejla's shoulder, he had. Still angry, he left in his car, speeding onto the interstate. He rolled down the window, blowing smoke into the cold night air. It started to snow and he flicked the wipers on.

Rakić drove around for another hour before he got the call. It was a potential homicide. Rakić suppressed his personal thoughts as he flipped on the lights and siren. The downtown city lights were a blur as he raced down the interstate on his way to the scene.

Chapter 7

Raif Rakić knelt on the frozen street next to the naked girl. Her face was turned toward him, one of her green eyes open, empty. The other had swollen shut back when she was alive. She was lying on her stomach, her left arm stretched out perpendicular to her body and her right arm folded in on itself like she was holding a football or a doll. He removed his winter glove and replaced it with one made of latex. Rakić felt her cheek. It was hard, frozen solid. He put his finger to her lips, but they were stuck in place. He closed his eyes for a moment, then stood up and walked around the other side of her frozen body. He glanced away from her, down the street blocked by police cruisers and emergency vehicles. It was a side street near downtown, just off a main drag. The houses up and down the block were lit up with faces peeking out of windows. How long did it take for a body to freeze solid? Was she dead when she was left here, naked and cold? Or had she been alive and died here?

"How long has she been here?" Rakić said, putting voice to the silent question hanging in the air.

"Hard to tell. A nurse on her way home from the hospital found her. Almost ran her over. Thought she was a snowdrift. Not too many other people around this time of night." The man speaking was a young uniformed officer. Rakić thought he'd been on the Des Moines force for a few years. Hansen might be his name.

"She was working, too," Rakić said.

"You think so? Why do you say that?" the young cop asked.

"Look where we are. Busted eye. The makeup. The hair. She was working."

The young cop bent over for a closer look. "I guess that makes sense. What happened? Guy didn't want to pay?"

"I don't know. Who doesn't pay up this time of year?" Rakić asked.

Rakić slowly walked around the girl again. They were in the middle of the block on a small incline. In one direction, the street descended toward the river. The other direction led to downtown.

"Maybe the bastard was just done with her. On his way home, maybe?" Rakić asked. Rakić looked at the houses with their darkened doors like gaping mouths in an expressionist painting from a hundred years ago. *Where was the painter from? Denmark? What a thought.* The painter didn't matter. The houses were there. The girl and the painter were gone, but the murderer was still alive, and so was he. The relatively peaceful, low conversations of the police and forensic teams were replaced by more excited murmurings. The gawkers had shown up. Cop scanner junkies, reporters, and neighbors. Maybe the bastard was one of them, watching right now.

"Anything on her?" Rakić asked Hansen.

"Nothing so far. We pulled up, closed the block off and waited for you guys to show up. Nothing has moved."

A forensic tech was snapping pictures of the girl, the flash going off in a staccato of blinding light. She stopped and looked into the view screen and flipped through the digital pictures. She had one of those names that always escaped him. He decided to go for it.

"You got what you need, Mckenzie?" She looked up from the camera and nodded.

"It's Makayla. Jesus, Raif."

"Sorry. Let's see if she's lying on anything," Rakić said as he knelt down and motioned for Hansen to help him. Rakić grabbed her around the ankles and Hansen gripped her under the shoulders. She didn't budge.

"Shit," Hansen said and fell back, losing his grip on the body.

"She's frozen into the damn street." Rakić sat down with her feet between his legs. The heat from her body had melted the snow and then had refrozen, bonding her to the street. Rakić had a sudden pit in his stomach. She had been alive, maybe. Then he noticed her feet. The soles were raw and bloody. He felt them with his latex covered finger. *Had she walked here? Had she been beaten up and then walked here in the sub-zero temps, become disoriented and lost her way, too weak or too scared to ask for help, and just curled up here on the street and died?*

Rakić stood up and searched her body again, his thoughts focused solely on what had killed her. He inspected her hair looking for any sign of a wound. Nothing. He checked for bruising on her neck and mouth. Not strangled. *What then? Frozen to death?* Then he noticed something on the back of her neck. It was a large red dot, like she had been stung by a bee or wasp, but larger.

"Hansen. What is this?" He pointed to the mark. Hansen came over and looked.

"Not sure. A needle mark. On the junk, maybe?" Hansen said.

Rakić leaned back on his haunches. "No, it's not a track mark. But maybe a needle. Come on, we can't leave her frozen to the ground." Rakić stood up and walked over to the first house and knocked on the door. A man in his fifties answered.

"Can I help you, officer?"

"Yeah. Do you have a portable heater?"

"Yes, I do. But what for? You guys can come inside to warm up."

Rakić thought about the girl walking down the street barefoot and cold and he tried to believe that this man would offer the dead girl the same sanctuary.

"She's frozen solid."

"Jesus. How long do you think she's been there?" the resident asked.

Rakić turned to the other cop. "Hansen, right? Take care of it, will ya?" And Rakić turned back to the street and the frozen girl. On his way there, Rakić stopped at his car, opened the trunk, and pulled out a plastic package. He walked between the cars with their flashing lights, back to the girl. He tore the plastic away and unfolded the shiny emergency blanket and spread it over her body. It dropped over her, covering her face. Rakić didn't like that. He pulled it down under her chin and tucked the fold into the stiff fingers of her right hand. He stood up and turned his back to her and walked over to the medical examiner who was leaning against the ambulance, talking to the driver.

"Hey, Terry," Rakić said. "I need this fast. I'm not sure it's a murder, but we need to get out in front and make sure. Signs of violence, but not sure on cause of death. Can't be sure yet anyway."

"Why not?" Terry had a small tight smile on his mouth. He was a prick, but he was good at what he did.

"She's stuck to the ground. Frozen."

"Shit. Prosticicle." The driver laughed. Rakić nodded twice, looking at his feet. Violence erupted inside his chest. This girl didn't deserve to have her death so crudely described. Control gone, he threw his right hand at the ambulance as hard as he could. His fist connected with the window of the back door, causing cracks to spider-web through the glass. The two men stood with their mouths open as Rakić shook his hand once.

"Like I said, we can't be sure. But the girl—" Rakić paused and stared at each of the men for a second. "The girl is frozen to the street. And she might not have been murdered. But there is a mark on her neck. Could be nothing. But I'd like to know what it is. And your full analysis as soon as possible."

"Jesus, Raif. Just say so."

"I did say so. Now do your fucking job." Rakić spun on his heel and walked back the short distance to the girl. Hansen had fired up a kerosene heater and was working to warm up the street. Rakić adjusted the angle of the heater, careful not to get too close to the body. Then Terry came over with the ambulance driver and started setting up a tent. They were able to arrange it around the body to effectively trap the warm air from the heater. It took close to an hour for the street to thaw enough to release her.

* * *

Moses had followed the trail behind Henry Duncan's house down a valley, through light woods, to a paved bike trail made on an abandoned railroad bed. The snowbound trail ran almost parallel with the Duncan house. It was harder to see down here under the tree limbs, as they blocked most of the moonlight, but he was able to follow the trail and was confident that Fred Dunsmore had stayed on the path.

His boots made a crunching sound on the frozen tracks which became slippery as the moon disappeared behind clouds and the snow began to fall. A few minutes later, he stopped where it looked like Dunsmore and his pursuer had left the main path. It was a small offshoot, a hiking trail or a game trail leading deeper into the woods that grew close to the river. The snow was fresh and unsullied except for the recent footprints. Moses glanced back and calculated how far he was from the barely-visible streetlight on Duncan's street. He thought he had gone about four hundred yards as he turned and plunged off the path and onto the trail.

He had gone twenty feet when he thought he heard something. He paused and waited. The sound didn't repeat, so he continued on, stuffing his hands into his pockets and wishing for a flashlight and a pair of gloves. A bare outline of the trail was all he could see this deep into the forest, but whoever he was following had trampled the dead, dried-out underbrush, giving him easy signposts to follow.

An engine revving split the silence, loud and urgent, and then it grew softer, idling. *It could be an off-road motorcycle.* Then the engine roared again. *No, definitely not a motorcycle or a snowmobile.* The sound grew loud and stayed loud. He counted the seconds. When he reached sixty, the engine idled again, and then it went silent. He started in the direction of the sound.

Moses moved as quickly as his footing would let him. Off the trail now, he weaved around fallen branches and hopped over brushy mounds. He paused to catch his breath. A faint trail was to his right in the direction of the engine and, without hesitation, he followed it toward the sound's origin.

Ahead, he could see fresh tracks through a deep snowdrift. He crouched and waited in the darkness. He blew on his hands, his breath a stream of white fog. His noticed he could see further now as his eyes had adjusted enough to the lack of light. From his vantage, he could see twenty feet down the trail before it disappeared behind the exposed roots of a fallen tree the diameter of a Volkswagen.

Moses caught his breath. A silhouette had appeared on the trail. It hadn't been there a moment before, but now it was and it was moving toward him. Panic gripped Moses as he finally felt the full brunt of fear at being alone in this desolate place so close to the river and the city full of people. The shape came into focus. It was a man carrying something across his shoulder. He seemed to glide upon the trail toward Moses. Moses smelled something. It was a musky, sweet smell, touched by a hint of decay. Then he heard the low rumble next to him, and he turned and saw a large black canine staring at him with jaws slightly opened, revealing jagged teeth. The time to run had passed.

"What is it?" The man from the trail asked.

Moses rose to his feet. "It's me."

The man calmly put down the large canvas bag that he was carrying. "That's too bad. I thought you were Elvis." The man's voice was deep and friendly.

"Elvis is dead."

"What? Oh. The singer. Yes." The man chuckled.

"What are you doing out here?" Moses asked.

"Are you police?"

"What are you doing out here?" Moses asked again.

The man stepped closer and leaned against a small tree as he fished in his pocket.

"Just cigarettes." The man waved, pulling a small package out of his pocket. The dog circled over to the man and sat next to him, its ghostly eyes never leaving Moses.

"You ask me what I am doing out here, but you are the one who is in the wrong place," the man said. He stuck a cigarette in his mouth, the flame from the lighter flickering over his face as he lit the smoke. Dark eyes glittered, then were gone, extinguished with the flame, back to darkness deeper than before.

"I was looking for a friend. He was supposed to meet me."

"Out here?" The man gestured with the cigarette.

"Yeah, maybe you've seen him. Tall, good looking. Dead, I'm guessing," Moses said.

The man sucked on the cigarette, casting a glow on his face from the bright red cherry.

"I have seen no one, but maybe Elvis has."

"Your dog can talk?" Moses asked.

"No. But he can," he said, pointing behind Moses.

Moses turned in time to see a blur and then a flash of light, and he was on his back. He felt his mind screaming somewhere in the darkness to get up and run. He clawed his way up the slippery black inkwell of his consciousness until he was staring at a boot print in the snow. He shoved himself to his feet, swinging his fist wildly. His foot slipped and he fell to the ground. On all fours, he frantically craned his head, looking for his attackers, but no one was there. They were gone, and he was alone in the woods.

Chapter 8

Raif Rakić was still at the scene with the frozen girl when he got the call and made his way to the residence of Mr. Henry Duncan. He had to order some officers to remain behind to finish up. Normally he would have gotten some argument. Everyone wanted to be at the next scene. That was the way it was. But the guys cut him a break. His hand still hurt from the ambulance door. He looked down at it on the steering wheel. Two knuckles were swollen, but other than that, it had held up all right.

A marked police cruiser was sitting in the driveway of the Duncan house with the emergency lights off. It was the same with the ambulance. Dispatch had said that the person injured had asked for him by name. Rakić walked up to a cluster of uniformed police huddled together on the driveway. He recognized Hansen and a few other familiar faces. "What do we got?" he asked.

"Some guy says he knows you."

"I don't know anyone that lives in this neighborhood," Rakić shot back.

The tension from the previous scene had evaporated. No one gave him a sideways look, even if by now the whole cop community had probably heard about his blowup.

"I do. Me and the governor are buddies," one of the men joked. The men chuckled, one of them coughing in the cold.

"He's inside," Hansen said.

"Thanks."

Rakić left the men to their bull session and made his way to the front door. He paused at the imposing wooden portal and then pushed his way inside. There was another uniformed police officer standing inside the door, talking with a well-dressed civilian.

"Are you the owner of the house, sir?" Rakić asked him.

"Yes, I'm Henry Duncan. The man you want to talk to is in the study. Let me show you."

The man led him deeper into the house until they were in a room with a fireplace. A man was sitting in an overstuffed chair next to the fireplace, wrapped in a blanket, being tended to by a paramedic. It was the private detective from the cabin.

"Rakić," he said.

"Mr. Winter. What happened?" Rakić said, gesturing at the bandage on his cheek.

"I think someone is trying to kill or has killed Fred Dunsmore."

"That's what he said when he pounded on my door," Henry Duncan said.

"And you found him like this?" Rakić asked, turning to Duncan.

"Yes."

"Mr. Winter, what happened to your face?" Rakić asked.

"I got hit."

"By what?"

Moses shook his head and then grabbed his head in pain.

"Take it easy. Why do you think someone is trying to kill Dunsmore?"

Moses went through the story of the phone call with Fred and the planned meeting at the address of Henry Duncan, and the subsequent encounter in the woods with the strange man and dog.

"So you know Duncan?" Rakić asked.

"No, I've never met him until tonight," Henry Duncan chimed in.

"He's right," Moses said.

"So you followed the tracks out to the forest by yourself?"

"Yeah, I saw his phone when I tried to call it and then the tracks."

"Where is it now?" Rakić asked.

Moses tilted his head to the side and felt his pockets. "It's gone. They must have taken it."

Rakić paced to the mantle, spreading his fingers in front of the fire. He removed a notebook and pen from an inner coat pocket. He opened the notebook to an empty page.

"Do you have your phone?" Rakić asked, keeping his back to Moses.

A pause then, "Yes, I still have mine."

Rakić scribbled the first word that came to mind on the page and then underlined it twice. The word was milk. He used this technique sometimes when he thought someone was lying to him. Sometimes the act of writing something down was enough to push the interviewee to talk. "And where did you get attacked?"

"Off the path, close to the river."

"When was this?"

"About an hour ago."

"How many?"

"Two, at least. And a dog."

"What kind of dog?" Rakić asked, turning toward Moses now. He absently flipped the notebook shut and stuffed it back in his pocket.

Moses turned pale and a tremor went through his body. "It was some monster of a dog. I couldn't really see it, but I could feel it beside me." Rakić nodded. Moses turned to him with wide eyes. "And you could smell it. The stench rolled off it in waves." Rakić leaned back and coughed. He felt a quick shiver run through his own body causing him to drop the pen in his hand. He bent quickly to retrieve it.

"One was named Elvis. The other called him Elvis anyway," Moses said.

"Elvis? What did he look like?" Rakić asked.

"I didn't see him. He hit me before I could get a look at him."

"And the other man again. What did he look like?"

"It was dark. But I think he had dark eyes, and he sounded older, raspy."

Rakić looked back to his notebook. He jotted down a few words. There was an Elvis he knew from the neighborhood. He was early twenties, barely old enough to remember the old world. The other man fit the description of most men he knew.

"Did you see anyone leave back this way?" Rakić looked at Duncan.

"No. I didn't see or hear anything. Fred's car is gone now, but I don't know who took it," Duncan said.

"Mr. Duncan, do you have any idea why Dunsmore would meet here?"

"We do business here sometimes, but he hadn't called to set anything up," Duncan said.

"What kind of business is Dunsmore in, if you don't mind me asking?"

"He is in the bar supply business. Other than that, I can't tell you much more due to attorney-client confidentiality," Duncan said.

"He sounded worried when I talked to him," Moses said.

"About what?" Rakić asked.

"He wanted to tell me something about his wife I think, but I don't know what it was," Moses said.

"Okay. I'm going to go over and check out the scene. Why don't you stay here until I get back?" Rakić asked.

"I'll go with you," Moses said, pushing off the chair.

Moses seemed to wobble for a moment, but then straightened up. *He's tough to take a shot like that and still be going*, Rakić thought.

"Okay. I'll see where K-9's at." Rakić walked out of the room with Moses and Duncan following him. He navigated his way back to the front door; the uniformed officer was still there.

"We got K-9 on the way?" Rakić asked.

"They got a drug call on the interstate, so they are going to be a while."

"Okay, just you and me, Moses. What do you say we get someone to carry a flashlight for us?" Rakić smiled.

"Hansen!" Rakić yelled as he stepped out the front door.

"Agent Rakić?"

"Get your gear. We are going to check out the scene."

Rakić let Moses and the police officer guide him down the bank to the trail and deeper into the gloomy woods. They plunged off the path and into the tangle of the forest, the beam of light from the flashlight bouncing with the steps of the officer, illuminating the swirling snow.

"Up here is where I started to hear the chainsaw."

"Chainsaw?"

"Yeah, I think it was a chainsaw. Nothing else makes sense," Moses said.

"Hmm. Yeah, I see what you mean," Rakić said. *Chainsaws? Hellhounds? Strange ghosts in the night? Was Moses' head injury worse than it looked?* His description of events certainly felt real in their detail, but it was a lot to take in.

"Then I found this other trail over here, after it got too thick going that way," Moses said. Moses' pace quickened and he ventured further ahead, at the edge of the light.

"Then I woke up here," Moses said, pointing to a bloody patch of snow, quickly filling in with fresh powder.

"Stand back," Rakić said as he pushed past Hansen. "Where were they standing when you saw them?"

"One was coming down this path here. The other one must have come up behind me," Moses said.

Rakić walked across the path and inspected the tracks. He found a set of boot tracks and dog tracks and an area that looked more packed down than the rest. Moses' story seemed to be holding up.

"Here?" Rakić called to Moses.

"Yeah. He leaned against the tree and lit a smoke." Rakić nodded and knelt with his flashlight, searching.

"Here we go," he said as he picked up a cigarette butt with his gloved hand and slipped it into an evidence baggy he pulled from his pocket. He stood up and started down toward the river when he saw something on the side of the trail. He toed at it with his boot and rolled it onto the trail. He turned the light on it. More like a small tree instead of a club. It was four feet long or so and narrowed to a nice handle. There was a dark splotch on the business end. He bent down and fingered it. It was sticky. He looked up at Moses.

"You're a tough bastard, I'll give you that."

Rakić motioned and they continued down the trail. It wound around the felled tree and then they were next to the river. Rakić looked out over the frozen water. He could hear the water babbling downstream, but in this part the river was frozen solid. It could be the dam, but it wasn't close enough. Maybe a hole in the ice nearby.

"Where is Dunsmore?" Rakić asked.

"I don't know. Maybe they took him with them?" Moses replied.

Rakić walked around the trunk of the tree again, kneeling down. There had definitely been some traffic here tonight, but no sign of blood, or a body, or anything for that matter, other than all of these tracks.

"We'll get the forensics in and figure out which boots are which. And maybe a dog if we ever get that lucky. Hansen, flag the blood so we don't lose it with this snow," Rakić said.

Made Safe

    What a night. First, a girl found frozen to the street and now his cousin's lover missing, last heard from by a private eye who was employed by the missing man's jealous wife. Rakić glanced at Moses, who was kneeling next to the riverbank. There was something about him. Something in his face made him feel like he could trust Moses. In the old world, his bullshit detector had served him well. The stakes were higher then. He could trust very few. Usually family, but even then, they still had to be vouched for. He looked up at the sky as the moon passed through a gap in the clouds. The snow had stopped, but he felt the cold seep through the layers of his clothes. It was going to be a bitter night.

Chapter 9

Moses left Raif Rakić with the understanding that Rakić would let him know if they found anything new. Moses had recovered enough to drive himself. The snow had tapered off and the streets were fairly clear as he drove to 35th Street, past his office and then under the freeway.

The man that had spoken to him out there by the river had been strangely familiar. He couldn't pin down what it was, but his voice and inflections reminded him of someone. He tried to remember anything he could before he got hit, some clue to what had happened to Fred Dunsmore, if he had really even been out there. What kind of dog was that? It wasn't like any dog he'd ever seen. A mix? He hadn't been much for dogs. He had one growing up, a little dog that barked a lot. The dog tonight had to weigh over a hundred pounds. It was dark and scary, not much to go on. The man had been very comfortable out there. The dark and cold seemed to be his native element. The other man too. He called him Elvis. That was something. The man that hit him was Elvis. Find Elvis, someone he hadn't even glimpsed.

He pulled Dunsmore's phone out of his pocket and looked at the display. He swiped his finger to unlock the phone, but was blocked by a pass code screen. He pulled over to the side of the road and flicked on the overhead lamp. Tilting the phone under the light he saw smudges where fingers had repeatedly tapped. He tried the first combo. 1-2-3-4. The screen shook as it rejected the numbers. He tried the reverse and was in. He navigated to the call log and thumbed through the list. He found his number and then two numbers that were dialed afterward. One was labeled. It was Henry Duncan's. So he wasn't telling the whole truth, but that didn't surprise him. The last number wasn't labeled. He pulled his Jeep into a driveway and spun the tires as he turned the vehicle around. He needed to find the last person Dunsmore had dialed before he disappeared.

* * *

Moses sat in his office on 35th and Rollins reading through an online search of phone numbers. It was one of his favorite applications. He paid a flat monthly fee and could look up as many phone numbers as he needed. It came in handy with infidelity cases and times like now. The phone number was registered to a convenience store as part of their inventory of pay–per-minute disposable phones. He tried another application he used to double-check the results and confirmed the dead end. If he was to believe the information, the phone was still sitting on a shelf in a New Mexico gas station. Moses leaned back in his chair. It had either been stolen or the inventory was off. He took Dunsmore's phone off his desk and turned on the display. He entered the unlock code and navigated to call history. He tapped on the last number in the call history. The phone rang. Two, three, four times, and then it went to voicemail. The current owner had not setup the voicemail message. He listened for a moment to the generic voice and then hung up the phone.

He redialed again, this time the phone rang once and a voice answered. "Yes?"

The voice on the phone was unmistakably feminine. Moses' voice caught in his throat. He shifted the phone to his other hand and grabbed a pen on his desk.

"Yes, hello," he said, his mind fumbling for a good line.

"Who is this?" she asked.

"Do you know this number?"

"Yes, I know the number," she said.

"Oh, good. I've been calling all the numbers on this phone I found, trying to figure out who it belongs to," Moses said. "Can you get it back to the owner?"

There was a long pause and then. "Yes. Meet me in an hour."

"Sure, where is good for you?" Moses asked.

"At the Zmaj. Do you know it?"

"No, I don't. What is that?" Moses asked.

"It's a bar. Ask for Majka."

She gave him the address and he scribbled it down. It was in the western suburbs. He said goodbye and tapped his hand on the desk and hopped up. Not much time, but he needed to stop at home first.

* * *

It was near midnight on Friday night, the day after the encounter at the cabin, when Moses arrived at the Zmaj. The Zmaj shared a strip mall with a Chinese restaurant and a hair salon. The bar was lit up in red and green neon above the heads of about twenty people standing in the cold waiting to get inside. Two big bouncers wearing black leather coats and slicked-back hair stood by the blacked-out glass door. Moses had been watching the bar for twenty minutes. In that time, he had seen half a dozen women bypass the line. There had been no signal or indication to the bouncers that he could see. They seemed to melt through the line and then the door opened for them and they were gone inside, leaving the others behind to wait.

Moses flicked his cigarette into a snowy patch of parking lot as he got out of his Jeep and started walking toward the strip mall. He navigated through the people and pushed through the door to the Chinese place. It was mostly deserted at this hour, but an old lady was behind the register.

"Order?" she asked smiling.

"Yeah. Mongolian beef and chicken fried rice," Moses said, pulling out his cash. He paid the lady, thanked her, and went to the glass door to wait for his food. A minute later, the lady brought him his food and he thanked her again. He pushed through the line of people at the Zmaj, then circled around toward the front door of the bar. He stood next to the rope on the opposite side of the line and got the attention of a bouncer.

"Order," Moses said showing him the bag.

The man couldn't be more than twenty-five, about Moses' height, and reminded him of a tank. The bouncer walked over to the rope and stuck his flashlight in the bag, then shined the light in Moses' face.

"What order?"

"This order. Someone inside ordered food," Moses said, shifting to the side and stamping his feet.

"Who ordered?" the man asked.

Moses paused and fished around inside the bag for the receipt, stalling. He couldn't find it, and then he had an idea.

"Elvis," he said.

The man took a step back and went to the other bouncer. He was a taller guy, but they could have been brothers. They talked for a few seconds, and then the man turned and came back toward Moses.

"Okay." He unlatched the rope and guided Moses toward the door. "Take it up to the bar."

"Okay," Moses said as the guard opened the door, and he walked inside the Zmaj. Moses wasn't sure why he hadn't asked for Majka or gone the frontal route. If Elvis and his partner were here, which it certainly seemed they might be, he wanted to see them before they saw him.

It was dark and crowded and smelled of booze, sweat, perfume, and smoke. The sound system was blasting a beat, melting all other sound into its constant stream. Several high-top tables were littered with drinks and twenty-somethings. He pushed by the throng of people not lucky enough to have a proper table and made his way to the back where he could see the long bar.

It was three deep when he got there. Even the waitress station was clogged. Moses pushed his way around until he found a gap and then wedged his way in. He set the food on the bar and tried to get the attention of one of the bartenders working the drinks.

"Hey!" he shouted when a bartender was close. The man leaned over and Moses gestured to the food. "Elvis," Moses said.

The man nodded and spun around, pulling out a bottle from the well and pouring and mixing a drink. Then he picked up a phone by the register and punched a button. He said a few words that Moses couldn't hear and then hung up.

"One minute," the man said and went on pouring drinks.

Moses nodded and turned around to take in the scene. He could see the dance floor now, filled with trendy men and women. Some were dancing in groups, others by themselves. The energy of the music and the room was tangible, breathing new energy into Moses' tired body. He unzipped his coat as he glanced in the other direction. Three women were walking his way. They were all very young and wearing the requisite risqué uniform of the time.

Moses locked eyes with the first. She smiled and kept walking, her friend close behind. The last one was looking down and held her arms over her stomach, shuffling more than walking. When she passed, he noticed how short and skinny she was. Then he looked back the way they had come and was face-to-face with a woman. She was just under his height and had long black hair, curled at the ends. She was smiling and was leaning in to talk to him, so close he could smell her perfume and a faint whiff of tobacco on her breath.

"Food?" she asked.

"Yes."

"Follow me," she said. She turned and began walking toward the back. Moses grabbed the food and hurried after her. She was making her way through the crowd toward the dance floor, fitting through seams and gaps in the people that didn't seem possible. She twisted her hip or put her hand on an arm and she was through without missing a beat. Moses had to jostle a few people to keep up with her and one man shouted something at him. She paused and looked back. He caught up to her and she slid her hand into his and smiled.

"Keep up."

And then she was pulling him through the crowd to a side door and out into a hallway. He tripped a little, and she caught him and pushed him up against the wall.

"Easy, Cowboy," she said, staring at his lips.

"Sorry." He couldn't seem to catch his breath.

She leaned back, looked up, and smiled that smile again. "Don't apologize. Come on."

She paused for a moment, then turned down the dimly lit hallway. Moses followed, holding the Chinese food and feeling like he was past the point of no return. There was nothing that would stop him from following this woman wherever she went and that was okay with him.

"In here," she said and opened another door, waiting for him. When he got to her, she entered and he followed. Inside, there were three men sitting at a small table sharing a strange bottle of booze. It could have been vodka, but the bottle had odd lettering so strange that Moses couldn't pronounce it even in his head. They were talking loudly in what sounded like an Eastern European language. When they saw Moses, they fell silent, staring blankly. One of the men flicked his hand at the woman and said something in clipped phrases. She responded and gestured at Moses. They went back and forth for a few seconds and then Moses' female guide spoke to him in English.

"Who is the food for?" she asked.

"Elvis. He hasn't paid either," Moses said.

She turned to the man doing the talking and they spoke again at length about Moses and the food, he imagined. "Wait here, I will get him," she said and left out of the door they had come in.

The men looked at him and sipped their drinks. Moses took in the room, trying to act like a good deliveryman, tapping his foot impatiently. There were kegs and empty boxes stacked along one wall and an old computer on a small desk shoved into a corner. The men started talking again and Moses watched the man that had spoken to the woman. He was about Moses' age with deep creases around the eyes and mouth, like a perpetual frown. But his dark eyes were the opposite, always smiling.

"You want a drink?" one of the other men asked.

"Yes, have a drink," the main man said, smiling.

"On duty, otherwise I'd love to," Moses said.

"Come on. We have whiskey," the first one said.

"You said the magic words," Moses replied. The main man pushed out an empty chair and gestured for Moses to sit across from him.

Moses took the seat and put the food on the table. The second talker leaned in and smelled the food deeply and then made a comment in the foreign language. The main man laughed and slapped Moses on the back.

"Here you go," the main man said as he set a shot glass in front of Moses and retrieved a bottle of whiskey from a shelf behind him. The man poured out a shot for himself, Moses, and the two other men.

"What do we drink to?" Moses asked.

"What would you like to drink to?"

The main man put his hand on Moses' shoulder. Then the woman reappeared.

"What are you doing to my cowboy?" she shouted. The men roared with laughter. She swatted the main man's hand away and sat down on Moses' lap.

"Cowboy drinks to me," she said.

Moses held her close with one arm and reached for the shot with the other. "Absolutely," Moses said.

"To Majka then," the man said, raising his glass.

"Majka!" the others echoed.

Moses paused. *So, this is Majka,* he thought and raised his glass. "Majka," he said. They slammed the shots in unison. Moses reached forward and set his glass on the table, squeezing Majka in the process.

"Easy," she whispered, looking back at him from her perch. Her eyes widened. "What happened to your face?" she asked, pushing his hat back on his head, exposing the bruise that ran across his cheek.

Moses glanced at the main man before answering. Their eyes met for moment before the other man continued his conversation. "Nothing, I ran into tree. They're always jumping out at me," he said, flashing a grin.

An eyebrow twitched higher and her lips tightened. "Vahid, pay this man. I don't think Elvis is coming," Majka said to the man that had done the talking until now.

Vahid grunted and pulled out his wallet. "How much is it, Cowboy?" he asked.

"Let's call it twenty," Moses said. Vahid tossed a twenty and a five on the table for Moses. Moses leaned over and picked up the cash and tucked it away.

"Do you want to try something good?" Vahid asked him.

"Sure. What do you have?" Moses asked.

"It is a drink from my country."

He grabbed the strange bottle from the table and poured out shots. Moses put the glass to his nose. It smelled dangerous. Something else tickled his brain. The way Vahid spoke was familiar to Moses. He thought he could be Elvis' friend with the dog. He needed to keep this going in hopes that Elvis would show. Then he would know for sure that he had found his assailants.

"Is it sweet?" Moses asked.

"Not really," Majka said.

"Okay, what do we drink to?" Moses asked.

"To Elvis," Vahid said, smiling.

"Yes, to Elvis," Moses said.

In unison, they raised their glasses and shouted. "Elvis!"

The drink was strangely sweet at first and then the raw alcohol surged to the forefront. He coughed a bit and set the glass down. He wiped his mouth with his hand and then grinned up at Majka who had twisted in his lap to watch him.

"Not bad," he said, with a catch in his throat.

The table burst into laughter and they poured another shot.

"I have to get back to work," Moses said.

"Okay, okay," Vahid said, "but one more," and he refilled Moses' glass.

Majka got off of Moses' lap and said something to Vahid in their language, and he shrugged in response.

"He's a grown man," Vahid said in English.

Majka crossed her arms and stood next to Moses. "Come on. Let's go, Cowboy. I'll show you out."

Moses stood up. "Just this one," he said, grabbing the glass.

Majka snorted and said something else he couldn't understand.

"Your funeral," she said in English.

Then the door opened and everyone turned. "Someone looking for me?" the new man asked. He was young, maybe twenty, and tall, with a disturbing, blank face.

"Elvis, we were just drinking to you," Vahid said.

"And here is your food," said another.

"What food?" Elvis asked.

"He had delivery for you," Vahid said, pointing at Moses.

Moses put the glass down, pushed his chair in, and picked up the food. "Here you go. Mongolian beef and chicken fried rice."

Elvis looked at him, and then the food. "I didn't order any food." Elvis looked back at Moses. "You think this guy is a delivery man for Chinese food?" Elvis asked.

Vahid paused and looked over at Moses and then back at Elvis.

"I just started," Moses said.

Elvis was still blocking the doorway and Majka was behind Moses. Everyone else was still sitting. Moses felt the air shift in the room. Sucked out was the merriment of a moment ago, replaced now with tense silence as faces drew tight and eyes narrowed. Moses glanced back one last time at Vahid, who was rising unsteadily to his feet.

"Listen guys, I just wanted to deliver this—" Moses said as he launched the bag of food at Elvis' head. Elvis ducked and Moses pushed him into the wall, knocking him to the floor. In a flash, Moses was past him into the hallway. The bar was too crowded, too easy to catch him in a scrum, he thought as he turned toward the back. He saw a red exit sign and made for it.

"Stop!" Majka shrieked. Moses kept running. "Stop, Cowboy!" Majka screamed again.

Moses was at the door and looked back. He could see Majka running after him and then he was outside on the backside of the strip mall. He sprinted down the long building and then down the side and was in the front parking lot again. The bouncers were still at the door, but now several other men were outside and scanning the lot. Moses stood behind an SUV for a minute catching his breath. Through the windshield of the car, he saw Vahid and Elvis burst through the front door of the bar. They were fanning out into the lot, cutting him off from his car. Stuffing his hands in his pockets, he turned and started walking the other direction. He was next to an office building further up the hill when he hurdled a snow bank and cut out to the street and started to cross. Down the hill, he saw a black sedan pulling out of the lot of the Zmaj, coming his way.

He started to run. *I can beat the car.* Then he stumbled. He righted himself, but then he stumbled again, barely catching himself. Disorganized thoughts crowded his mind as he struggled to concentrate on reaching the median. Slowed down to barely a jog now, the car closed in. As he approached the median, he felt the street slide out from under him, no longer where his feet expected it. He pitched forward in a desperate attempt to avoid the oncoming car. Smashing his ribs on the jutting, dirty snowbank, he scrambled out of the street as the car flew past. Moses rolled over to watch as the taillights of the car lit up and the car started backing towards him. Struggling like his body was caught in something gooey, Moses fought his way to his feet as the car slid to a stop next to him.

The driver's side door flew open. "Cowboy!"

It was Majka. Moses started laughing. "I can't get rid of you!" he said.

"No, you can't, Cowboy. Get in!" She shouted back from the driver's side of the car. Moses leaned on the car and looked inside. She was alone. "Get in," she said, scooting over to the passenger side.

"Where are we going?"

"My place. You drive."

"What about Elvis and Vahid?"

"Don't worry about them."

Moses looked back at the Zmaj and then down at Majka. He knew this was a bad idea, but he needed to get off the street. "What about my car?"

"We'll get it tomorrow," she said.

"You better drive, I'm not feeling so good," Moses said, using the car to steady himself. She slid behind the wheel and he got in the passenger side.

"I was afraid of that," Majka said, putting her hand on his neck and giving him a concerned look as they sped off toward the glowing green stoplights of the intersection ahead. Moses fought the slow ebb of his consciousness that he vaguely realized had started inside the Zmaj. But he didn't care now as he drifted into oblivion, Majka's warm hand stroking his neck.

Chapter 10

Raif Rakić needed to check on Šejla. She had been out of jail for a few hours now, but she worried him. She wasn't being herself. He had left the scene after it was secured. Nothing could be done there until daylight. He parked his car in his mother's driveway and walked up the steps to the entry. He pushed through the unlocked door and into the parlor.

"*Mother*," Rakić called in his native tongue.

His mother entered the living room from the kitchen and offered him her cheek. He kissed her and squeezed her shoulders.

"*Hello, my dear boy*," she responded in the same language.

"*Where is Šejla?*"

"I am here," she said in English from the kitchen.

Rakić's mother frowned in her direction and turned back to him. "*Have you eaten?*"

He slapped his stomach and shook his head. "*No, Mother, but I can't stay long. Important case. I came to check on her*," he said with a nod toward the kitchen. "How is she?"

Rakić's mother shrugged. "*The same. She talks only of this Freddy and how she hates his wife.*" She frowned again. "*She should be with a man her own age.*"

Rakić nodded and then kissed his mother on the forehead, left her, and went to the kitchen.

"Šejla," he said.

She was sitting at a small round table smoking a cigarette. "Raif," she said.

"How are you?" he said, in English now.

"I am fine. I can't get ahold of Freddy. He left the hospital. Did you know that?"

Rakić paused, pulled out a chair, and sat across from her. "Yes, I wanted to talk to you about that."

"What is it?" She leaned forward. "Did that bitch get to him?"

Rakić shook his head. Then he paused, thinking. "Why would you say that?" Rakić asked.

"Why would I say what?"

"You think that he is in danger from his wife?"

"She almost killed him," she responded.

"Good point, but she is in jail."

Šejla sighed and took a drag on her smoke. Rakić felt something strange about her, something he wasn't seeing. Was she relieved? That would make sense; Mrs. Dunsmore had assaulted her. But there was something else dancing on the edge of his thoughts.

"Fred is missing," he said.

"I know, I can't reach him."

"No, listen. We think he may have been attacked."

Šejla's eyes widened mid-inhale as she choked, coughing up puffs of smoke. Rakić stood and slammed her on the back a few times. She started breathing easier and pushed his hand away.

"Who?" she asked.

"We aren't sure," Rakić said sitting down. "Do you know something?" Rakić asked. Šejla went back to smoking her cigarette and shook her head. "I know Fred means something to you," he said. Šejla nodded.

"I will find him and clear this all up. Don't worry," he said, putting his hand on hers. "Now get some rest."

He stood and buttoned his coat and then glanced around the kitchen. "*And help your aunt a little. She is helping you,*" he said, in Bosnian now.

Šejla nodded and put out her cigarette. She stood and folded her arms over her chest. "*Find him for me,*" she said in Bosnian.

He nodded and squeezed her arm. He said goodbye to his mother and kissed her on the way out, and then he was in his car and back on the street. The sky was starting to brighten and he felt better knowing that his family was okay. He hoped Fred Dunsmore was alive somewhere, for Šejla's sake. Her worried eyes burned in his mind and looked at him from the rearview mirror as he drove the night streets.

*　*　*

Moses awoke to the slamming of a car trunk. His mind was foggy and he needed a moment to remember. It came to him. The memory of the men in the back of the strange bar in the suburbs and the woman who had helped him get away. He was in her car, Majka's car, in what looked like an underground parking garage. Craning his neck, he was able to see Majka walking toward him between her car and the one next to it. Smiling, she leaned over and tapped on the glass.

Moses waved her back and opened the car door. "Where are we?" he asked.

"My place, come on." She practically dragged him from the car, led him to the elevator, and punched the button. When the doors opened, Majka pulled him inside and Moses leaned into the corner. She followed him, laying her head on his shoulder as they rode to the top.

Moses had seen Elvis and hadn't been able to do anything about it, but now, at least, he knew what he looked like. He couldn't be certain, but he thought that Vahid was the other man who had attacked him, the dog owner. And Majka, this woman who was so friendly, what did she have to do with this? They all knew each other, worked together, and she was connected to Fred Dunsmore somehow.

The door opened and Majka pulled him out and down the hall. One of the doors opened and a girl stuck her head out and said something to Majka in the neighborhood of Russian. Majka responded sharply and the girl shut the door. The encounter with the girl topped off a night that felt like it had taken place in Central Europe, not Des Moines. Majka led him further down the hall and stopped at 810.

"This is us," she said, unlocking the door. "Cheer up, Cowboy," she said, smiling. She always seemed to be smiling. She pushed the door in and was dragging Moses after her again. The space was large and open. The kitchen was to the right, resplendent with granite counters and stainless steel appliances. She led him down a hall to a bedroom with exposed brick and a large king-sized bed, nestled between two corner windows. The view matched, overlooking the frozen river and the ballpark next to it with its marquee shining brightly against the dark river.

"This will make you feel better," she said, jumping on the bed and laughing.

Moses stood there looking at her. She was gorgeous. Her legs were long and smooth, reflecting the glimmer of the ballpark's neon lights. What was she doing? What was her part in this? He wasn't going to let her make him a fool.

"Come here," she said as she kicked her shoes off and shrugged out of her coat.

He walked forward and stood in front of her. There was no doubt in his mind that she knew something. *She probably had set up Fred. Why was he still here with her?*

"Sit down," she said and he did. She straddled him, pulling at his coat. "Relax." His mind was still hazy. Anything she said, he did. Answers would have to wait.

* * *

Moses was lying on the bed with Majka next to him facing away, nestled into his body. He raised his head and looked down at her face.

"You awake?" he asked.

"No," she said and pulled the blanket up to her chin and pushed back into him. He looked down at her and then reached to the floor for his coat. He fished in the pocket, pulling out a cell phone.

"I was going to give this to you," Moses said.

"What?" she asked, not opening her eyes.

"This phone," Moses said.

She groaned and pulled the blanket over her head. She pulled the cover down to her nose and cracked one eye open and looked back up at him.

"What fucking phone?" she asked.

The way she said fuck made his skin tingle. Moses unlocked the phone and redialed the last number. The phone lit up and started ringing. A moment passed and then a dance beat from a pop song began playing from the kitchen.

Majka jumped out of bed naked and dashed to the kitchen to find the source of the music. Moses propped himself up on the pillows and watched. She leaned over the island counter and fished inside her handbag and pulled out her phone.

"Hello?" she said.

Moses hit cancel on the phone. Majka turned to face him. She tossed her phone on the counter and walked slowly back to the bed, standing over Moses. "You were the one from earlier?"

"Yes."

"Why do you have Freddy's phone?"

"Why did he call you?"

"We work together. Where did you get his phone?"

"I found it. It was in a snowbank next to a mansion south of Grand. Do you know the place?"

"Maybe. When did you find it?"

"Tonight—I think he's hurt and I can't find him. What did he say to you?"

"Nothing. The connection was bad," she said.

Moses checked the call log on the phone. The call had lasted twenty seconds. "You didn't hear anything he said?"

"He said something about Šejla."

"Do you know her?" he asked.

"Yes, she works for me."

"What does she do?"

"She's a waitress," she said.

"At the Zmaj?" She nodded. "Does that mean something? Zmaj?"

"Everything means something. It means dragon."

"Fred didn't say anything?"

"Most of it was cutting out. He said he needed to talk to a lawyer, I think."

"Henry Duncan?"

"Maybe that is his lawyer."

"What business does Mr. Dunsmore have with you?" Moses asked.

"Tell me why you care, Cowboy?"

"I work for his wife."

"Oh, her," she said, taking a drag on her cigarette. "We buy and sell things to each other for the bar. He has cheap sources," she said. A pair of fine curved lines formed at the corners of her mouth. The lines made her seem to have a perpetual half pout and they deepened when she shrugged, a gesture that seemed to both emphasize her sentence while at the same time dismissing his question.

"Did you know Šejla and Fred Dunsmore were together?"

Majka sighed and looked away. "I tried to tell her to date someone else," she said.

"It's hard to tell someone who to love," Moses said.

"She said something like that. I told her to grow up." Majka shrugged again.

"What did you mean in the car when you said you were afraid of that?" Moses asked.

Majka reached over him to the nightstand and retrieved her cigarettes and lighter. Sticking one between her teeth she answered, "I've seen them do it before."

"Do what before?"

"What they did to you. The drink, the glass, the drug."

"So that's why I feel like I got run over by a pack of elephants," Moses said. "Who have they done this to before?"

Majka flicked the lighter and raised the flame to her cigarette. The dim light made her face glow as her eyes narrowed. She killed the flame so only the amber of the cigarette and the neon light from the window illuminated her face.

"People they didn't like," she said.

"You?" he asked. She shook her head. "How did they do it?"

"I'm not sure. Something with the glasses. They keep a *special* one."

"Who is Vahid?"

"He does business at the Zmaj sometimes."

"Why do you let him?"

"I have no choice."

"Was he there all night tonight?" She shook her head, bringing the cigarette down to her opposite elbow as she crossed her arms over her naked navel.

"Where did he go?" Moses asked.

"I don't ask," she said, blowing a long stream of smoke out of the corner of her mouth. She reached her arm up across her chest, scratching her back, causing her breasts to shake. Moses must have been staring. "You are done with the questioning then?" she asked, smiling. Moses couldn't contain his own smile. He reached for her, pulling her down to the bed. She kissed him.

He was thinking about how good she tasted when his phone began to ring. He tried to ignore it. He looked out the window, still holding the kiss. The river was starting to glow from the brightening eastern sky. It would be dawn soon, and they might have found Fred Dunsmore and were calling him. He rolled Majka over and kissed her one last time. He stood up and she tried to pull him back down. He struggled and she fell back on the soft bed. He scrambled for his pants and found his phone.

"Moses. It's Rakić. Get back here. We got something I want to show you."

Moses turned to Majka, "Take me to my car."

Chapter 11

Rakić stuffed his cell phone in his pocket and put his glove back on. He turned to the river where the crime scene techs were working in the early morning light. When the sun rose behind the white clouds, they found the blood and the tracks. It was a small splatter, almost obscured by the previous night's snowfall near a massive tree stump by the river. The large tree was downed next to the stump, extending into the nearby river. The chainsaw cut was recent.

"Are those dog tracks or some other animal?" Rakić asked. The tracks were more obvious in the light, only partially filled in with snow.

"Dog, no question," said the woman taking pictures of the tracks. Mckenzie? Why was it so hard to remember their names?

"What kind?" Rakić asked.

"Tough to say. It's big though. Probably over a hundred pounds."

The team had brought in ATVs with plow attachments the city used to clear the trails of snow. They had cleared paths adjacent to the crime scenes allowing easy access. Without them, half of the staff wouldn't have been able to do their jobs.

"You seen the K-9 yet?"

The other man shook his head. Johnson or Jackson. Rakić knew the face, but doubted the name. Rakić paced back down to where Moses had been attacked. The teams were gone from this area now, on to the hotter site that Rakić had just left.

Rakić tried to put together the events. Moses Winter, no friend of Fred Dunsmore, had taken Sharon Dunsmore to confront him less than twenty-four hours prior. Aided her, but he wasn't complicit. Poor judgment, definitely, but Moses didn't have malice toward Fred. Still, he wouldn't call them friends. So why would Fred Dunsmore reach out to Moses Winter? How had Fred gotten here, if he *was* out here? He rubbed his gloved hands together. It felt like Fred was here. He couldn't point to a single fact, but he knew they were missing a body and he was starting to believe it was Fred's.

Rakić stood on the path next to the small game trail and looked at the route Moses had taken, where he had stopped, where he claimed to have talked to this mysterious man. It was still gloomy here, under the trees, in the early morning. There was now a small red flag in the spot where Rakić had found the cigarette. The tracks of the smoking man left the river and walked back this direction with the dog. There had been three sets of human tracks that converged by the river. Then there had been a lot of traffic and the individual tracks were lost in the area around the tree stump. Two sets of tracks returned this way. Not the other set of tracks. The third set was missing. Then the two remaining sets of tracks split from each other again. If these were Elvis' tracks, he had gone on ahead and then had come back.

Rakić walked back to the river and looked at the tree again. *Why in hell had they cut it down?* The tree was huge. It was probably five feet thick and was now partially submerged and frozen in the river. A thin band of water remained unfrozen like a dark halo around the tree.

"How cold is it?" Rakić asked.

"Nine degrees," a city cop answered from the seat of one of the ATVs.

"Nine," Rakić said. He walked closer to the river. They had found two sets of tracks going down the small trail to the river itself. The same two that had left under their own power.

A voice came over Rakić's police radio. "Rakić. We have something." The voice on the other end directed him to look south and southwest. Rakić scanned that direction until he saw a blue coat waving at him about 50 yards away. There was no direct path there, so he trudged through the heavy snow until he was nearly breathless when he finally reached him.

"See that," DCI Agent Thomas said. He was pointing at a shotgun shell casing. Fresh too. There was only a small dusting of snow covering it.

"Nice spot," Rakić said.

He pressed the button on the handset and spoke, calling for more people to canvas the new area. He slapped the man on the back and trudged back the way he came. It was looking more and more like Fred Dunsmore had been murdered. All they were missing was the body.

* * *

"I want you to walk me through this again," Rakić said to Moses.

They had been out in the cold for hours and still had no body. The sun had risen, but was doing little to warm the air. Moses was cold and getting tired of explaining his brief encounter with the mysterious men. He wasn't sure that Rakić believed him.

"Listen. I told you. I only saw him from a distance and I didn't see the other guy," Moses said.

"Okay. Let's mix it up. Follow me," Rakić said. Moses followed him down the plowed path towards the river. There was a group of cops leaning against an ATV near the fallen tree and stump.

"Why do you think they cut this down?" Rakić asked.

Moses walked closer to the edge of the bank and looked at the small opening in the ice that wasn't frozen around the trunk of the tree. "To make a hole to dump Fred's body," Moses said.

"That's what I think. But why go to all the trouble? They didn't know you were here," Rakić said.

"I don't know. Maybe they really didn't want him found," Moses said.

"Yes. Maybe. But in the spring the body would be found. If not here, then the dam downstream. Maybe further, if they get lucky. But the body will get found."

"They didn't seem like this was their first rodeo. Maybe they were cutting him up," Moses said.

"What?" Rakić asked.

"They didn't seem nervous. Very professional. Maybe they dumped him in pieces," Moses said.

"Ah. Yeah. Professionals. Well they did leave the cigarette and the shells. And you alive," Rakić said.

Moses kicked the snow. *Was he accusing him of being involved?* "I have no idea who those guys were," Moses said.

Rakić nodded and walked over to the ATV where the other cops were congregated, huddling together trying to keep warm. Moses fished in his pocket and pulled out his pack of smokes. He lit up and walked down the river a bit. Something didn't seem right. He had heard the chainsaw. Then he had run into the man in the darkness. Probably Vahid. It seemed fast. Cut down a tree. Break the ice. Cut up the body and dump it in the river. Maybe he was already cut up. Maybe that was the last piece. He imagined the chain cutting into Dunsmore's neck or maybe his thigh. He forced himself to focus on the details. Cutting him up made sense. This tree didn't for some reason. He walked over to it again and looked at the cut. Then he looked down at the river. Dump the body in the hole. He knelt down and rested his hand on the stump and took the last drag of the smoke. He pushed the cigarette down into the snow next to the exposed root of the tree. He rubbed his head and closed his eyes.

"What did you do?" Rakić asked.

Moses shook his head. His last comment had stuck with him and now anger lurched through his veins. What the hell was he accusing him of now? He stood up with an insult on his tongue, but Rakić's expression stopped him cold. He was looking down at the stump where Moses had knelt. Moses looked down. There was a black hole in the snow the size of a fist. It was gaping, dark, and unnatural. Anger was replaced by excitement.

"I think I found something," Moses said.

Chapter 12

It took the better part of the next two hours for the city employees to find enough chains and rope to attach to the tree stump. In that time, a K-9 unit had arrived and confirmed a hit on the tree stump. Rakić had said that it was lucky that they had a K-9 that could detect drugs, blood, and even a person hiding. The dog was a German Shorthaired Pointer, sleek white along her flanks and back with an all chocolate face. The dog turned his direction and winked each warm eye in turn before looking away, and Moses thought she would be impossible to see against the snow if he didn't know where to look.

Rakić had asked Moses to stay and Moses was glad even if it was to keep an eye on him. But, if Fred was there, he wanted to know. Three ATVs were attached by chain to the stump and a half dozen people, a mix of city employees and cops, were ready with ropes to guide the stump out of the hole. The tree had apparently fallen over some time ago, the sandy soil no longer able to bear the stress of the massive weight of the old tree.

Now they were finally ready to pull the stump out of the hole. The signal was given and the ATVs pulled slowly in unison to remove the slack in the chains. Then, on a signal from a city worker, they gunned the engines. The stump leaned and then tilted and started to slowly slide up the hole. The tires of the ATVs started to spin in the snow, throwing it back against the stump and coating it with white powder. The men strained against the ropes, adding their own weight to the effort. Now the heated rubber tires threw dirt and mud, the tire-chains biting into the frozen earth. Moses trudged closer. Rakić followed and Moses found himself standing with him. Moses saw an empty spot on one of the ropes and grabbed on, pulling as hard as he could. The muscles in his arms burned and his head ached where he'd been hit the day before. He grunted and leaned back.

"Let up!" a voice shouted.

The ATVs idled and let the stump slide back into the pit. The men holding the ropes were dragged forward. Moses let the rope slide through his gloved hands and then patted the back of the man in front of him to let him know he was there. He glanced over and saw that Rakić had jumped on another line a few feet over.

"Okay, one more time, people!" the same city worker shouted.

Moses watched as Rakić picked up his rope and started pulling with the ATVs. Moses did the same, and then they were all pulling. He could hear the engines roaring behind him and he realized he was holding his breath as he strained against the rope, unable to inhale or he might collapse from the relief in pressure. One of the roots groaned and snapped against the chain and then the tree slid out of the hole, twisting violently. Moses and Raif and the other straining men and women were flattened to the ground like poorly placed dominos. The chain pulled out from underneath them with the sudden slack in the rope. A man fell on top of Moses and he pushed him to the side. One of the chains snapped like a whip and then went slack, as the driver of the ATV it was attached to idled the engine. Moses got to his feet and lurched forward toward the stump. Rakić was next to him and they both looked down into the pit where the stump had been a moment before.

There are many shades of white in the world. The white of the snow. The white of a cloudy winter sky. The white of bone. The last was what Rakić and Moses saw when they looked down into the earthen hole. The white stood out in the red of the blood and the dark color of the woolen winter coat. The flesh on the upper shoulder of Fred Dunsmore had been completely ripped away. He lay on his side, facing away from them, looking like a discarded toy. His legs were unnaturally contorted with one booted foot pointing the wrong direction. His dark hair was uncovered, except for the blood that had leaked onto it from the stump of his torn ear. One eye stared blankly at Moses, the other obscured by mangled meat.

"Dunsmore," Rakić said.

"No fucking way. Can a dog do that?" Moses asked.

"I've seen it. A dog can," Rakić said. "Boys. We got a body!"

A group of paramedics came to the pit, and one jumped in and went to work. Moses leaned back against the tree stump and looked away. He had been so close to the men who had done this and they had gotten away. Now Fred was at the bottom of a pit, dead and defiled.

Rakić walked over, leaned next to Moses, and offered him a cigarette. Moses took it and let Rakić light it for him.

"I know you think you can stop this, but you can't. People are going to kill each other. It happens. You could fast forward a thousand years and we will still have murder and cops trying to stop it," Rakić said and then lit his own smoke.

"I let this one happen," Moses said.

Rakić nodded and Moses felt him pat his back. "I let this happen too," Rakić said.

"What do you mean?" Moses asked.

"We all let this happen. Everyday." Moses wasn't sure what Rakić was talking about right now and he didn't care. Moses had allowed the events to unfold until they were digging Fred out of a hole in the ground. Rakić stood up and walked back over to the hole. He flicked his cigarette to the side, and he looked at Moses with wide eyes. Then he looked back to the man in the pit.

"Is he alive?" Rakić asked.

"Barely," the paramedic answered.

Moses' stomach burned and his throat went dry. He ran to Rakić's side. In the pit, one paramedic was now working a manual respirator attached to the mangled face of Fred Dunsmore as another frantically administered bandages to the gaping wounds on his body. He did the math. Dunsmore had been in the frozen pit under tons of tree for over twelve hours.

Rakić jumped down beside them and Moses followed. Moses assisted the medic wherever he could, holding a bandage or working the respirator. In minutes, Rakić and Moses were on either side of a gurney straining to pull Fred out of the pit. The paramedics strapped Dunsmore to the front of an ATV and rushed him off.

Moses looked at Rakić. He had blood on his face and was sweating in the cold air. Moses looked at his bare hands. He'd taken his gloves off to help the paramedics and now they were stained dark with the life of Fred Dunsmore for the second time.

"Did we crush him?" Moses asked.

"We saved him," Rakić said, wiping his hands in the snow, leaving a pair of crimson crescents.

Chapter 13

Moses was sitting in his favorite bar in Des Moines nursing a domestic full-bodied pint. The Oak Barrel was in the basement of an old three-story brick warehouse downtown. They served food and tap beer and even had a few televisions. This was a good place to think and Liz was good company when she wasn't too busy with customers.

The crisp, cool beer tasted better than normal as it hit his tongue. Something Fred might never experience again, he thought. The events of the previous few days pushed thoughts of the beer aside.

Sharon and he had confronted Fred and Šejla. Fred was wounded and was in the hospital for less than a day, then was so scared that he left. In that time, he made three phone calls. One was to his lawyer. One was to Moses, and one was to Majka. The lawyer call added up. The call to Moses was a little more of a stretch, but the really fishy one was the call Fred made to Majka. *What tie did Fred have to her? He didn't call Šejla, but he called Majka. Why?*

Then Fred went to see his lawyer, Duncan. Duncan was crooked, but how crooked? Fred either talked to him or didn't have a chance. Then he was chased into the woods. Attacked, mangled, and buried alive and not found for most of a day, barely hanging on.

"Hey, Liz. What city is this?" Moses asked.

"What do you mean? It's Des Moines, dummy." One of the nice things about Liz was the way she was easy to talk to. No pretense, no bullshit.

"Just checking. When you get a chance," he said, tipping his empty glass.

Liz grabbed the glass and began pouring from the tap next to him.

"Something happen?" she asked.

"Yeah, just a case," he said.

"Well, don't bring down the whole place with your sour puss," she said.

Moses nodded and managed a grin. Liz put the beer in front of him and went to the next order. Moses had a few more until he was nice and warm and the crowd had gotten bigger.

Fred had said something about Sharon. He couldn't remember. Something about her. He was afraid of her. Moses couldn't figure that out. She was a decent person from what he could tell. She had been nice enough to him. Had paid him on time. Moses looked at his watch. He needed some sleep. He would visit her in jail tomorrow; she must know something.

* * *

It was late when Rakić finally left the crime scene, but the excitement of finding Fred Dunsmore had left him wired. He had never heard of a person being found like this. It was the work of a brutal killer. The tree thing hadn't been an accident. The killer or killers had scouted and planned the disposal of the body well in advance. It made Rakić wonder how many other bodies were buried out there by the river. He hadn't been thinking of where he was going. On automatic, he pulled his police cruiser onto the gravel access road running parallel to the westernmost Des Moines International Airport runway. He parked the car at the locked utility gate as a large UPS cargo plane roared down the runway toward him. The nose of the great plane tilted up and then the rear landing gear came off the tarmac and the plane was over him and gone. The roar was still in his ears as he thought of the girl frozen to the street.

The scene had gotten to him in a different way than finding Fred had. Why? He could guess. She was young. And the color of her hair. It was the same as his mother's and sister's. Maybe it was her hair, and her age, and something in the goddamn water or the food. Or the situation with Šejla and Fred Dunsmore. He heard another plane revving its engines on the adjacent runway, but he couldn't see it yet. Maybe she was his sister. He didn't believe in shit like that. She had died a long time ago in Sarajevo. But maybe she was, in some strange way. This girl hadn't made it across the street either.

Why else had he reacted to Terry's joke the way he had? He'd heard a million jokes like that at a crime scene. It's how people dealt with it. It's how he usually dealt with it. It's either laugh or cry with tragedy like that. Maybe because it was Christmastime and she was alone, naked, and dead on the street. And he couldn't call her people. He didn't know who she was or who her people were. They might be sitting somewhere right now, waiting for her to call. He missed his sister. That, and he didn't have anyone to tell—to go home to, squeeze, and hold—who could help him forget about it. The police radio crackled. He turned it up. He sighed; it wasn't for him. It was a car accident somewhere on the north side. He sat for a while on the dark road, watching the shining aluminum planes take off into the cold Iowa air.

Some time later, his phone vibrated in the car's cup holder. He picked it up and answered. "Rakić speaking."

"Rakić, this is Hansen. You assigned me to guard Dunsmore."

"I remember," Rakić said.

"Well, he didn't make it. I wanted you to know ASAP."

"Thanks." Rakić ended the call. He turned the car around and made for the city and his mother's house. He knew he had a duty to Fred, but he couldn't care about him as much as that poor girl in the street and it made sense now. He knew why it hurt. This girl mattered even though no one cared. He would care. He would find out what happened to her and who she was no matter how long it took. First, he had to talk to Šejla.

He arrived back at his mother's house. The moon was still bright in the sky, just shy of full, waning. He opened the door and called for his mother.

"Yes, Raif," she said as she appeared and then pulled him into a hug.

"Šejla?" he asked.

She pointed back to her room down the hall from the parlor. Rakić nodded at her and offered a tired smile as he squeezed her arms. He walked down the hall and knocked softly on Šejla's door.

"Šejla," Rakić said.

"Yes," she answered.

"Can I come in?"

"Yes."

Rakić opened the door and saw Šejla sitting on her bed. Her eyes were red and her nose was running. Rakić sat next to her and held her hand. He felt an overwhelming guilt. This man had meant something to his cousin.

"I'm sorry. How did you hear?"

"A girl from work."

"At Zmaj? Or the grocery store?" Rakić asked.

"Zmaj."

Rakić put his arm around her shoulders and she rested her head against him. She started sobbing. He squeezed her tighter and tried to think about catching the bastards that had done this to his cousin. Rakić brushed his hand across his face and pushed Šejla away a bit.

"*Tell me, Šejla. Who is the girl that told you this?*" Rakić said in Bosnian.

"*Her name is Biba. She is a friend. Don't cause her trouble, okay?*" she replied in the same tongue.

"*I know this girl. Don't worry,*" Rakić said, squeezing her close again. "*You are a strong woman.*" Šejla nodded into his chest. "*Some things I thought were left behind for us, but it seems we must endure some more. I wished to stop you from having to feel more like this in your life. But we are strong and we will continue.*" She nodded again, and he gave her one more squeeze and stood up.

"*Don't go,*" she said.

"*I will be here tonight. Right out there on the couch,*" he said. "*Try to smile once for me tomorrow.*"

"*Okay.*"

"*Good night.*"

"*Good night,*" he said, pulling the door shut. He walked back to the parlor and found his mother sitting in a chair reading a *Time* magazine. She put it down and sat up as he came in. "I am staying here tonight, Mother."

She smiled a little and nodded. "You can take my room."

"No, Mother. I will sleep on the couch," he said, leaning over and patting her hand.

"I will make a big breakfast for us in the morning. All will seem better then," she said.

"Yes, Mother." *All will seem better then.* How often had his mother uttered those words in Sarajevo? Sometime in the future it will be better. This will pass. We survive. Rakić pulled his boots off and stretched out on the couch. He laced his fingers behind his head as he thought. Someone at the Zmaj had known about Fred's death almost before the police did.

Chapter 14

Two days later Moses was waiting for Sharon in the visiting room of the county jail. He had been turned away the day before. No visitors on Sundays. Sharon Dunsmore looked tired, he thought, as she was led into the visitation room. She sat down across from him at the small table and the guard left them. Moses wasn't sure how to start. *She must know that her husband was dead, didn't she?*

"He's dead. I know. They told me," she said.

Moses shifted in his seat and crossed his arms. "They found him two days ago," Moses said.

"They are going to let me out now. The lawyer said it was so I could make arrangements. And I guess the other stuff doesn't matter as much now."

"I suppose not. Do you have any idea what he was up to out there?" Moses asked.

She shook her head and put both hands to her mouth. Moses leaned forward and put his hand in front of her. He glanced at the guard by the door. He was looking away. Moses reached forward and pulled her hand into his.

"Hey, it's okay." He pulled his hand back and she quickly wiped her eyes.

"He had business partners."

"In real estate?"

"Yes. But he had other side businesses," she said.

"Bar supplies?" Moses asked.

"Yes. Did you follow him to some of those places?" she asked.

"No. I found his phone the night before we found him."

"Oh, did you find something out?"

"Not really. Traced it back to a bar. Zmaj. Did Fred ever talk about it?"

"I have heard of it. Fred never talked about it, but a girlfriend of mine has been there."

"What is her name?" Moses asked.

"Megan. Why?"

Moses shook his head. "Just curious. What's her last name?"

"I don't see how this matters. Listen, I've talked to the cops all day yesterday. What are you trying to do?"

"Nothing. Sorry, just trying to help. I feel like I caused this somehow."

Sharon's face softened and she leaned forward and put her hand out. "Listen, Moses. You did what I asked you to do. This isn't your fault. The cops will find the people that did this."

"He called me before he died," Moses said.

She pulled her hand back. "He did? What did he say?"

"Not much. He wanted to meet at his lawyer's. He sounded afraid of you."

Sharon laughed, a dry jarring sound, on the edge of crying. "He would be."

"Why?"

"No reason. He was just a nervous guy," Sharon said.

Moses leaned back and shifted gears. "Did he ever mention an Elvis?"

"He liked his music, but there was a kid I think he worked with named Elvis. Bosnian kid."

"Visiting time is over," the guard announced.

Sharon stood up and Moses followed suit.

"I can take you home if you want," Moses said.

"I have a ride. Thank you, Moses." Sharon turned and walked out the door.

* * *

Majka had answered the phone on the first ring and agreed to come over to Moses' apartment; now they were lying in bed naked and smoking. Moses flicked his cigarette into an ashtray resting on his stomach. Majka lounged against his side with her cigarette held close to her mouth. She raised her hand to flick an ash when he noticed the missing portion of her ring finger.

"How'd that happen?" Moses asked.

"What?"

"Your finger."

"I'm thirsty," Majka said. Putting the cigarette in her mouth, she pushed off of his chest and vaulted over him on her way to the kitchen. Moses watched as she found a glass, and then she moved out of sight. He stared up at the ceiling, feeling relaxed for once. It was nice having her around, he thought as he listened to the sounds of her in the kitchen: her bare feet padding on the linoleum floor, the ice tinkling in the glass, liquid pouring.

"What is this? Are you some Nazi lover?" Majka asked, standing in the doorway holding his gun in one hand and a glass of ice water in the other, her cigarette dangling from her lips.

Moses stubbed his cigarette out in the ashtray and moved it to the nightstand. He sat up and held out his hand. "Bring it to me." Majka shifted the gun forward so now the barrel was pointing just to the side of Moses, and her face became expressionless. In stark contrast to the smile of a moment before, it seemed a robot had taken her place. "I said, bring it to me," he said.

Majka let the gun drop to her thigh and she struggled to keep the cigarette in its place as her mouth split into a gleaming smile, her body shaking with silent laughter. "Your face, Cowboy." She raised the glass of ice water to her cheek, shaking her head.

"Give it to me," he said again.

Majka stopped smiling. "What is the big deal, Cowboy? Don't you trust me?"

"It's not about trust. That gun is all I have left."

"All you have left of what?"

"Give it to me."

"First you tell me why it is important."

Moses rose to his feet and took a step toward her. "No," he said.

Majka studied him for a moment and then, with a shrug, tossed the gun on the bed. Raising the glass to her lips, she took a long drink.

Moses fought the urgency he felt and forced himself to slowly retrieve the gun. He released the clip and worked the action. He caught a round as it was expelled from the chamber of the gun. He flipped the safety off and then on again, put the weapon on the nightstand next to the ashtray, and sat on the bed staring at it.

Majka came over and sat next to him. She leaned against him and snaked her arm around his hip. "Tell me about it."

"It was my grandfather's."

"Who was your grandfather?"

Moses looked at her. *Who was his grandfather? How could he explain?* "He was in World War II, Europe. He got the gun close to the end."

"American side?" Majka asked.

"Yeah, of course."

"My grandfather was made to be Nazi."

"*Made?*"

"Everyone had to fight back then. There was only one choice where I am from. Fascist pigs. How did he get it?" Majka asked, pointing at the gun.

"At the end, the Germans sent everyone that could walk to the front. Boys, old men, everyone. My grandfather was in the infantry. 'Those guys walked into Germany,' he liked to say. But he only ever told me about the gun one time."

"Why did he tell you?"

"I don't know. He was older. Maybe he wanted the story to go along with the gun." Moses lit a cigarette and leaned back, feeling relaxed again with her arm around him. "But he told me. Like I said, it was toward the end. Things were getting desperate. Nazi's were trying to make their escape like rats running from a burning barn. He was part of Seventh Army who made the push all the way to Salzburg."

"Austria?"

"Yeah. They were in Bavaria where a lot of Nazis had holed up. They came across this village near an airfield they were supposed to secure. They stopped and, like he said, they usually got treated pretty well by the Bavarians. The people came out and gave them some food and water. It was late, so they camped out on the edge of town. Grandpa had the 3:00 a.m. watch with another guy. Close to 4:00 a.m., a carload of Germans came through. It was a family. Two kids, a mom, and a dad dressed like regular civilians. Grandpa and his partner stopped the car and had them all get out. The dad and the kids acted normal, but the mom looked like she was ready to keel over. Grandpa kept them talking and motioned for his partner to check the trunk and backseat."

"Where were they going?"

"They looked like they were just out for a drive. No baggage strapped to the roof. They weren't refugees or anything. But the mom was acting weird and now the dad was starting to get agitated, looking back and forth from Grandpa to his partner. Then he suddenly made a break. The man ran at a dead sprint past my Grandpa, so he took off after him. The man ran into a house and up the stairs. By the time Grandpa got there, he had that Luger pointed at the head of a fifteen-year-old girl."

Majka gasped. "No! He doesn't kill her, does he?"

Moses continued, "Grandpa didn't know any German and the man holding the gun was only speaking in German. He was yelling and waving the gun and pointing it at this girl. The rest of the house was awake now and the family was standing behind my Grandpa, screaming at him. Grandpa didn't know what to do. He was just a twenty-one-year-old kid from Iowa. But he kept yelling at the man to calm down. Then the woman from the car pushed her way through and talked to the man. She said a few words, but the man didn't budge. She said them again. Now the German man had tears streaming down his cheeks. Finally, he handed over the gun to the woman. The man let the girl go and he hugged the woman, and she patted his head like it was nothing. And then she raised the gun to the man's head, and before Grandpa could do anything, she pulled the trigger. Blam, his brains all over the wall."

"No, she didn't."

"Yeah, she did."

"Why?" Majka asked.

"At this point, they didn't know what to do. But the lady just handed him the gun and left the room. They got back to the car and the mom and Grandpa's partner wave him over. Stuffed down underneath where the kids were sitting was the body of a man. Turned out it was that lady's husband. The man she had shot was a Nazi trying to get to the airfield to fly to Italy and then Argentina or somewhere."

"Bastard. What did she say to him to get the gun?"

"That's what I wondered. Grandpa thought she said it was okay, but they didn't really know."

"What happened to her?"

"They let her go, her and her family. No idea what happened to them."

"Why did he keep it?" she asked.

"I don't know. He said it reminded him."

"You loved your grandfather very much?"

"Yeah, when he died, he wanted me to have the gun."

"What do you think it means?"

"I don't know. The story is just a story, but it was my grandfather's gun and he was the most decent and honest man I've ever known."

"What did he do for work?"

"He farmed and raised cattle."

"What about your father?" she asked.

"He and my mom broke up when I was young."

"I see."

They both looked at the gun until finally Moses looked at Majka and said, "Now your finger."

"I cut it peeling potatoes," Majka said.

"Sure you did." Moses sat smoking his cigarette, thinking about his Grandfather.

"Why is it all you have?"

"No reason. I had to say something to get it back." Moses felt like changing the subject. "I went to see Fred's wife today," Moses said.

"What for?"

"To see if she knew the people that did this to Fred."

"Did she?"

"I don't know."

"What did she say?"

"Nothing much. She seemed sad enough about everything. I don't know." Majka rolled back so she was lying on the bed behind him now. "Fred was afraid of Sharon. I'm sure of it. I just can't figure out why."

"Fred was a nervous guy," Majka said.

"That's what Sharon said. Have you talked to Šejla?"

"No."

"It's probably hitting her hard," Moses said.

"She is a strong girl."

"I need to talk to her. Maybe she knows what Fred was doing that night. Do you know where she is?"

"Yes, she is staying at her aunt's house."

"Will you show me?"

"Anything for you, Cowboy," Majka said.

Chapter 15

Moses and Majka were at the door to the house where Šejla Tahirović was staying. It was the same house Moses had followed Rakić to before he'd gotten the call from Fred. Moses glanced at Majka and then pressed the doorbell. He could faintly hear the chime deep inside the house. Majka shuffled a little and turned away from the door. Moses put his hand on her shoulder and she covered it with her own.

The door opened, and a short woman with wrinkles bunched at her eyes and a pale face split by a proud nose stuck her head out.

"Yes?" she asked.

"Hello, ma'am. We are here to see your niece. Šejla Tahirović," Moses said.

"Why?" The word passed between her closed lips and her eyes began to smoke.

"I'd rather tell her in person, ma'am."

She was silent for a beat, absorbing Moses from behind her crossed arms. She allowed Majka a flick of her eyes and then was back on Moses.

"What is your name?" she asked.

"I'm Moses Winter."

"Of course. Come in." She stepped out into the night and shooed them inside. "Here, give me coats. I'm Edina," she said.

Moses pulled his gloves off and stuffed them inside his coat pockets and let Edina take it from him. He turned to help Majka with her coat. She removed her scarf and let Moses pull the coat down her arms. She finished hanging Moses' coat and turned to take Majka's, but dropped it.

"Oh, I'm sorry, my dear. It almost burned my fingers," she said.

Majka smiled with her lips and Moses was certain he'd missed something. Edina led them into her parlor and sat them down on the couch.

"Let me get Šejla," she said and disappeared down the hallway.

"We should be quick," Majka said.

"Why? What's wrong?" Moses asked.

Majka's face was tight. She shook her head and then Šejla was in the room with Edina close behind her. Moses stood up and stuck his hand out.

"What are you doing here?" Šejla asked.

"I'm sorry, I'm sure I'm the last person you wanted to see," Moses said.

Šejla crossed her arms and then saw Majka sitting down on the couch behind him. "And you brought her?" Edina stepped forward and spoke in a gentle tone to Šejla in Bosnian. Šejla answered her in the same tongue. They had a terse exchange. Moses heard Majka snort at one point, then she fell silent.

"Why don't I make tea?" the old woman said in English.

Šejla, appearing mollified, sat in a chair and pointed at the couch for Moses to sit.

"What do you want?"

"I know this is tough. Sorry for your loss. But if you don't mind, I wanted to talk to you about what Fred was doing that night. The night he went missing."

Šejla's face turned a little paler than before as her eyes began to water, and the arm of the chair creaked under the stress of her white-knuckled grip. She opened her mouth to begin talking and then closed it as Edina reappeared.

"The water is on. It will only be a few minutes," she said.

Then she looked at Šejla, who was blinking furiously, and at Moses, who was leaning forward.

"What has happened?" Edina asked.

Šejla didn't speak, and Moses leaned forward further on the couch, almost standing up. "I came here to ask her about her friend that passed away," Moses said.

"It is okay," Šejla said, placing her hand on Edina's arm.

Now Šejla was speaking quickly to Edina in Bosnian again. Edina nodded and went back to the kitchen.

"Why did you bring her?" Šejla asked, jerking her head in Majka's direction.

"She knew where you were," Moses said.

"How did she know that, I wonder?"

Majka leaned forward and said a few short words in Bosnian.

"Say it again," Šejla said. Her eyes were clear now, her jaw set.

Majka shrugged, leaned back, and crossed her legs.

"What did she say?" Moses asked.

"This woman that you brought into my aunt's house says that I should mind my own business."

Majka said a word. Then said another. And finally another, drawing out the syllables like she was teaching a child. Šejla flew from her chair and onto Majka in a blur of motion. She grabbed Majka by her slender neck and forced her knee into Majka's stomach. Spit dangled from Šejla's lip as she squeezed the blood in Majka's neck to a cold stop. Moses grabbed Šejla's shoulders, trying to pry her off of Majka. He heard the old woman screaming something behind him. Then he was on the floor on his back with Šejla sitting on his chest. She launched herself off the floor, breaking Moses' grip. Rolling to the side, he found his feet in time to see Majka slugging Šejla in the gut. The air rushed out of her lungs with a groan as she crumpled to the floor. Majka stood over her, but Šejla had recovered quickly and was almost to her feet. Moses pushed Majka away. Now he was between them. Šejla took a swing and caught Moses in the face with her ringed hand. He felt a sting under his eye and knew that he was cut.

Then a voice was shouting, "Šejla! Stop!"

Raif Rakić slammed the front door behind him. Šejla slumped against the wall, her chest heaving, and she put her hands to her hips. Moses felt Majka relax behind him. The house was as quiet as it had been loud a second before. A high-pitched wail broke the silence. The water was done. Edina ran back to the kitchen as Rakić stepped into the parlor.

"What are you doing here?" Rakić demanded.

Moses couldn't think of anything to say. *What was Rakić doing here?* Rakić walked over to Šejla and grabbed her by the shoulders.

"Are you hurt?" Rakić asked.

She shook her head. Rakić let her go and turned to Moses.

"Is this your house? I came to ask her about Fred," Moses said.

"My mother's. Šejla doesn't know anything. I already talked to her. I think you better go."

"I think you're right." Moses took Majka by the arm and led her to the door. Edina came back from the kitchen as Moses and Majka were putting their coats on. She made a sign and spoke some harsh foreign words.

"Mother, please. That is enough," Rakić said. Edina shot him a withering look and then returned to the kitchen, muttering under her breath.

"Sorry for the trouble," Moses said as he pulled the front door closed behind them.

Majka walked in front of him and got into the Jeep. Moses started the car and backed out of the driveway. He pulled a smoke out of his pocket and lit it up. He glanced over at Majka, but she was looking out the window.

"What was that about?" Moses asked.

"What was what?"

"That lady acted like you were the Devil or something."

Majka looked at Moses and shrugged. She snagged the cigarette from his mouth and took a drag, holding the smoke in her lungs. She closed her eyes and let it slowly exit her mouth in one long, white tendril. She leaned over the center console and put the smoke back to his lips. He glanced down at her and took a puff. She pulled the cigarette back to her lips and then put both arms around his torso, leaning her head against his chest.

"Not everyone looks at me like you do, Cowboy."

"I guess not," he said. He took the cigarette from her mouth and stuck it back in his face. Majka pushed away from him and went back to her corner of the car. She made a small indignant noise and pulled out her pack of smokes and lit her own cigarette.

"Raif is related to Šejla?"

"They are cousins," Majka said, staring out the window at the night.

"I think Vahid and Elvis killed Fred Dunsmore."

Majka sighed heavily. "They probably did."

"You think they did it, too? Why didn't you say something?"

"I don't want to get in the middle."

Moses nailed the brakes and the car slid to stop.

"Wake the fuck up, Majka! You already are!" Her nose twisted to the side as she exhaled smoke from her nostrils, staring at him dead-eyed. Moses wanted to slap her, but instead, he slammed his fist on the dashboard. He exhaled and tried to forget she was in the car and started driving again. "Where can I find them?"

"You won't. No one will talk."

"Like you, I guess?"

"Listen, Cowboy. This is something you should stay out of."

"I'll take you to your car," Moses said.

"Take me to the Zmaj. I'll get my car later."

"You got it."

Moses made his way through town to the Zmaj. Stay out of it. That was one option, but not for him. He had to find out what had happened to Fred. Someone knew. Someone had answers. Maybe it was Majka. He looked at her again. Looking back to the street, he thought about Šejla and Rakić. He was protecting her. Was he blinded by his family connection? Moses needed to do some more work. For now, he'd start with the lawyer.

Chapter 16

Rakić and Wilson sat in Sharon Dunsmore's living room, waiting for her to return from the kitchen with coffee. Wilson sat in an armchair as relaxed as if he were waiting for the next basketball game to come on the television. Rakić sat on a couch next to Wilson, flipping through his notebook.

"Here you go, gentlemen," Sharon said, placing a tray with three coffees on the end table between Wilson and Rakić.

"Thank you," Rakić said. Wilson took his coffee and began stirring it.

"Is it alright?" Sharon asked.

"Yeah, it's fine, ma'am," Wilson said, not looking up from his drink.

"Mrs. Dunsmore. Thanks for taking the time to meet with us. We know you have to plan for things, to make arrangements, and that this is a tough time, but we need to ask you about Fred and his business ties."

"I understand. Anything I can do," she said, sitting down in a chair across from them.

Rakić glanced at Wilson, who seemed to be more interested in his coffee at the moment than interviewing a murder victim's spouse. "Let's start with Fred's private life. Other than Ms. Tahirović, did Fred have any other…" Rakić let the question hang for a moment, "relationships?"

Sharon shifted in her seat, looking out the window at the view of the ice-covered cul-de-sac. "Not that I am aware of," she said, finally.

"Sorry, we had to ask." Rakić flipped to another page in his notebook. "Are you aware of any business associates or contacts that Fred was having trouble with, or had any sort of disagreement with?" Sharon shook her head. Rakić stood up and paced to the window. Looking out on the view of the street, he asked, "What about Duncan?"

"What about him?"

"Why was he going to meet him?"

"I don't know, you'll have to ask him."

"We will." Rakić turned toward her. "Did he ever mention a young guy by the name of Elvis?"

Sharon looked at him with a flash of recognition in her eyes. "Yes, Elvis. Yes, I overheard that name."

"You did?" Rakić asked, sticking out his lower lip and nodding. "When was this?"

"I don't remember much about it. It was a phone conversation, but I definitely remember the name Elvis coming up."

"Fred was talking to this Elvis?" Wilson asked, setting his coffee down on the table.

"This is really important, Sharon. Do you remember when you overheard this conversation?" Rakić asked.

"It was the night before the cabin. We were driving somewhere together, to pick up the kids, I think."

"I see. Did the name Vahid, or did Mr. Duncan come up at all?" Rakić asked. Sharon shook her head.

"We are going to need to see your financial records," Wilson said.

"Is that really necessary?" Sharon asked.

"I'm afraid so. We need to rule out any of Mr. Dunsmore's business relationships having a motive," Wilson said.

"I'll get you what you need," Sharon said.

"Thank you, ma'am. We won't take up any more of your time," Rakić said.

"When can I get my husband back?" Sharon asked.

Rakić paused, not sure how to answer. Sharon's expression was a mixture of exhaustion and fatigue. "The county medical examiner hasn't released him yet," he said.

"I know. We need to bury him. The kids need to say goodbye to their father."

"I'm sorry, ma'am. Believe me, as soon as they can, they will give him back to you."

"Thank you," she said, looking like she was close to tears. Rakić went to her and put a hand on her shoulder. She put her hand over his and he felt her shudder beneath his touch. After a moment, he gently pulled his hand away and motioned to Wilson that they should leave.

Wilson and Rakić left the house with Rakić still thinking about Sharon. Then he thought about Elvis and how Fred was connected to him. When they got to the car, he asked Wilson, "You got the financial end?"

"Yeah, I got it, Raif," Wilson said.

"Alright, I'll keep digging on this Elvis kid. Let me know what you find."

* * *

Moses parked his Jeep next to the long driveway of Duncan's house, on the spot that Fred's SUV had recently occupied. Henry Duncan was one of the last people to talk to Fred Dunsmore, and Moses was sure he was hiding something.

The driveway wasn't empty. A gray Toyota pickup was parked close to the house. It was a relatively new model, but looked like it had seen its fair share of use. Moses peeked in the passenger window, but other than a pack of smokes, he didn't see anything interesting, so he went to the front door of the mansion.

Moses slammed the massive knocker against the huge, ancient door of Henry Duncan's house. He waited in the cold darkness, watching his breath float in wispy white streams before disappearing. Three times he watched his breath disappear before he pounded his fist against the door. He faced the street and stamped his feet. Then he heard the bolt slide and turned back to the door as it swung open. Standing in front of him was a young man he had seen before.

"Elvis!" Moses said.

The kid turned and fled down the hallway into the manor. Moses recovered from the shock of being face-to-face with a suspected killer and chased after him. Left. Right. Long hall. Bouncing off a swinging door and into a room with a roaring fireplace and another familiar face, Vahid. Elvis shouted something and then Moses was chasing both of them as they fled the room.

"Help," a voice croaked behind him. Moses skidded to a stop on the polished stone floor.

"Help," the voice said again. Moses located the source. Duncan was lying on the floor, blood running down his face, his hands tied behind his back with a plastic zip tie. Moses glanced back the way Vahid and Elvis had gone.

"Sit tight, Duncan, I'll be right back." Moses sprinted out the door and down another hallway, then paused, listening. He heard a door clank open and ran in its direction. He found himself back at the front door. Rubber whirred on the icy pavement. Moses ran down the driveway and onto the street as the taillights disappeared around the corner.

Moses bent over, gasping for air. He let his lungs catch up and turned back to the house. He found Duncan sitting up now and knelt down to free him from the plastic ties.

"Looks like someone else had some questions for you," Moses said as he worked the blade of a utility tool he always carried against the plastic. The blade was dull, but the bindings finally gave way.

Duncan grunted and rubbed his wrists. "We need to call the police. There is a landline in the next room."

"Not quite yet. Do you know those guys?" Moses asked.

Duncan slumped into a nearby chair and put his hand to his forehead. He was dressed for bed; his feet were bare and he wore monogrammed pajamas. Moses checked his watch and realized it was much later than he thought. Duncan looked a little older than last time he'd seen him, like his face was falling off, his fleshy cheeks bunching and pinching in deep crevices around his mouth. This might be the best time to get some answers.

"I think I've seen them before and I'm pretty sure they are the guys that I saw out in the woods…the killers," Moses said.

Duncan was staring into the fire now. Moses found another chair and dragged it over to Duncan and sat down. Duncan was shaken up. He didn't blame him. Elvis and Vahid had buried a man alive recently and were back. *Why?*

"These bastards are going to pay," Duncan said.

Moses leaned back in his chair. "Who were they?"

"Messengers."

"For?"

"That bitch," Duncan said.

"What's her name?" Moses asked.

Duncan stopped staring into the flames and looked at Moses with an expression of surprise, like he had forgotten that he wasn't alone.

"Sorry, what did you say?"

"What's her name?" Moses asked again.

"I don't know. Don't listen to me. Maybe they are just thugs looking to score on a rich old man's house."

Moses stood up and leaned over Duncan. "Stop bullshitting me, Duncan. What are you hiding? Dunsmore is dead and you know something. What is it?"

Duncan shook his head. "My business. I'll take care of it," Duncan said.

"It's not your business anymore. It's mine. But you want to end up under a tree somewhere, be my guest," Moses said.

"When I need help, I'll ask for it. I've done this all myself for this long. I don't need you," Duncan said, his voice barely a whisper.

"You sure?" Moses asked, pacing the room. "How'd they get in?"

"I don't know. They probably broke a window. Or the back door was open. I don't know."

"You don't have an alarm on this place?" Duncan shifted in his chair. "You let them in, didn't you? You know exactly who they are. Can't control the beast now that it is out of the cage, can you?"

"Things are changing. I've handled change before and I'll handle it now. This won't be figured out on a conference call or over email. It'll be handled at night, by men." Life seemed to flow back into Duncan's body and he looked vibrant again. Moses was a little on edge by the sudden transformation. It was like a retired boxer answering the bell in his sleep, not yet aware that he no longer possessed the weapons of his youth, but still dangerous enough that he couldn't be ignored. Moses was getting somewhere. He just needed to keep him talking. Down the street, he heard sirens.

"Did you call the police?"

"No. I've been here with you."

"Tell me who's in charge. Is it Vahid?"

"Vahid? No. He is a thug. A smart thug, but not the boss."

"Then who?" Moses heard voices down the hall and knew there was no time to talk to Duncan. Soon the police would be asking the questions.

"Give me something," Moses said. He could hear scuffling and shouting now inside the house. He had to try to push one more time. He leaned over Duncan again. "Come on, you bastard. Talk!"

Duncan shook his head. Police officers burst into the room and threw Moses to the ground. Duncan protested loudly and finally they let Moses back up. They questioned him, took his statement, and told him to leave. Moses tried to talk to Duncan, but medics and police surrounded him. He walked to the front door and almost ran into Rakić as he was on his way in.

"What the hell are you doing here?" Rakić asked.

"I came to talk to Duncan and ran into Elvis and his friend. Listen, I need to talk to you. Got a minute?" Rakić nodded and followed Moses outside. "Sorry about earlier with your family. I was just trying to help."

Rakić nodded. "It gets to be a little volatile when you involve the different clans in town. What the hell happened?"

"Yeah, sorry. I didn't realize. But here's the deal. I think that Duncan is involved in Dunsmore's murder. These guys that broke into Duncan's house are the same guys that I saw in the woods. They were at the Zmaj the other night."

"This Elvis guy?"

"Yeah, Elvis and Vahid. Do you think Šejla can help us figure out who these guys are, where we can find them?"

Rakić stuck his hands in his pockets and shook his head. "I don't want her mixed up with this stuff. I think I might tell her to take a vacation."

"Yeah. You're probably right. Listen, there is something I didn't tell the other cops."

"What's that?"

"I got a plate on that truck."

Rakić's eyes widened and then narrowed. "Why didn't you report it?"

"I don't know. Hard to know who to trust. The plate was XYU-896."

Rakić pulled out a notebook and scribbled it down. "Alright, I'll tell you if we get a hit on it."

"Thanks, Rakić." Rakić nodded. Moses got in his car and drove off, watching Rakić in the rearview. Rakić waited in the driveway until Moses had pulled away, then turned and walked back toward the Duncan house.

Chapter 17

Duncan had answered Rakić's questions, but offered no new explanation as to why the two men had broken into his house. Rakić left Wilson to finish up the scene. He had checked the plate on the truck, but it had come back as stolen a week ago. He flagged it so he would be notified if it came up on any of the various traffic cameras throughout the city. After that dead end, he decided to come here, the grocery store on 86th Street. It was time to work his contacts in the neighborhood, something he hated to do. Authority, even without a uniform, was regarded with a base level of suspicion. Pushed a degree and it could be met with open scorn and any injustice, perceived or real, could spark violent retaliation. Top that off with the widely-held belief that the criminals were somehow justified in what they did.

Rakić was looking for Biba. He had found her car easily enough and had parked next to it under a flickering streetlight, facing the side entrance to the large supermarket. He checked the time on his watch, then pulled out his wallet and started discarding business cards and receipts into a pile on the passenger seat. Satisfied, he stuffed his wallet back into his pocket. He pulled out his cigarettes and shook one loose from the pack into his mouth. Rakić pressed the car's cigarette lighter and waited for the click. The door to the store swung open and three women bundled against the cold stepped outside and lit cigarettes, waving goodbye as they made their way to their cars.

Rakić put his unlit cigarette into the cup holder and stepped out of the car.

"Biba," he said.

Biba, almost to her car, stopped. She pulled the cigarette from her mouth and exhaled a smoky cloud. The other two women paused at their cars, watching.

"What do you want?"

Rakić motioned to the passenger side of the car. "Get in."

Biba nodded back to the other two and, her steps shortened by the cold, pulled open the passenger door of the squad car. Rakić got back in and cleared the passenger seat of his mess.

Rakić resumed lighting his cigarette and cracked the window as Biba got in. She put her cigarette in her mouth and sat down, putting her purse on her lap, folding her hands on top of it.

"What do you want, Raif?"

"You still working with Šejla at the Zmaj?"

Biba shrugged. "You know I am."

"Were you working last Saturday?"

"I work every Friday and Saturday night, why?"

"Who was talking of death?" Rakić asked.

"Who was talking of death?" Biba laughed. "No one talks like this. Why are you so strange?"

"Don't laugh. This is my work. It is serious."

"You are just on a power trip. I don't know what you are talking about, 'death.' What does that mean?"

"There was someone killed in a very gruesome way. Someone at the Zmaj was talking. Someone said you heard about it."

Biba laughed again. "You are insane. Listen to yourself. In a million years, I would never talk about such things even if I knew."

"Not even to Šejla, if it was her lover? I am not so sure. You have been close."

Biba took the cigarette from her mouth and smoothed her lips with her hand. "Freddy is dead?"

Rakić shifted in his seat leaning closer to Biba. "Don't fuck with me, Biba. This is serious."

Biba shook her head. "I'm not, Raif. I really did not know. I haven't been to the Zmaj since Saturday and I haven't talked to Šejla."

Rakić leaned back. "So, you didn't hear anything the other night?" Biba shook her head. "Do you know an Elvis or a Vahid?" She put the cigarette back in her mouth and looked out the window. He could see her eyes reflected in the glass of the window. "So you do. That is okay. I know how it is. It is as it was in the old country. No one trusts the authorities. I get it."

Rakić drew on his cigarette one last time and then tossed it out the crack in the window. "It is different here, though. You work how many jobs?"

"You know how many. Two," she said, her eyes looking tired now. Rakić felt guilty at watching her without her knowing.

"Not bad. Do these worthless ones work at all? Do they only prey upon us like it was before? The difference is here that they don't get away with it. You can't kill here. No one lets you kill here and just bury the body and forget about it. You can do a lot, but you can't kill. These people that you protect don't care, but I don't need your help; I will find them."

"Do you still watch the planes?" she asked, and her eyes changed. Before, they were looking at the nothing of the nearly-empty, dirty-snow-covered parking lot, dead. But only able to see a glimmer of her through the reflection, he thought maybe her eyes were seeing something beautiful.

"Sometimes."

"I don't. Not anymore. I can go?" she asked, turning now to look at him.

"Just one thing. You don't have to tell me anything about them. But if they come in again, send me a text and let me know. Just one text. It is not much." Rakić pulled out a card from the discards he had cleared from the seat, found a pen in the console, and wrote his number on the back.

"You make speeches, but I don't see the difference. The world is the same everywhere."

"If you say so," he said, offering her the card.

She opened the door and got out. Then she stuck her hand back in. "Give it to me."

Chapter 18

Moses sat in his car watching the back door of the Zmaj from a lot a few hundred feet away. It was Christmas Eve day, shortly after noon, and there had been very little activity. The cleaning crew had left an hour ago and since then the place had been quiet. He opened the center console, located a small black sleeve the size of a reporter's notebook and a small flashlight, and stuffed them in his coat pocket. He left the engine running and got out. He zipped the cowl of his coat over his mouth and pulled on a gray stocking hat as he made his way down the snowy bank to the backdoor of the Zmaj.

A quick glance left and right and he tried the door. Locked. He knelt down, removing the black sleeve from his pocket and unfolding it on the icy asphalt of the lot. He pulled off his gloves and selected two tools from their plastic sheathes.

He inserted the first small metal tool and pulled the tip across the top of the lock, setting the tumblers. He inserted the other L-shaped tool and turned it slightly to put tension on the lock. His fingertips were beginning to numb from the cold breeze as he inserted the first tool again. This was the rake that he had the most success with and he hoped it would work quickly. He rocked the pick up and down, starting with the tumbler furthest from him and working his way out. The tumblers gave way and the tension wrench spun the bolt open. He put the tools away, stashed them back in his pocket, and slipped inside. He quietly closed the door and paused a moment while his eyes adjusted to the dim corridor. No alarms sounded and no one came rushing into the hallway to find him. So far, so good. He took his flashlight from his coat pocket and flicked it on. He focused the beam on the floor as he made his way deeper into the bar. The door to the room where he'd drank the strange liquor with

Vahid and Majka was closed. He ignored it for now and continued into the main bar to make sure he was alone.

The place seemed closed up. The bar was reset and restocked, the glasses stacked neatly on the counter. Moses walked to the front window and looked out. Checking the parking lot and seeing nothing, he returned to the office in the back. He tried the door. Locked. He bent down and looked. It was a simple lock. He pulled out his tool set again and this time selected a thin metal card in the shape of a credit card. Moses pulled hard on the knob creating space between the frame and the door, slid the card between the catch, and the door sprang open. He flipped the light on.

Inside, the room was very much the way he had seen it the last time he was there. A deck of cards was stacked next to a half-full ashtray. A newspaper and the bottle of the strange liquor were off to the side. He spun the bottle around and flipped the paper over. It was a few days old. Hanging from a nail on the wall was a clipboard. It looked like a schedule of some sort. He took his cell phone out and snapped a picture. He went through the shelves. There was a stack of beer boxes on one. He tapped them. They seemed empty, but the weight was off. He pulled the top box off, put it on the table, and opened it. Inside, right on top, was a bank bag. He emptied it on the table. A large roll of cash fell out, along with some rolls of change. He stuffed the money back in the bag and put it away, re-stacking the boxes. Up against the wall was a four-drawer filing cabinet with a Christmas present on top. He pulled on the first drawer and was glad to find it unlocked. Inside, he found a folder marked "receipts." He set the folder down on the table and started flipping through it. It was mostly delivery stuff. He went back to the file cabinet and went through the rest of the drawers. On the bottom drawer, he found an expandable file underneath some hanging folders. He unwound the cord tying it shut and emptied the contents on the table. They appeared to be legal documents for incorporation of a business in the state. He flipped to the end of the first document where the represented parties were listed. He recognized one of the names. Fred Dunsmore. He snapped pictures of the documents, stuffed them back in the folder, and returned it to its place underneath the hanging folder.

He took one last look around the office and then left. He locked the door and closed it behind him. He froze. Something had changed. He felt the back of his neck turn to gooseflesh. He turned toward the bar and saw shadows dancing on the wall in the hallway. Then the lights came on and he was exposed in the bright electric light. He heard soft talking and then a chuckle. The voices were faint, but he could hear no trace of alarm in them and was able to breathe easier. They didn't know he was there. He crept toward the bar to get a look at the visitors. Moses cracked the door open, revealing a sliver of the room and a stranger. He was an old, tall man whom he didn't recognize. Then a second person came into view. It was Majka. She was smiling brightly at the old man. Moses watched her as she went behind the bar and poured drinks. She returned and set a drink in front of the man. She lingered and the man returned the smile. He had a small, angular face, a long thin nose, a chin that disappeared into his long neck, and a pony tail falling down his back. Even from Moses' vantage, he could see the man's teeth were yellowed and large, jutting out from thin lips. His hollow cheeks completed his lupine visage. Moses thought he looked like a lean old coyote.

"Drink this. I will get it," Majka said, gesturing to the glass.

Majka started walking toward Moses. He felt his heart jump a beat, but was able to slowly let the door close. He fell back into the shadows in the corner behind the door, forcing himself to breath slowly. Majka walked through the door a second later, rushing past Moses down the hall, her heels clacking on the linoleum floor. Then she disappeared into the office. A few seconds passed. Moses felt a moment of panic. He was trapped between Majka and the Coyote with nowhere to go. *Had he returned everything to its place?* A rogue thought entered his mind. *Was she seeing this man as well? Was this business? It felt like business.* Moses waited, watching, and shifted his position, concealing himself behind a stack of kegs. Majka returned and walked past him, back into the bar carrying the gift-wrapped box from the office. Moses rushed back to his observation point and cracked the door again.

"Here you are." Majka placed the box in front of the old man.

"Ah. Perfect." The man pulled the top of the box off and leaned over to look inside. "Good. Well, I have to get going," he said, putting the top back on the box and tucking it under his arm.

"Are you sure?" Majka said, grabbing his arm in hers and walking him to the front door. The lights went out, the door closing behind her as she exited. The deadbolt clinked home and Moses was alone again.

Moses leaned back against the wall, feeling some of the tension release. Loneliness filled him and a weak part of him wished he had been discovered. He felt no energy in his limbs, only dead weight. As quickly as the loneliness had arrived it was replaced with anger. *Who was that guy?* With a sudden burst of energy, Moses dashed through the bar to the front window. The old Coyote was driving off in a large shuttle van, heading west out of the lot. There was no sign of Majka. Moses ran back down the hallway and out the back door to his Jeep. His foot slipped on a patch of ice and he nearly slid under the vehicle. Cursing, he got into the Jeep and yanked the shifter into gear. He jumped the curb, drove down the bank, cut through another lot, and was on the street speeding after the man with the box.

He crested the hill and spotted the van ahead of him cruising through an intersection at the bottom of the hill. Moses squinted in the brightness, straining to read the license plate number. He stomped on the gas, now able to make it out, and started to repeat it to himself, "XFZ-896. XFZ-896. XFZ-896."

Moses let the van get farther ahead as his mind started to drift. The man had a box. *Was it drugs? Cash? Maybe the Coyote was delivering it to the boss. Drugs or cash.* He couldn't think of anything else it could be. *Kittens.* Moses smiled to himself. *XFZ-896. XFZ-896. Delivering to the boss would be good.* He wanted that meeting more than anything. He still had a blind spot for Majka. He knew she was somehow involved now, *but how? At what level?* He didn't believe she knew anything about Fred's murder, *but what was her connection?*

The Coyote took a left at the light and Moses found himself farther back than he should be, chasing a yellow light. He stepped on the accelerator, the rear end of his Jeep slid around, and he gunned the engine through the turn, barely in control, but still on the tail of the Coyote. He followed him south and then west, farther away from the city, into the newer part of the suburb. They were stuck at a light for a moment and Moses pulled his cell phone out of his pocket. No missed calls or messages. He should call Rakić. No, he didn't really have anything. He had an old man with a Christmas present in a van. It could be he was taking the gift to a charity drive. It didn't feel like this guy was Santa, but cops need a reason, even these days. He had a feeling that he had lucked into something big, something that couldn't be planned for. He had caught them out in the open, exposed, by coincidence. It would take months of police work to get a sniff of a bagman like this, on his way to a delivery and even then, it would be lucky. He was lucky.

The van pulled off the street and into a shopping mall parking lot. Moses kept going to the next entrance and then cut through a roundabout. It was one of those new walking malls. Three-story buildings with apartments on top and high-end boutiques on the main floor. Moses lost sight of the van as he continued on a parallel path. Emerging from the storefronts and out into the open space of the larger parking lot, he searched for the van. It was not where it should be; the entire lot was virtually empty except for a few stray cars covered in snow. He drove around the other side where the van had entered and backtracked toward the street. Nothing. It felt like he had lost a winning lottery ticket. He circled around one more time and decided to park in the lot. He positioned his car so it faced the storefronts with the road between him and the building. The van must have pulled into one of the subterranean garages that were below the storefronts, the parking for the apartments above.

The big fish got away, he thought. Or he could have just been coming here. This could be his destination. He noted the addresses of the potential apartments that the Coyote could have entered and the license plate of the van in his notebook. He pulled out his smokes and lit one. He watched the garages for half a cigarette. Then the garage directly in front of his car began to open.

"Shit." The van barreled out of the garage and was coming right at him. Moses drew in his breath and held it. He instinctively tried to remain quiet and not move, as if a deadly predator was charging him. If he could attain complete stillness, he wouldn't be seen and mauled. The van passed by and Moses saw the Coyote inside. He laughed at himself and started breathing again. Moses pulled the car out of the lot and followed the Coyote again. This time they didn't stick to the side streets. In less than a minute, they were speeding down the freeway, headed into the heart of the city. He was tight on him and hoped that he hadn't been made. He tried to keep some cars between himself and the Coyote, but there wasn't much traffic. They were off on 42nd street and headed south past Grand Avenue. Moses had a sinking feeling. It was too much of a coincidence. They could only be going one place. After the next turn, Moses was sure. He let the van get way ahead, then took a side street, and went around the block on a different route. He drove slowly down the street, seeing the van in the driveway and the Coyote walking to the door of the Duncan house carrying the Christmas present.

"Bastard is running the whole damn thing," Moses whispered to himself. He found a place to park around the curve in the road, facing away from the Duncan house, but with full view in his mirrors. This is what Duncan was talking about. *Had Fred been part of an organized crime syndicate? What was the crime? Drugs. Bars like to have drugs available. It could be drugs. Cheap black market booze? Maybe. Protection?* Moses settled into his seat further and tried to get comfortable.

He had been in his Jeep a while. Gas was running low. The gauge was on the orange part of the last quarter. He killed the engine to conserve gas. The sky was starting to darken and it looked more and more like the night Moses had run into Vahid and Elvis. Movement in the side mirror caught his attention. The front door of the house opened and the Coyote walked briskly to his van carrying the present.

What's in the damn present? The van pulled out of the driveway and zoomed past Moses, headed back down the street. Moses hesitated. He could talk to Duncan or keep on the tail. Duncan would keep. The Coyote could get away. He jerked the Jeep into gear and sped after the disappearing van.

Moses followed the van as the Coyote retraced his route to the freeway. On the freeway, they curved through the downtown skyline as they traveled toward the northeast edge of the city. A few minutes later, Moses followed the van off an exit to a truck stop. The truck stop was massive due to its location at the intersection of two major interstate highways. The Coyote steered the van toward a group of parked livestock tractor trailers parked at an angle, facing the pumps. The van backed into an open space between two of the trucks. Moses swung the Jeep around and parked by the entrance to the cafe, affording him a view of the front of the van and semis. The Coyote got out of the van and walked to the truck parked on the passenger side of his van. It was a red Mack. The license plate was from Iowa. TNN-762. Moses marked it down next to the van's plate number in his notebook.

The Coyote stood on the fuel tank of the truck and pulled the door open. He seemed to say something and then nodded his head and shut the door. In a minute, he returned with the present and passed it up to the person in the cab. Then he stepped down and walked over to his van and leaned his shoulder on the passenger side door, waiting. A minute passed and then a big, middle-aged man in a tan Carhartt jacket got out of the cab. He said something to the Coyote and they both walked to the back of the trailer.

"Dammit," Moses said as they disappeared behind the trailer of the semi. Moses checked his gas tank. It seemed to be in the same spot. He should get gas now in case he had to follow the Coyote or the truck.

He shut the engine off and got out of the Jeep. He walked around the gas pumps and made a beeline to the parked trucks, giving himself a cushion of a few trucks between him, the Coyote, and the Big Man. Moses walked down the line of semis until he was standing next to the red Mack truck. The cab appeared empty. He walked down the length of the livestock trailer on the driver's side, all the openings in the sheet metal along the trailer's length making it look like a giant cheese grater. The gravel popped underneath his feet with every step, making him nervous of being discovered. When he reached the rear of the trailer, he knelt down and peered underneath, looking for anyone or anything on the other side. Wet noses made snuffling noises as the cows inside the trailer pressed against the ventilation holes of the trailer, eager to assess him.

Moses continued around the back of the trailer and found the spring-loaded door was raised, allowing a view of the inside. There were three rows of stalls. The stalls on the exterior walls of the trailer were packed with cows but the center stall was empty. He heard steps on the gravel on the opposite side of the trailer and he peered around the end so he could see the passenger side. The Coyote and the Big Man were helping a girl into the back of the Coyote's van where other girls were seated. The girl they were helping was dressed in a winter coat and was wearing a pink pair of ski pants. Blonde hair stuck out of a knit hat, then she was gone inside the van and they shut the door behind her. The Coyote and the Big Man talked for a bit; Moses couldn't hear the words.

The two finished talking and the Big Man started walking toward Moses.

"Shit," he whispered to himself. He scrambled up the back of the trailer, looking to evade notice, but he was too late.

"Hey! What are you doing on my truck?" said a masculine voice that sounded like it had gone through its fair share of beechwood aging.

Moses turned and looked down into the face of the Big Man, his gloved hands balled up into fists. Moses jumped down the side and put a step between him and the truck driver. The Big Man stepped toward him. Moses took a step back.

"Just wondering what kind of steaks you had in there," Moses said.

"Steaks, huh? Come here, I'll show you."

Moses turned and ran down the side of the semi at a dead sprint. He cleared the front of the truck in time to see the Coyote leaving in his van. Moses chanced a look back and didn't see the Big Man. He must have chalked him up to a truck stop weirdo. Moses jogged the rest of the way to his Jeep. When he arrived at the Jeep, he paused a moment, leaning against the car door as he gasped for air. He reached in his pocket, found his pack of smokes, and lit one up. The smoke calmed him as he got inside and started the car. He had to stay on the Coyote. He put the car in gear and raced out of the lot after the van.

What was going on? Were humans just bought and sold? He had heard stories of human trafficking, but not here. Not in Iowa. He tried to wrap his head around it. Had Fred been the kingpin of a trafficking ring? That didn't seem right. Had he wanted out of it? Had he been the money? Duncan was involved, with apparent ties to the west-side clubs and an important vein of influence ran right through Majka and the Zmaj. Moses stubbed out his cigarette in the ashtray and cracked his window. He was a few hundred feet back from the Coyote, the highway nearly deserted. Light snow began to fall. They continued north and exited westbound on the mixmaster, the convergence of two major interstates and the freeway loop through Des Moines. Moses pulled his hat back, letting the cold air hit him in the face. When he figured out where they were taking these poor girls, he was going to have a talk with Majka and Duncan, but first he needed something he could take to Rakić.

As the Coyote exited northbound on Highway 49, Moses closed the gap between them. The Coyote turned into an old motel within sight of the interstate called the Center Line Inn. It was two stories, with an office in the corner of the L-shaped building. The rooms all had doors facing the lot. It was the type of place on the edge of town where you could find a cheap room, a place that took cash and didn't care who it came from.

The Coyote pulled the van around the corner of the office and parked in front of the last room at the end. Moses pulled into a spot closer to the office and shut the engine off. The Coyote got out of the van and slid the side door open. The first person to step out of the van was small. Her long black hair fell over the fur lining of her heavy winter coat, her pale face almost glowing in the dimly lit parking lot. A man stepped out of the room, startling the girl. She fell back, almost falling into the van. The Coyote pulled her out by her arms, lifting her off the ground, and pushed her toward the man. The man caught her and pulled her inside the room.

The Coyote waited until the man returned and then pushed the next girl to him. The same scene played out for the next eight women and girls. Moses tried to keep track of what they looked like. He wished for a better camera, cursing his cheap cell phone.

In the end, he had to go by hair color. He counted six blondes and four brunettes. He thought that there were at least five underage girls fifteen or younger, probably more. He picked up his phone again. He didn't want to call the police. Something was telling him to wait. If this was a citywide human trafficking ring, he wanted to bring down the entire network.

He put the phone back in the console and zipped his coat up to his mouth. He couldn't run the engine or he'd risk running out of gas. He tested the air inside the Jeep with a puff of breath; it came out in smoky vapor.

An hour had passed since the two men had gone inside the hotel room with the ten women and girls. The snow was falling faster now. Moses could still see the room but it was harder to see the office and the rest of the hotel.

The Coyote had been outside for a few puffs of a cigarette a while ago, but since then, it had been quiet. Moses started the engine and let it run. He needed to warm up or he might fall asleep. Lights flashed across his rearview mirror, blinding him momentarily. The lights swung past his car and turned down the L of the motel toward the van and the Coyote. The source of the lights was a white SUV stretch limo. The limo turned around and parked behind the van, facing the exit of the parking lot, the lights flooding the interior of Moses' Jeep. The license plate holder on the limo was empty.

The driver-side door opened and a man popped out. Moses' face tensed and his veins pulsed with blood. He recognized the man. Elvis trotted up to the door and knocked, glanced around, and then disappeared inside.

A few minutes later, the motel door opened and Elvis trotted back to the limo and opened the back passenger doors. The Coyote walked out of the motel, waving to the motel door in a shooing motion toward the car. Out came a blonde girl wearing a short skirt and high heels. She had on a tiny fur coat and her hair was done up big. She took several quick steps and let Elvis help her into the limo. Then another came out dressed in a similar way. She had blonde hair as well. Then came a brunette. These seemed closer in age to women than girls. The other man followed the last girl out. He leaned against the doorframe and watched as Elvis herded them into the limo. All told, six of the ten got into the limo. The Coyote got into the van and waited as Elvis pulled the limo ahead. Then the Coyote backed his van out and left, Moses slunk down in his seat as he went by. He didn't know where to find the Coyote, but he knew who did. Moses wanted to know where Elvis was taking the girls.

Elvis got out of the driver's side and into the back of the limo with the girls. The other man went back into the motel and shut the door. A minute passed, then Elvis was outside again and into the driver's seat of the limo, barreling past him on his way to the street. Moses pulled the Jeep out after him. Moses tried not to think about what was going on behind that motel room door.

They were back on the interstate and headed west in seconds. Moses had to stay closer now that the snow was falling harder and starting to blow. He let the limo drift ahead until the vehicle was mostly obscured by the swirling snow, visible only by the glow of its burning red taillights. Now it was two vehicles, Moses in the Jeep and Elvis driving the girls in the limo, locked together by the snow and forty feet of visibility. It was close to 9:00 p.m.

They exited two miles down, headed north, on the edge of the city. Elvis took a right turn and pulled into a large, nearly-empty lot. He pulled the limo around the side of the large warehouse-type building and parked next to a side entrance. Elvis got out, opened the car door, and the women poured out. Elvis ushered them into the building. Moses picked up his phone and dialed.

"This is Rakić."

"Rakić, this is Winter. I can't explain, but I think you need to come down to the Devil's Playhouse."

"The strip club? It's Christmas Eve. What are you talking about?"

"Just get down here. There are some women who shouldn't be here. I think they are kidnapped and I'm looking right at Elvis."

"Elvis? Got any proof?"

"Nope. I just saw them get off a semi-truck and get dropped off here. Either way, don't you want to talk to him?"

"Stay put. It's not that far. I can make it in twenty."

"This is only part of them. Listen, there are six at the strip club. The other four are at a motel called the Center Line Inn, room fifteen on Highway 49. Know it?"

"Yeah, I know it."

"The ones there are young. I need to go check on them."

"Okay, I'll send some backup that way. Winter, don't do anything stupid."

"Yeah." Moses ended the call. He pulled his Jeep out of the lot and headed back to the Center Line Inn. He had to get there before they left and he lost them forever. It seemed to take longer than five minutes, but he was back in the lot of the Center Line. Moses shut off the engine and got out of the car. He walked up to the office and down the boardwalk that ran the length of the motel rooms. He knew there was at least one man, but he had no way of knowing if there were more inside. Moses slowed his pace and tried to muffle his footfalls as he got closer. He crept up to the window of the room and looked through the gap in the blinds.

Inside, Moses saw the man from before and three of the girls. The man had black-framed glasses on a wax face and thick, premature gray hair greased into a part. He was wearing corduroys and a sweater with a collared shirt sticking out of the V neck. He would be right at home in any office. His light blue eyes were focused, magnified by the lenses of his glasses, making it seem like Moses was the one behind the glass. His attention was on the girl sitting on the bed. The other two were standing to the side like they were in line at the grocery store. The man leaned over the girl on the bed, holding her hair off her neck. The girl winced and the man raised his hand, holding a large syringe with the plunger depressed. The tube was empty. Whatever the contents had been were now inside the girl. He patted her on the back and she stood up. He gestured for the next girl to sit down. He picked up a notepad from the bed and scribbled something on it, then tossed the syringe in a small garbage bin. He picked up a package containing another syringe and repeated the process. *Was he doping them up? Giving them some sort of inoculation?* Only three of the girls were in sight. Where was the fourth? There was a door on the far wall that had to lead to the bathroom. She must be in there. The third girl was getting her shot when the door to the bathroom opened. Out came the girl with the long dark hair. Her eyes were bright and her lips were set in a thin line. The man seemed oblivious to her presence as he administered the injection to the final subject. The girl from the bathroom moved slowly to the end of the bed and leaned down. She stood up, holding an electrical cord. She slowly wrapped it around her small hand, picked up the lamp that it belonged to, and glided behind the man. Finished with the shot, the man turned toward the girl with the dark hair. She bared her teeth as she swung the lamp in a merciless arc toward the man's head. The shade crumpled against his skull. Glass from the light bulb rained over the bed as the man collapsed in a heap on the floor. The girl sprang onto the bed, over it, and flung the exterior door open. Moses was now face-to-face with her. She showed her teeth again, freezing him in his tracks long enough for her to dart past Moses into the parking lot. Then the man emerged from the room, leaning on the doorframe and holding his forehead, his glasses gone.

"What's up, doc?" Moses asked.

The man turned at Moses' voice, squinting. "What do you want?"

"Wanted to ask you about these girls you have here."

"My daughters? What about them?"

"Daughters? I don't think so. What are you putting in their necks?" Moses bulled forward and the man retreated into the room, his hand inching toward his back.

"Don't go for a gun if that's what you're thinking. The cops are already here. And they don't like other people with guns. People get shot that way."

The man seemed to relax. "So, you're not the police."

Moses cursed himself silently. He needed to keep this man in the room until the cops showed up. "Just friendly toward the law and don't like seeing girls taken advantage of." Moses took a second to look at the girls. Their eyes seemed clear and bright. Whatever the man had given them wasn't doping them up yet.

"If you are not police then you have to go. Leave me and my girls alone." The man reached behind his back again. Moses jumped at him. He twisted, and Moses tripped him and they fell onto the bed. Moses got on top of him and pinned him down.

"Run!" Moses shouted at the girls. They stood there, wide-eyed, mouths open. Moses yelled again and pointed to the door. They came unstuck and were gone in a swirl of hair, elbows, and shrill chatter. He turned back to the man, shaking him.

"What did you put in them?" Moses twisted the man's arm until he screamed.

"It's nothing. Nothing. Ahhh!" the man cried out and Moses let up a degree.

White light flashed across the wall. Moses smiled. "Now the cops are here." Moses reached into the man's belt and pulled out the 9mm pistol he'd been reaching for. He shoved the man down and walked to the door. As he stepped outside, the headlights went dark and Moses realized it wasn't the cops. It was the white van. The passenger and driver doors opened and the Coyote and Vahid stepped out. Vahid shouted something and reached for his belt. Moses jerked to the right, down the boardwalk, ducking as he ran.

Crack. Crack. Crack.

Urgent barks of gunfire erupted into the night. Moses veered through the lot toward his Jeep. More gunfire.

Crack. Crack.

He was almost to his Jeep when he saw a figure dart toward him. He aimed the gun at center mass, then pointed it away when he recognized her. It was the dark-haired girl, running with him.

Moses jerked the Jeep door open and shoved the girl inside, almost throwing her over the console into the passenger seat. He turned the key in the ignition and the engine growled to life. He pulled the shifter into drive and the tires grabbed the pavement as he hit the gas. The Jeep careened wildly toward the lot's exit. He looked in the rearview and saw a man chasing them with fire flashing from his raised arm. Moses pushed the girl's head down below the dash, then they were out on the street, racing away. Moses tossed the gun on the dash.

"You okay?" Moses pulled her head back up. "You okay?"

She just looked at him. "Okay?" he asked again. She shook her head.

Moses scoured her body for any sign of blood. Seeing none, it dawned on him. She probably didn't speak a word of English. He steered the Jeep onto the interstate and put the gas pedal to the floor as they sped toward the northwest suburbs. He checked the rearview. Empty. He looked down at the girl. She was huddled into the corner of the seat with her knees up to her chin. He reached over and pulled the seatbelt, motioning for her to put it on. She gave him a look that seemed to say there were more likely ways they would die tonight, but then she pulled the belt over her shoulder, latching it in place. Moses sighed and, finding his smokes in the cup holder, he lit up. The girl leaned over and pulled one out of the pack. Moses swatted it out of her hand and shook his head at her. She pulled away, sticking out her lower lip. Jesus, she was young.

"What's your name?"

"Brooklyn," she said.

"Holy shit, I didn't expect an answer. Where are you from?"

"Savage Lake." Brooklyn said.

Minnesota. She was from Minnesota.

Moses checked the rearview again. Lights.

"Shit."

He tried to push his foot through the floor. He checked his speed. The needle read 100mph. He thought the lights were getting further away. Then he felt the steering wheel go stiff. Lights lit up on the dash. The engine was dead and they began to decelerate.

"Shit! Shit! Shit!"

"Shit," the girl repeated.

Moses shot her a look and she clapped her hand over her mouth. They were passing an off-ramp and Moses pulled the Jeep through the warning lines and off onto the Merle Hay Avenue exit. He put the shifter in neutral and let the Jeep coast. The lights on the highway were closer now and followed him onto the exit ramp. They were sitting ducks, no place to go. The Jeep ran out of momentum thirty yards from the street. He managed to pull over to the shoulder. Now the lights were close, slowing down. His last hope that it was another car and not the Coyote went as the lights pulled in behind them.

"Down," Moses said, pointing to the floor. He grabbed the 9mm off the dash as the girl slouched down below the seatback. Moses watched in the rearview as the passenger door opened and a shadow passed in front of the headlights. Moses opened his door and stepped out.

"Cowboy, don't shoot. We just want the girl," Vahid said.

"Stay where you are."

"Don't be like this, Cowboy. It is business and I like you."

Moses flipped the safety off the gun. "Stay back or I'll shoot, Vahid. This girl isn't going anywhere." Moses felt a tremor start in his elbow and travel all the way to his forefinger, resting on the trigger. He shrugged his shoulder as it passed, the weight of the gun dragging on his arm, making him feel weak. The barrel dipped lower and lower. His lungs were cold, his breath shallow.

Vahid took a step. "Don't shoot. Let's talk."

Vahid was a silhouette in front of him, bulky in his winter coat. Steam from his body heat illuminated in the headlights of the van. If Moses screwed up, the girl would be his and would be gone. Something would be stuck in her neck and she'd be driven to the closest strip club or whorehouse or street corner to sell her body to hungry, desperate men. The anger pushed away the other thing and he felt power return to his arm. He raised the gun again, then turned and fired it to the side.

"I know you, Vahid. I'll find you. I'll kill you. You killed Fred. I have no problem returning the favor. Leave now and leave this girl with me and I'll forget we ever met."

Vahid put his hands up and retreated, walking backwards to the other side of the van, and Moses thought maybe he would. Then the driver side door opened and the Coyote leaned out with a shotgun. Moses dove back into the Jeep.

"Stay down!" he shouted to the girl as he ducked. The shotgun blast shattered the back window of the Jeep. Headlights flashed across the backseat as the van reversed. Moses reached outside and fired twice into the center of the lights. The lights stopped retreating. Maybe I got the engine, he thought.

They started moving again toward the Jeep, picking up speed. Moses pulled the girl upright and yanked the seatbelt tight. He leaned out of the door and emptied the gun toward the onrushing van. He had a fraction of a second to brace himself against the wheel.

"Shit," he whispered and managed one last look at the girl. Then he was floating, suspended as his ribs went numb. His head bounced off the dash. Somehow, his foot kicked the ceiling of the car and his legs were in the front seat. His torso wedged in the footwell of the backseat, and he forgot everything for a while.

Chapter 19

Ten minutes earlier than he thought possible, Raif Rakić pulled his police car into the lot of the Devil's Playhouse. The urgency in Moses' voice had compelled him here on Christmas Eve. He had run the lights and siren until he was on the interstate. Now they were dark and quiet as he eased his car toward the side of the building. One of the few days out of the year this place was closed was tonight. It would be open tomorrow night, the lot would be full of cars, and there would be a line outside of the building to get inside. But now it was empty. He pulled up to the side entrance and parked. He got out and walked to the windowless metal door and pounded on it with his fist. He waited for a minute, but there was no response. He pounded again and then tried it. Locked. He stepped back and looked up and down the building. The place looked deserted. He got back in his car and drove around back, but it was deserted as well. Rakić sighed. All he had to go on was Moses' word that he saw girls going into the club. That was not that unusual, other than the day and Moses' instincts, but he couldn't get a search warrant on a private detective's gut. He pulled around the lot and parked the car in front. He pulled his cell phone out and dialed Moses' number. It rang. He got his voice mail.

"Moses. It's Rakić. I don't see anything here at the club. I'm going to the motel. Call me back."

Rakić ended the call, left the lot, and headed back to the interstate. Back east toward the Center Line Inn. Rakić had called into the Des Moines PD night sergeant about the motel and the suspicious activity, but he didn't get the feeling that it was getting a high priority. It was on the edge of town with no real evidence. The shift was light anyway. Most were home with their families. He thought about calling the county in, but he still wasn't sure what he had.

Rakić passed an exit and saw a stopped vehicle on the opposite shoulder of the westbound exit ramp. Not thinking anyone was still with the car, he slowed down anyway and looked. The Jeep was like the one Moses drove, same color, but this one had been in an accident. The whole back end was smashed in. It was too much to be coincidence. I'm too late, he thought.

"Son of a bitch." He would have to go to the next exit to turn around. The concrete barrier that separated the lanes didn't have any breaks on this side of town. The car accelerated back to a highway speed and then beyond. Rakić needed to find out if Moses was still with his car and still okay. The exit was over three miles down the road and seemed to take an eternity to reach. He ran the light on the exit, turned around, and entered the on-ramp to the westbound lane.

"Come on. Come on." Then his training took over and he grabbed his radio. "This is Agent Rakić, DCI. I need EMT to westbound Merle Hay Road off-ramp. Looks like a hit and run. Unknown if occupants remain in the vehicle, over."

The operator was confirming the information when his headlights flashed on a dark shape in the passing lane. Too late for Rakić to stop, he swerved to the other lane and slammed on the brake pedal. The brakes vibrated under his foot as the automatic braking system ground the car to a stop. He looked in the rearview and saw the lights of another vehicle a good distance behind him.

"Sir, are you—" the operator's voice was cut off as Rakić flung the handset onto the dash of the car and shifted into reverse. He looked over his shoulder, using the back window to navigate. He wasn't sure what he saw, but it was moving slowly, in a jerking manner. It could be a drunk. It wouldn't be the first time someone was hit on the interstate after having one too many and wandering into traffic. He pulled up next to the shambling shape and realized who it was. He parked the car on the shoulder and flipped his emergency lights on. Rakić flung the door open.

"Moses! Can you hear me, Moses?"

Moses Winter, his face covered in blood and clutching his right side, stumbled forward like a zombie headed east toward the inn.

"Moses!" Rakić ran to him and pulled his hand away from his side. He couldn't see any blood. He glanced back and saw the lights getting closer. He checked Moses' face. The whites of his eyes were stark, gleaming between dark caked blood from a cut on his forehead and his black pupils. Moses stopped walking as recognition flickered in his eyes.

"Rakić." Moses smiled, showing blood-streaked teeth. Moses lunged forward and grabbed Rakić's arm. Rakić tried to pull away, afraid Moses would drag him to the ground, but Moses' grip was too strong. "They took her. They took them," Moses said.

"I know. I know." Rakić didn't know who he was talking about, but he had to get him off the road. He broke Moses' grip, grabbed him by the wrist, threw Moses' arm over his shoulder, and began the odyssey of dragging the bigger man across the twenty feet of pavement to the shoulder of the road.

"You gotta help me a little here, Moses," Rakić said as he saw the headlights closing in. "Do they not see the fucking lights?" he whispered. Finally, the last five feet within reach, Rakić lunged forward, pushing Moses toward the back of the car. Rakić jumped after him, the horn of a car honking behind him as it zoomed past.

"Your lucky night." Rakić memorized the plate, promising himself he would find out who it was when he had a chance. Moses had slumped to the ground, leaning on the bumper of the car, one hand holding his head and the other his side. Rakić knelt down and checked him more closely. He looked unharmed except for the cut on his head. Moses couldn't have been outside for much more than twenty minutes at the max, and he was dressed for the dangerously cold temperatures. Something else was wrong.

"Okay. On your feet, soldier." Rakić reached down and pulled Moses to his feet and propelled him toward the passenger seat. He opened the door and helped Moses inside. Rakić got in the driver seat and pulled back onto the highway.

He checked on Moses. He was leaning his head back and still clutching his side. *Don't die on me.* "Hang in there, buddy. We'll be at the hospital in a minute."

Moses snapped his head forward. "No. We have to go to the inn. We have to go to the inn."

"You're in no shape. We gotta get you to a doctor."

"No." Moses leaned over and grabbed the wheel. "They are still there! We have time. I just need to catch my breath. If we don't go and let those girls disappear…"

Rakić put his hand on Moses' shoulder and pushed him back into his seat. Rakić pulled off on the Merle Hay exit past the Jeep, under the interstate overpass and down the on-ramp, heading back to the Center Line Inn. An explanation on what had happened would wait.

"Don't die on me." Rakić glanced in Moses' direction.

"I promise," Moses said, and seemed to relax. "As long as you got a smoke."

Rakić couldn't stop the grin that spread across his face as he fished in his pocket for a cigarette.

* * *

"Moses."

Moses jerked awake, his side erupting in agony. He half-stifled a groan. He was in the passenger seat of Rakić's car. Now he remembered. He felt the cigarette between his fingers and brought it up to his mouth. His throat burned with a mix of smoke and blood. The headlights of the car were shining on number fifteen. They were there. Moses fumbled with the door latch. He felt a hand on his shoulder.

"Let me go first," Rakić said.

Moses glanced at Rakić, nodded, and got out of the car. Rakić was already walking to the door, Moses steadied himself on the car and then followed. Rakić glanced back at him, his hand on his holstered gun. A thin sliver of light escaped from the partially cracked-open door. Rakić drew his pistol and pushed lightly on the door with his off hand. It swung open and Rakić rushed into the room. Moses lurched forward and followed him. Rakić cleared the main room and then kicked the bathroom door open.

"Shit," Rakić said.

"They're gone. They are long gone," Moses said.

Moses shut the door behind him and leaned his back on it, taking a few quick, shallow breaths. The room smelled. The obvious scent of beauty products was undercut by a more powerful and deeply embedded odor of use and decay. Rakić walked around the room saying something, but Moses couldn't concentrate on what it was. He had lost them. Lost all of them. He had saved one for a minute, but he had lost her, too. They had taken her and he had let them. He couldn't save even one girl. Moses walked forward and sat on the bed facing the door, his back to Rakić.

"You didn't find them at the strip club?" Moses asked, already knowing he hadn't.

"No. The place was deserted," Rakić said.

Moses nodded as he tried to piece together what had happened in his head. *Elvis. Vahid. And Majka.* He could hear Rakić searching the room as he sat there. *Elvis. Vahid and Majka. And this Coyote man and a farmer with cattle. With cattle and girls. Cattle and girls and syringes and guns and immigrants and refugees and a doctor and a strip club. What in the good goddamn was happening in his city? This was Des Moines.* Moses lurched up and grabbed a lamp from the nightstand and hurled it against the wall.

"Ahhhh!" Moses couldn't stay balanced and his momentum took him into the wall. He put his hands against it, hanging his head.

"You alright?" He heard Rakić say.

"What is going on in this fucking place? They are treating those girls like animals. They put them in a livestock trailer. They pumped God-knows-what into their necks with those syringes."

"What syringes?" Rakić asked. Moses looked over at him. The last one he had seen was in the doctor man's hand, but he had been throwing them away in a bin.

"There was a trash bin. He threw them away."

Rakić found it next to a dresser and dumped it on the bed. What came out was a jumble of syringes, gauze, and fast food bags.

"How many are there?" Moses asked.

Rakić pulled out a pair of blue latex gloves from his pocket and put them on. He carefully removed the needles from the pile and placed them in a row on the bed.

"Ten."

"That's one for each then. They all got whatever it was." Moses felt stronger and pushed himself toward the bed. Still wearing his winter gloves, Moses picked one of the needles up and inspected the tip. It was easily two inches long and thick.

"What do you use this for? Why is it so big?"

"I don't know." Rakić shook his head. Moses picked up a soda bottle and used it to push the debris from the can around.

"No packages."

"What?" Rakić asked.

"The syringes all came in packages. But they took them. Why?" Moses lurched around the bed and into the bathroom. He opened the medicine cabinet. It was empty. He found a trashcan under the sink, but all it contained was a cardboard toilet paper roll. He came back out into the main room and got on his knees, feeling under the bed.

"What are you doing?"

"The packages. There must be something on the packages."

Rakić got down and started helping him. Moses started around the other side and then retraced. He found a sock and tossed it into the bathroom.

"I have something." Rakić said. Moses rose up and leaned on the bed. Rakić put the scrap of cardboard in front of him. It was a small scrap with the letters F I N and another small piece of a letter. Bellow the letters was part of a barcode.

"Could be anything," Moses said. He took the scrap and one of the syringes and wrapped them up in a piece of the fast food bag and put it in his pocket.

"Let's go," Moses said as he stood up.

"Where are we going to go?"

"We are going to find the girls."

"Moses, you need to see a doctor. Let the police handle this."

"What are you going to tell them? That you found some needles at a shitbox motel on the edge of town? And that some girls are missing? You think that will hit the top of the list?"

Rakić looked away. "Let's get something solid then. Where to?" he said.

"The Zmaj. The last place I saw Majka. She's part of this and she is going to give up Vahid and Elvis and that Coyote and that fucking doctor and the farmer. And then…" Moses couldn't catch his breath. He felt his knee buckle and put his hand out to catch himself. Rakić caught him and helped him sit on the bed.

Moses grabbed Rakić's shoulder. "No doctors," Moses said, putting out his hand. Rakić took it and pulled him to his feet.

"Yeah. We'll see." Rakić helped him outside and into the car. Moses noticed it had stopped snowing as Rakić drove him away from the motel.

Chapter 20

Rakić helped Moses up the two steps to his mother's front door. It had been all he could do to keep Moses awake on the short trip across town. Rakić had decided to take him to his mother's almost as soon as they'd pulled out of the motel lot. Moses was in no shape for anything and needed rest and someone to watch his back. As they reached the door, Moses went limp and Rakić struggled to say upright.

"Help me out here," Rakić said, hoping that Moses could still hear him. Rakić fished his keys out of his pocket and adjusted Moses' limp form. He managed to unlock the door and drag Moses inside.

"Mother!" Rakić shouted, as he dumped the lifeless Moses onto the couch.

The light flipped on in the hallway and his mother appeared dressed in a robe. "*It is late. What is it?*" she asked in Bosnian.

Rakić gestured at the couch. "*He's hurt. Get some towels and water.*" His mother nodded and disappeared back down the hallway. She returned shortly with the supplies. They turned Moses over and placed a sheet under him and then rolled him back and began stripping him down, searching for any signs of injury. They were able to clean the gash on his forehead and bandage it.

"He doesn't look that bad," Rakić said.

"It's his ribs," she said, pointing out the dark bruising on his right side. Rakić probed the bruise with his fingers as gently as he could.

"Maahh!" Moses moaned.

"They are either broken or cracked," Rakić said.

"He needs a doctor, *sin*." She said, mixing in the Bosnian word for son.

"He asked me not to."

"What do you care? This man lives with doctor or dies on my couch."

"This man asked me not to take him to the doctor. He is hurt and he needs our help."

"If he dies, you are buying me a new couch. I will not sit on a dead man's couch in my living room."

Rakić sighed. His mother was right. There was something keeping Rakić from taking this man to the emergency room. *What was it?* He had known the man for only a few days. *Was he worried that he wouldn't be safe in a hospital?*

"You don't have to be responsible for him. He is grown man," she said.

"I will get you your new couch, but let me be for now, Mother."

He felt her stiffen and then she rubbed his shoulder and left the room. Rakić shut the light off and moved into the armchair next to the couch and slouched down, trying to get comfortable. Moses' labored breathing filled the room as Rakić sat watching his chest rise and fall beneath the blanket.

* * *

Rakić awoke to his cell phone ringing in his pocket. He rubbed his eyes and checked on Moses. He seemed the same: pale, his breathing as ragged as before. He checked his cell phone and answered it.

"This is Rakić."

"Rakić, we got one. West of downtown." It was Kenny, the desk sergeant.

"Got any details?"

"To be honest?"

"Yeah."

"Sounds like an accident, but you're on. Christmas."

"All right, what's the address?" Rakić jotted it down on a magazine he found on the coffee table. "Okay. I'll be there in twenty." Rakić ended the call. He noted the time on the screen: 4:12 a.m. He went to his mother's room and tapped on the door and opened it a crack.

"Mother, I need to go out. Watch over him." She was awake in an instant and out of bed, pushing past him and out to the parlor, nodding the whole while and muttering about coffee. Rakić followed her into the parlor and watched as she took the bandage from Moses' head and cleaned the wound. Rakić couldn't help smiling. It was nice that now the biggest problems in her life were small. Although, not tonight. Tonight, he needed his strong mother to watch over Moses.

"I'll be back soon," he said and kissed her on top of her head. She waved him off.

"Go. I will watch him."

Rakić paused for a second at the door and then went outside into the cold, dark morning, racing to another dead body in his city.

Chapter 21

The minute Rakić arrived at the scene, he knew it was an accident. The man looked like a jackknifed truck with his chin tucked at an impossible angle under his shoulder, a bone from his broken neck threatening to rip through his skin. One black high-heeled shoe remained on his left foot; the other still on the seventh step of the staircase as if the person wearing it had simply vanished with its twin. But that person hadn't vanished, he had fallen headfirst down the stairs and jammed into the corner of the wall next to the doorway, breaking his neck. Dressed in one shoe and a pair of white Jockey shorts, the man had died alone.

Rakić looked at Wilson standing across the living room of the house laughing with another cop about something. He looked back to the man on the floor, watching as the forensic team did their work. The front door opened and a frozen-looking Hansen stepped inside, brushing snow from his winter issue hat.

"Neighbors know anything?" Rakić asked.

"Not much. Say he lived alone. Quiet guy," Hansen said, moving to stand shoulder to shoulder with Rakić, joining him in watching the techs collect fiber evidence.

"Look like murder to you?"

"Not unless someone else was here. Forensics will know."

"Yeah, I suppose so." A long silence and then, "The night Fred died, did anyone visit before he passed away?" Rakić asked.

Hansen lowered his head bringing his hand to his chin. "The night commander showed up for a minute to talk to me and Wilson."

"Wilson? Agent Wilson?"

"Yeah, Wilson went into the room for five minutes, maybe." Hansen said.

"Did Fred wake up? Was he ever conscious?"

"Not that I know. You think something is up?"

Rakić glanced at Wilson across the room, still laughing it up with the other cops. Then he looked at Hansen and his worried expression. "Nah, he told me about it. I was just curious if he told you anything. Sometimes he forgets to write all the details in his reports." Rakić patted him on the shoulder and walked into the living room where Wilson was now leaning on a couch. The lie to Hansen was part of the code. If Wilson was up to something, he would cover for him until he found out what it was. Partners were a weird thing. Wilson was never that fond of Rakić and the feeling was returned, but they had closed some cases and he was serviceable as a cop. More than could be said for some. *The devil you know.*

"Wilson, you got a second?" Rakić asked, pointing toward the kitchen.

"Sure, Raif." Wilson followed him into the kitchen. "What's up?"

"Nothing. You know that Hansen kid? Uni?"

"Yeah, sure. He's alright. You been really training him up, I hear. He making the transfer into DCI?"

"Maybe, what do you think of him?"

"I said he's alright. Don't really know him."

"Were you at the hospital the other night? To talk to Fred Dunsmore?"

"Yeah, I was there. Didn't talk to him though. He never woke up."

"Fucked up thing, isn't it?"

"What?"

"How he died, that dog tearing him apart like that."

Wilson leaned against the kitchen counter, tapping his knuckles on the granite. "I guess so. We've seen stranger ways to go," he said, jerking a thumb toward the dead man in the other room.

"Hah, you're right, we have." Rakić leaned forward and slapped him on the shoulder.

"That it?"

"Yeah, that's it. I was just curious why you didn't tell me you went to see Fred Dunsmore?"

"I filed the fucking report, Raif, can't you read?"

"Alright, alright, go fuck yourself. Let's get back out there before they think you're blowin' me."

"Jesus, alright. And they'd think that you were blowin' *me*, anyway."

Rakić's phone buzzed in his pocket. He pulled it out and answered it, waving Wilson away with a grin. "Hello, Mother."

"He is gone," she said.

"What? Are you okay?" Rakić thought the worst. Someone had come to the house looking for Moses.

"Yes, why? Of course. He just got up and left. I asked him to stay, but he refused."

"Did he walk?"

"No, a woman picked him up."

"Okay, Mother. I will come over later. No new couch, eh."

"Yes, no new couch." They said goodbye and Rakić left the kitchen, back to the scene in the other room.

* * *

Moses called the only person he could think of that would pick him up at 7:00 a.m. on Christmas morning. Claudia lived down the hall from him. She hadn't questioned him on the phone and now they were driving back to the converted Victorian house where they each had a small apartment.

"What happened? Who did this to you?" Claudia asked.

"Long story. Thanks for picking me up. I know it's Christmas."

"I owe you anyway. Jimmy was still sleeping. Teenagers, you know."

"Yeah. Sleep while you can," he said.

Claudia laughed a little. "You know, a few people have been stopping by at weird hours."

"My place?"

"Yeah. Well, I think you were home one time. A woman. Dark hair."

"Ah, yeah. She is a work friend," Moses said.

"Oh. You got a case with her? Someone cheating on her?"

"Yeah. Sort of. Who else has been around?"

"A kid, not much older than Jimmy. Strange-looking though, somehow."

Could be Elvis, Moses thought. "How is Jimmy? Is he going to get that scholarship?"

"We interview in a few weeks. You know Jimmy. He takes care of me, it seems like, more and more."

"Yeah. He's a good kid." They drove on for a few blocks when a squirrel jumped in front of the car. Claudia jerked the wheel slightly to miss it. Moses braced himself with his arm, but the extra stress on his ribs flashed a stabbing pain through his head, traveling down to his stomach. He looked down at the floor of the car and swallowed hard, holding himself together with spit.

"I'm sorry, Mos. Are you okay? I should take you to the hospital."

Moses just motioned forward, shaking his head. Finally, he managed, "I'm okay."

Claudia's eyes were wide and her lips parted, wanting to say more. He could tell she was worried about him, but this wasn't her problem. Moses managed to smile at her and she relaxed a little. They drove on in silence for the remainder of the short trip. Claudia drove slower and shot glances at him whenever they hit a small bump. Moses could feel the exhaustion building like a vice—squeezing down on the edges of his eyes, darkness closing in—but he only had a few hours to rest. Those girls were out there alone, with no one to help them.

* * *

Sleep had come easy even with the pain. But now Moses was awake. He checked the clock by his bed. It flashed 3:34 a.m. He forgot to reset it. The power was always flickering on and off in this old apartment. He reached for his cell phone next to the alarm clock. Pain shot up his side. He grimaced and finally reached the phone. He fell back into the bed, recoiling from the burning in his ribs. It was just after 11:00 a.m. according to his phone. Something had stirred in the other room. He rolled off the bed, trying to be quiet as he pushed himself to his feet, but he couldn't suppress a gasp when he straightened up. He found a pair of jogging pants and was finally able to get them on after several attempts, trying to avoid aggravating his stiff and sore abdomen. After the trial of the sweatpants, he thought a shirt was pushing it and decided to brave the other room without it. He put his hand on the door, ready to face the next room when he had a thought. *The gun. Where did he put the gun?* He glanced back at his bed and then the dresser. *The freezer*. He had hidden it there. Bad place. He pushed the door open and stepped into the next room.

The other room served as his living room and kitchen. It also had the only exit door. A couch was along the wall shared with his bedroom and a tube TV was sitting on a box in the opposite corner. A small kitchenette was off to the side with a refrigerator/freezer and a small range and sink. Moses could smell the cigarette. It was different than his standard Marlboro tobacco and it was mixed with her perfume, which made it all the more interesting.

"Cowboy," she said, not sounding happy to see him. She had a way of injecting derision, or if she wanted, the opposite into every word she spoke.

"Majka," he said as he made his way slowly to the kitchen. He had no way of knowing why she was here, but he was glad she was. He was going to see her anyway. He opened a cabinet and pulled out a glass. He set it on the counter and then opened the freezer.

"What happened to you?" she asked.

"Car accident. Hit and run," Moses said over his shoulder. "I need a drink. You thirsty?" Moses asked.

When he turned his head, he felt a sharp pain in his neck. He rubbed it and checked for blood. His hand came away clean, but the pain persisted for a few seconds before finally subsiding into a manageable ache.

"Sure. One drink on Christmas," Majka said, and went back to smoking her cigarette.

Moses opened the freezer door and pulled out the ice tray. He glanced at Majka. She was not paying attention. He pulled the door open, shielding him from her view and reached for the box of breakfast waffles. He pulled it out and set it on the counter with the ice. It felt too light. *It had to be in the box*. He popped a few ice cubes from the tray and clanked them into a glass. He reached into the box and felt for the gun. Nothing. He pulled the bag of waffles out of the box and looked inside, not believing it. Empty. *Where was the gun?* Shit, he remembered. Vahid. He had the gun with him when he was attacked. *Did Vahid have it now? Was it still in the car somewhere?*

"How about that drink, Cowboy?"

"Coming up," Moses said and stuffed the waffles back into the freezer. He made a whiskey for himself and Majka and brought them out to her. He sat next to her and raised his glass.

"Merry Christmas," Moses said. Majka raised her drink and took a sip.

"You know, I'm Muslim, but Christmas is fun."

"I guess I didn't think of it."

She shrugged. "How badly are you hurt?" she asked.

"Not bad."

"Good." She moved closer and put her hand on his thigh. "We should celebrate."

"I don't feel that good," Moses said.

Majka moved away and crossed her legs so they pointed away from him and folded her arms.

"Fine, Cowboy. You don't like me anymore? Because I am heathen?" Moses wished that was true because it would be easier that way.

"I don't think we are the same people."

"Because of my heritage." Majka's eyebrows danced above her eyes.

"God, no, I don't give a shit about that."

"Funny words."

"Yeah, I guess. I wouldn't care if you were a Martian."

"Then what is it?" she asked.

"You tell me a story and I'll see if I like it or not," Moses said.

"A story about what?"

Moses stood up, putting himself between Majka and the door. "A story about a present full of money. A trailer full of girls. And a hit man named Vahid. And an old dog-looking van driver." He decided to hold back on the doctor for now.

Majka leaped to her feet snarling. "How dare you!" Moses ducked under the glass of whiskey as it hurtled over his head. Majka was on her feet and trying to push past him as the glass shattered on the floor of the kitchen.

"No, you don't. Time for running away is over." Moses caught her at the door and spun her around. "Tell me all you know." Majka slumped back against the door, staring up at him.

"I don't know nothin', copper." The accent and the smirk on her face made him think he was Bogart for a second. But this wasn't some black and white movie from seventy years ago. She was making a fool of him.

"Fuck you. You know about a man and a van. I know you do. I saw it."

"You think you saw something, Cowboy? It is all in your head. Maybe, if you keep talking about it, you won't be troubled by it for very long." Majka said the last words almost sweetly.

"Here is me talking about it," Moses said, staring into her eyes. "You want to know what it is? I think a poor immigrant lady decided to exploit refugees, girls that had the same type of shitty luck that she did. Girls that are vulnerable and weak. She decided to buy them and sell them. Why? Money. Money and power." Majka's face was blank except for her eyes. Her eyes had widened as he spoke. The only hint that she had heard a word he'd said.

"How far does the ring go? All the way through Des Moines. Is it regional? Maybe it is. Maybe she takes trips and sets up franchises in Minneapolis and Kansas City. Majka's Pussy Pit. Now she's got the connection and the money. The sky's the limit. The American dream. Build something and grow it. The land of opportunity." Majka's eyes narrowed at his last words and a small smirk began to play around the corners of her mouth.

He continued, "But not for those girls. The land of the free skipped them on that part, didn't it? How close am I? Warm enough? So, if that was some threat to shut me up or get me out of the way, do it. The more people you send my way, the closer I'll get to taking it all down. I hope you aren't the ringleader. I want you to look at me and understand."

"You know why I like you, Cowboy? You're like a dog I had. He never knew how small he was. Until he chased a car one too many times."

"Get out."

Moses pulled the door open and gestured for her to leave. Majka took her time, pulling her coat on, and winked at him on the way out of the apartment. Moses shut the door behind her and slumped to the floor, holding his side. He sat there for a few seconds, not sure if he could get up. There was a soft knock on the door. Moses sighed, gathering his strength until he was able to get back to his feet. He opened the door, ready for anything. Moses almost started laughing when he saw Claudia holding a steaming plate of turkey and ham with all the fixings.

"We eat early. Jimmy is at his Dad's this afternoon." Moses nodded and took the plate.

"Thanks, Claud. You want to come in?"

"No, I should get back. My sister is here with her kids. I'm not snooping. I was just worried about you with all that racket and that woman."

"Thanks, Claud. Don't worry about me. That was just some unfinished business."

"Is it all done then? With her?" Claudia tilted her head to the side.

"If I had my way it would be, but I still have to straighten a few things out."

"Oh. Okay." She paused at the door, looking at her feet. "I'll get the plate later." Claudia whisked down the hallway. Moses leaned out of his doorway, watching her disappear through the door to her apartment. *Why did he always do that?* He looked down at the plate of food, picked a piece of turkey loose, and stuffed it in his mouth. No doubt she could cook. Food could wait, but now he needed to put the pieces together. He walked over to his coat lying on a small chair in the kitchen and pulled out a scrap of paper from an inner pocket. XFZ-896 was scribbled on the top and TNN-762 below it. These two sets of characters would tell him who owned the vehicles and lead him to the girls. He needed to get to his office and do some work. He set the paper and the plate down and rushed as best he could to his bedroom to get dressed.

Chapter 22

Moses had been at his computer for a few hours, running down the plates on the van and Mack truck. The van was a slow lead. It would take legwork to track it down. It was a fleet vehicle owned by a local high-end hotel. He would have to make some calls and probably wouldn't get any answers on the holiday. The Mack truck had been a better lead so far. A local farm owned it. Sunshine Del Farms and Produce was the name his search pulled up. It was an LLC with the managing partner named Delbert Williams. The address was about a thirty-minute drive from the city. The name was familiar. Moses had grown up in the area, but he hadn't recognized the truck driver. *Why would the Coyote and Vahid use a truck from so far away?* There were plenty of semis to be had in the city. The answer to that question would require a trip to see Delbert Williams. Moses switched back to the van. The van was, at least, in the city. He needed an extra set of eyes. There wasn't time to run down both these leads. The girls would be gone. They might be already.

His cell phone buzzed on his desk. He popped it open. It was Rakić. "This is Moses."

"Moses. Rakić here. Where are you?"

"My office."

"Where's that? I'm stopping by."

Moses told him the address and clicked the phone off. He leaned back in his chair and lit a cigarette. The van was registered to a hotel. Anyone from a bellhop to a manager or a front desk clerk could have access to it. Maybe the Coyote did pickups for the hotel. Maybe it was that easy. The bells hanging from the door jingled as Raif Rakić stepped into his office. Moses got to his feet and pointed at the chair in front of his desk. Rakić slumped into it.

Moses sat down and lit up another cigarette. Rakić looked worse than Moses felt. The dark circles wouldn't be so bad if he wasn't so pale, his nose bright pink from the cold. Rakić fumbled in his pocket and pulled out his pack of smokes, lit one, and tossed the pack on the desk in front of him.

"How are you feeling?" Rakić asked.

"I'll live."

Rakić smirked, then leaned forward and raked his fingers through his thick black hair.

"Fucking city, Moses. It's falling apart."

"What now?"

"I think there are more than just the girls from last night."

Moses sat up. "Why is that?"

"I didn't put it together until now. The ME just called me back, made me think of your story about last night. We found a girl frozen to the street. Over south of downtown the other day."

"Frozen how?" Moses asked.

"Naked, frozen right into the street. Snow melted and refroze to her."

"What puts them together?"

Rakić pointed to the back of his neck. "She's got one of those holes in her neck."

"Do you know what it is?" Moses asked. Rakić shook his head. Moses gripped the edge of the desk. The girls from last night were just the latest shipment. Who knew how many there were.

"How did she die?"

"Froze to death, we think. She was naked, Moses. Bare feet. No clothes. We think she got lost." Rakić put his head down on the desk.

Moses spun to the side and watched him out of the corner of his eye. He hadn't known Rakić long, but seeing him like this worried him.

"Listen, we are going to find these monsters," Moses started to say, but was interrupted.

"Ahhhh!" Rakić screamed. He was on his feet with a burst of energy, ripping at his coat collar like it was choking him. "How the fuck do they do this? This is America. We are the land of the free. Slavery is over. I left this shit. Treating people as less than human. I left it on the other side of the goddamn ocean. And now, I'm here and a slave girl dies in the street. In Iowa. The Heartland of America." He slumped back into the chair, deflated.

Moses sat there, feeling shame and guilt wash over him. He felt the emotion in his gut and fought back the urge to throw his chair through the window. Moses stood up and paced to the back of the office, his body tight after sitting. His ribs felt okay if he wasn't moving. Rakić was right. The papers and news wouldn't write it that way, but he was right. A runaway slave girl had just died in the streets of an American city. *How did we let it happen?* Indifference. Greed. Turning a blind eye. Moses paced back to his desk.

"America is an idea. You've probably heard that. It means different things to different people, but mostly it is hope. You can go to America and get a fair shake at a better life for you and your family. America is a work in progress that's for sure, but these bastards aren't a part of my America. If you don't want to be a part of that, then we have remedies. Prison is one," Moses said.

"I'm an American. I came here not that long ago from a place where hope was destroyed. But we have a commonality with each other, a sense of community. When someone does something wrong, we help them. But when they cannot stop themselves from doing wrong, action must be taken," Rakić said.

Moses wasn't sure what Rakić meant, but he looked better. He had a spark in his eye again. "I need to see the girl."

Rakić scowled. "Why? She is dead. The ME is working on her. He owes me so he's putting in a shift on Christmas."

"I need to see her face."

"Why?"

"I just need to," Moses said.

Rakić watched him a long time. Moses couldn't explain why he needed to see her face, and he didn't think he could try.

Then Rakić said, "Let's go."

* * *

Moses followed Rakić through the dark chambers of the county morgue. An antiseptic smell permeated the air, their footfalls muffled by their blue disposable booties. They made a final turn, pushing through a heavy double door into a small, glaringly white room. A white sheet covered a body on a gurney in the center of the room.

"This is her. They just got done with the autopsy." Moses could feel the blood draining from his face and the tension building in his body. The tendons in his neck felt like they would crush his collarbones into powder. He looked to Rakić, his face covered with a surgical mask, head and body with a light blue cap and gown. Rakić pulled the sheet back with a rubber-gloved hand, revealing the youthful face of a teenage girl. Moses stared at her one open eye. It was light blue. Death had done little to rob the girl of her beauty; even the black eye wasn't ugly. She had fine, blonde hair and a small, sharp-featured face reminding him of an elf in one of those movies with orcs and dragons. But she didn't need to worry about make-believe dangers. She had met real-life monsters. Her lips were a light pink; she looked as if she were just ready to say something.

Moses was drawn back to her eyes. The one blue, the other black. She was so young. She had been someone's hope. She had been someone's future. She had taken a wrong turn on a street in Prague, Sarajevo, or Davenport, and then a final one on a street in Des Moines. She didn't deserve to be left to die in the middle of a city of hundreds of thousands, cold and alone. Getting tired, her feet hurting until, slowly at first, the frozen snow of the street started to feel warm and it spread to her legs and her whole body was warm. And finally, she laid down and died. Hugging the frozen street and its false promise of warmth. Her voice silenced forever.

Rakić coughed. "We don't have any other info than that thing on her neck."
"You'll let me know when you find out what it is?" Moses asked.
"Yeah. You'll be the first."
"Good." Moses stroked the girl's hair with his gloved hand, deploring the clinical barrier between them. Then he covered her face with the sheet. They left the room and made the long journey back out. "I need your help with something else," Moses said.
"What is it?"
"I need your help finding this van." Moses handed him a piece of paper with a license plate number scrawled across it. "I traced it to the Mayan Hotel but that is as far as I got."
Rakić looked at the plate number. "What are you going to do?"
"I have to go visit a farmer."

Chapter 23

The trip out to the farm was a short one. Moses had driven by the house a lot in his youth, but had never been inside. It was a classic foursquare farmhouse, at least a hundred years old, two and a half stories with a big porch and an inviting driveway. Moses climbed the steps to the porch and looked inside the window. A woman was tending to a pot on the stove with her back to him. She had short, reddish-brown hair with streaks of gray and was decked out in red and green for the season. Moses knocked on the door and turned to look at his rental car. Luckily, the airport rental office had been open today. The tiny car looked out of place on the farm. The door opened with a squeak and Moses turned to look down into the round, smiling face of the lady from the kitchen.

"Hello, what can I do for you? On Christmas at that."

"Yeah, sorry about that. I'm actually here to talk to Delbert. Is he around?"

"Del is down in the shed. I'll call him. Come in, come in. What's your name?"

"Moses Winter."

"Jim Winter's boy?"

"Yes, ma'am."

She shooed him inside. Moses stepped into the entry area. There was a mat in front of a bench with boots underneath and hooks for coats above. He stomped his feet on the mat and stood, shifting his weight from foot to foot. She went into the kitchen and picked up the phone. The cut on his forehead burned. He scratched at it next to the bandage, but got too close. The tape holding it in place gave way and the bandage flapped down over his eyes. The wound pulsed with pain as he pushed the bandage back into place. He heard the woman talking on the phone and then heard the phone clang on its cradle.

"Del says come down. There's a path— What is on your—come in here. We need to get that cleaned up." The woman grabbed his arm, pulled him into the kitchen, and pushed him into a chair. She dabbed at his forehead with a paper towel. It came away with pieces of dark, coagulated blood and fresh, brighter blood.

"What have you gotten into?" she asked. She put his hand on the paper towel to keep pressure on the gash. She darted over to the sink and opened a cabinet at her knees. She pulled out a large first-aid kit and was back at his side.

"Keep this here for Del. He's had his share of nasty cuts and scrapes out here," she said as she hummed notes that seemed to be thoughts more than an actual song. From the first-aid kit, she fished out a piece of gauze and some tape. Her small, strong hands worked quickly and then she was pulling him to his feet. "Good as new. Now listen. You need to change the bandage every day and clean it out. You don't want an infection."

Moses nodded, but his eyes were looking past her at the stove. It was covered with pots and pans. All the fixings for Christmas dinner were coming together. Moses looked at his watch: 3:45 p.m. "I'm sorry, ma'am. I didn't realize it was this late and you have Christmas."

"It's alright, Del won't mind and I don't mind. Now, get going, I have stuff to do." She smiled and pushed him out the door. Moses made his way around the house and followed a path in the snow that led to another driveway and the shed. It was a massive shed, a hundred feet or more in length with two sets of enormous sliding doors and a smaller door to the side. As he approached the smaller side door, it swung open and a wiry man with weathered skin and dark hair peeking out from a seed hat stepped out to meet him.

"You Winter?"

"Yes, sir."

"Get in here out of the cold." Moses stepped inside and the man followed. The size of the shed was hard to grasp from the outside. But now inside, he found the towering implements made him feel slightly claustrophobic. The king of them all was a massive combine parked in front of a set of large doors on the far side of the building. And there, right in front of him, was parked the Mack truck that he had seen the night before with the plate TNN-762.

Francis Sparks

The ceiling was strange. Moses had never seen anything like it before. Instead of exposed beams and the underside of the aluminum roof, it was a flat plywood ceiling running the entire length of the building. Off to the side there was a set of stairs that climbed upward, leading up into a hatch in the ceiling. Moses felt a little dizzy and put his hand on the long wooden workbench to his right.

"I've never seen that before," Moses said. Delbert Williams glanced up the stairs and nodded as he put a cigarette to his mouth. "Put that in myself. Use it for storing smaller things. Used to have a basketball court up there for the kids. But not anymore. Now, what can I do for you?"

"Yes, sir. I got a question or two to ask you. This truck right here, where was it last night?"

"This truck? Are you with the police, son? I don't think you are. Sounds like a police question."

"No, sir. I am private investigator. I'm trying to figure out what happened to some girls that were kidnapped."

"Girls? What girls?"

"Some girls about fourteen to twenty in ages."

"What does that have to do with my truck?" Delbert asked.

"That's it. I saw them getting pulled out of a trailer that this truck was pulling last night."

"Bullshit. This trailer was hauling cattle yesterday."

"Where was it hauling them to?" Moses asked.

"Up north. We have a contract with the packing plant. We were picking them up to fatten," Del said.

"How far north?"

"Marshalltown."

"Who drove? Wasn't you. I saw the man. Tall, kind of hefty guy." Moses said. Delbert took a long drag on his smoke and let it hang in his mouth, his eyes narrowed. "How else would you describe this fella?"

"Big, wearing overalls. About like every farmer, I guess." Delbert laughed at that, slapping his knee.

Made Safe

"Well, we do look alike, don't we?" The small door swung open, flooding the dimly lit building with the light of the setting sun. The figure in the door was a large shadow, then the door shut and Moses' eyes adjusted.

"Yeah, you do. But he's the guy."

The Big Man looked at Moses and then at Delbert. "What's going on, Del?"

"This guy says he saw you yesterday. Something about some girls. Know what he's talking about?"

The Big Man shook his head. "No, Del. I don't. I picked cattle up in Marshalltown and came right back."

"Yeah. You came back. Seemed like it was taking you longer than usual though."

Moses watched Delbert. He still had his cigarette in his mouth, but he had crossed his arms. The Big Man was looking down and kicking his feet.

"Yeah. The lady called me," the Big Man said.

"The lady called?" Delbert leaned forward, his voice rising slightly. "She called you?" Delbert asked.

"Yes," the Big Man answered.

"And what did she want?" Delbert asked.

"To make a pickup."

"Where?"

"Clear Lake."

"Holy shit. I'd say that's an extra run with my truck. Why'd she call you?"

"Said you didn't need to know," the Big Man said.

Delbert turned his back on Moses and the Big Man and spiked his cigarette into the floor, sending sparks bouncing off the concrete. He spun on his heel and walked toward Moses. Moses tensed as the man approached with clenched fists. The sudden movement caught Moses flatfooted as the older man charged at him. Moses pushed himself to the side as Delbert lunged at the bench. But instead of attacking Moses, he grabbed a huge wrench and threw it across the floor in the direction of the truck. The Big Man flinched as the metallic clatter echoed in the building.

Delbert stood glaring at the Big Man. The Big Man stuffed his hands in his pockets and looked at Moses, back at Delbert, and then to his boots. Delbert waited, poised as his violent outburst reverberated through the room, echoing off the aluminum walls, letting the Big Man squirm. A lean animal waiting, seething, chomping to tear into the other man. Moses felt like he should leave them alone, like he was out of place watching this silent exchange. Finally, Delbert broke his silence.

"What are you thinking, you big idiot? That's my truck. Not your truck. If some good-looking lady calls up, you do whatever she says? Is that how this works? I don't think so. You work for me. You do what I say or you're done." Delbert had walked closer to the Big Man with every word and now he was toe-to-toe with the Big Man. The Big Man averted his eyes. Delbert took a deep breath and stepped back.

"Now, what did she have you do?"

"Pick up the girls and drive them to the truck stop," the Big Man said.

Moses blinked rapidly. The way he said "girls." The man was a little slow, there was no doubt of that now, but the way he said it still made Moses fantasize of new ways to make him hurt.

"What are they going to do with them, do you know?" Moses shouted. The Big Man flinched as if he had been struck.

"The lady said they get jobs and get to make money here," the Big Man said.

"Do you know what kind of jobs?" Moses asked. The Big Man shook his head. "Strippers and prostitutes. You know what that kind of work is like?" Moses started toward the Big Man, but Delbert stepped in front of him.

"Easy, Moses. He's a little slow. He made a dumb mistake." Moses clenched his fists and stepped away.

"What lady is he talking about? Do you do regular business with her?" Moses asked.

Delbert turned to the Big Man. "Go up to the house and tell Jeanie I'll be up. We'll have a talk about this truck business." The Big Man nodded and almost ran out of the shed.

When he was gone, Delbert turned to Moses, calm again. "I do business with her. But she's new. Only been a few months."

"What kind of business?"

"None of yours. But never this stuff with girls. This is the first I've heard of it." Moses nodded and thought he believed him.

"They are just kids…children. One can't be more than thirteen."

Made Safe

Delbert sighed and rubbed his eyes. "Shit. All I can give you is a number. She's new, like I said. I used to work with a different guy, but this lady took over a few months back."

"Listen, I don't bullshit. If I find out you knew about this, I'll be back," Moses said.

"I'm not worried, my nose is clean. Let me get that number for you." Delbert pulled out a cell phone and read the numbers to Moses. Moses couldn't help thinking that he knew who was going to answer when he called.

* * *

Moses was driving back into the city at almost 5:00 p.m. on Christmas night. His mind swirled with thoughts about how to handle this. He glanced at the phone number written on a piece of paper on the passenger seat. If he called the number, Majka might answer. If she did, then he would have to confront his own complicity and guilt. He had shared a bed and his body with her. *If she was buying and selling girls...* He merged off the interstate and down the street to his favorite place. The Oak Barrel opened at 2:00 p.m. on Christmas. Moses pushed through the front door and jogged down the narrow flight of stairs. The place already had the regulars scattered along the long bar and Liz was working. Moses found a stool near the taps. He set his phone and a scrap of paper on the bar and waved to Liz as she came up with his beer. He said hello, but she was off to a table to take an order. It was busy even with the holiday. He rubbed the bandage on his forehead. At least he didn't have to explain his face to Liz. She was too easy for that.

He flipped his phone around and drank his beer. The number on the paper was local. He should look it up at his office. He ordered another drink. *Maybe it wasn't Majka. You're an idiot. You saw her give the money to the Coyote. She knows Vahid and Elvis. What are you doing? You might as well have been driving the van, pressed the plungers on the syringes buried in their necks. You are responsible. You let it happen.* He waved Liz down as he finished his beer.

"Can I use your phone?"

He was going to put his suspicions to rest, but he didn't want to tip her off. He got lucky with the Fred dial, but she knew him now. A call to another number of hers would be it. She might get spooked.

"Sure, Mos." Liz pulled the phone over from the counter behind the bar and set it in front of him. Moses dialed the number. The phone rang. Two. Three rings.

"Hello." Moses paused. It didn't sound like Majka. But he couldn't be sure. He needed to say something to keep the conversation going.

Moses coughed and made his voice more gravelly. "Yes. Can I speak with Majka?"

"Who is this? Who's Majka?"

Moses hung on the line for a moment, too shocked to say anything, and then hung up. He picked up his cell phone and threw twenty dollars on the bar, put his coat on, and was out front lighting a cigarette in the cold wind before Liz noticed he was leaving. He knew that voice.

Chapter 24

Raif Rakić was sitting in the general manager's office of the Mayan Hotel. When he had flashed his badge and started asking questions about the van, the front desk staff whisked him inside the back office and asked him to wait. He checked his cell phone and noticed a message. It was Terry; he must have news on the girl. Rakić hit "call back."

"Terry, it's Rakić. What do you got?"

"This is weird. She died of hypothermia."

"What about the thing on her neck?"

"That's the weird part. It's some sort of electronic device. Small. Really small. I sent it over to tech for them to check it out."

"Any idea what it is?"

"I've never seen anything like it."

"Okay. Thanks, Terry. What with Christmas and all."

"No problem, Rakić. Sorry about the scene. It has been bothering me. That was unprofessional." His tone was mechanically sincere. It probably wasn't the easiest thing for him to say.

"Forget it, Terry, it's what we do. Sorry I got upset. This one is burning me."

"Yeah, it's an odd one. Take care, Raif."

Rakić hung up as the door to the office opened and a woman stepped in. She was good-looking, probably in her late twenties or early thirties. Rakić stood up and stuck his hand out. "Raif Rakić. Iowa Division of Criminal Investigation."

She shook his hand, smiling. "Hello, Mr. Rakić. I'm Amy Strauss, assistant manager. With the holiday, you know, the manager is out, but what can the Mayan do for you today?" She motioned for him to take a chair and she sat down behind the desk.

Rakić sat on the edge of the chair. "Here it is. We have a delicate situation. We are working an undercover sting operation and we had some interference from a vehicle of yours last night. We are hopeful that the driver may have some information for us."

"Our vehicle?"

"Here's the plate." Rakić pushed a piece of paper across the desk to her. She picked it up, glanced at it, and set it back down.

"We have several vehicles. What type of vehicle was it? I can track down who was driving it." She shifted to the side, tapped on her keyboard, and glanced at him, waiting.

"A shuttle van. The kind you'd use to take guests to the airport."

"Okay." She bit her lower lip as she typed. Then she smiled. "Here we go. It looks like it was signed out at 8:00 a.m. yesterday and…" Her brow crinkled up. "But it hasn't been signed in yet."

"Maybe someone took it home for Christmas?"

"That would be out of the norm. Staff should check vehicles back in the same day. Where did you see our vehicle?"

"Can't say, ma'am. There could be damage to the vehicle, but that is all I can say."

"Hmm. Well, I can tell you who signed it out."

"Great. What's the name?" Rakić pulled a notebook from his front pocket.

"Elvis Sidran. I'm not familiar with him, but he seems to have a good record here. We try to help them, you know, they had it so rough."

Rakić wrote the name down, bottling up the excitement he felt in his stomach. He was so excited he barely registered her statement. "Who's that, ma'am?"

"You know, the Bosnians. Even if they are Muslim, I don't judge."

"Best to leave that to God," Rakić said, letting his accent play loud and clear through his words, his mouth twisted in a tight smile.

"Oh, I'm sorry. I didn't know. I am so, so embarrassed." Her pale winter skin flushed a light pink. Rakić thought it was good on her.

"How could you? Don't worry about it." He let his mouth relax. It wasn't her fault. People were people everywhere. "Now, do you have an address for Elvis?"

Amy Strauss stuck her tongue in her cheek and twisted her lips to the side. "Do you have a warrant? I don't believe we normally give out this information without some sort of documentation," she said, tilting her head back, her confidence restored.

Rakić leaned forward and raised his pen to his cheek. "I totally understand. We wouldn't normally even ask without a warrant, but the sensitive nature of the investigation…" He paused and, angling his head to the side, he leaned forward and lowered is voice. "Ms. Strauss. This is an undercover operation. It is highly important that we discuss what this gentleman saw last night. I can give you my word." Rakić pulled out a card, put it on her desk and pushed it toward her. "If you have any concerns, call me directly. That has my personal cell phone." Rakić smiled as Amy Strauss picked up the card and nodded.

"Is it terrorism?"

"Can't say, ma'am, but believe me, Ms. Strauss, you would be doing the government a favor." He flashed a genuine grin. She sighed and gave him a small smile and relaxed, apparently convinced.

"Okay. Well, just leave the Mayan out of it if you can. We don't believe the nonsense of any press is good press." Rakić nodded and chuckled a little. Amy Strauss read off the address and phone number of Elvis Sidran. Rakić flipped his notebook shut and rushed out the door of the office saying thank you over his shoulder. He hurried to his car. He now knew where one of the murderers lived and he wasn't going to waste any more time. He checked his watch. It was just after 4:00 p.m. He dialed Moses' number. Voicemail. He ended the call. He'd try him again later. He needed to get to Elvis' house

Chapter 25

Moses had been watching the Dunsmore house for a little over an hour. It was a big house among big houses, set back off a cul-de-sac. He had watched a neighbor drop off a casserole a few hours ago. Sharon had barely popped her head out the door. Yet, he strained to see her face for that brief instant. To read it. To find some sign that she was the Queen of the Slaves. She didn't look like it, still in her pajamas and a robe.

Since then, nothing had stirred in the house. Moses' mind drifted back to the girl in the morgue and the girl he had failed to save at the motel. He could still remember her excited expression as they fled from Vahid and the Coyote. He gripped the steering wheel of the rental car harder, and the rage passed. He relaxed a little and lit a smoke.

His phone rang. It was Rakić. "Rakić, what do you got?" Moses asked.

"I got an address for Elvis from the hotel records. He works there. Must have checked out the van and used it for the night. I'm at the address, but no sign of him."

Moses' mind raced. If they had Elvis, they could get to Vahid and possibly the girls. The garage door of the Dunsmore house opened. Moses straightened up as a gray minivan slowly backed toward him down the driveway. He slumped down and put the car into gear. The van drove around the curved drive of the cul-de-sac until it was coming toward him. It was her, Sharon. Moses sat low as she passed. After giving her a few seconds head start, he followed.

"You still there?" Rakić asked.

"Listen, there's been a development I have to run down. I'm on a tail right now. Don't, whatever you do, let Elvis get away if he shows. He can get us to the girls. If he shows up, call me back." Moses ended the call and checked the time: 7:00 p.m. He tossed the phone in the console of the car and sped after Sharon.

She took him east into the cit to another house. Moses parked down the street as he watched Sharon get out of the car. She was dressed for something. She wore red high-heels and a knee-length fashionable winter coat and scarf. Even from this distance, he could see she had done the full works on her face and hair. Sharon opened the sliding door of the van and her two small children hopped out. She led them to the front door where an older woman met her. She leaned over and kissed them each on the cheek, then pushed them inside after the woman. Then she was back in her car and zooming past him. Moses turned the car around and was back on her as she led him to the interstate.

Soon they were exiting in the middle of the city, heading south. They made a few turns and Moses could guess where they were going. A few minutes later, Sharon pulled her minivan down the long driveway of the Duncan estate and disappeared around back. Moses stopped well short of where Fred had parked that night only six days ago. This still wasn't enough to hang her, but it was certainly peculiar. Sharon had legitimate business with Duncan. He was Fred's attorney and she was in the process of settling the estate. But the hour and date were odd at best.

Moses checked his watch. It was 7:30 p.m. Small, powdery snowflakes began to swirl around the car. He hunched down in his seat. Another car zipped by, turned onto the Duncan driveway, and disappeared. He pulled a pen out of his pocket and scribbled the plate number in his notebook. In the next few minutes, three more luxury SUVs disappeared down the Duncan driveway and Moses managed to write them all down. After ten minutes passed without any activity, Moses got out of the car, bracing himself against the stiffening wind. Head lowered against the pelting snow, he advanced toward the Duncan house. Off the sidewalk now, he slogged through the calf-deep snow toward the side of the house on a line near where he had found Fred's phone. He reached the window on the corner of the house and peered inside. Inside was a small antechamber. A door to the side might lead to the large room where he had found Duncan days before. He crept down the side of the house and peeked in the next set of windows. The room was shrouded in deep shadows, lit by the glow of a roaring fire in the fireplace and sconces on the wall. It was a large, empty room, big enough for ballroom dancing. The arrangement was odd, like it was setup for a show. Six chairs were placed in a single row in front of a portable stage in the middle of the room. Moses started to move on to the next set of windows when the door on the far wall opened. A large group of people filed in. He counted thirteen. Moses recognized three of them. Duncan, Sharon, and Vahid.

Moses felt his skin start to burn and he briefly toyed with the idea of smashing the window and leaping inside. Sharon seemed very comfortable in the company she was keeping. The snow swirled around him as he unzipped his coat to relieve the heat building in his face. The group seemed to make small talk before taking their places. Sharon and Duncan sat next to each other while Vahid stood behind Sharon. The rest filed in, principals sitting and subordinates standing. When everyone was settled, Sharon stood up and spoke to the group. The door opened again and a stream of girls walked into the room, single file. Moses counted twenty-nine. He searched their faces. They were all young, as young as the girls from yesterday. All of them were dressed in white terrycloth robes. They filed onto the stage and then turned in unison toward the seated people. Except for one. It was the girl from his Jeep. It was obvious that her face was swollen under the paint and makeup. She was far away, but Moses thought her eyes still glowed with the same tough inner spirit he had witnessed at the motel and during their brief escape. Then Moses saw a woman wearing a black dress standing off to the side. Majka. Majka dashed onto the stage and pushed the girl into alignment and left just as quickly. Moses leaned forward and grabbed snow with his bare hands, grinding the freezing powder into his palms in an effort to calm himself. The pain focused him, and he dropped the snow, returning his attention to the vile proceedings. With a nod from Majka, the girls untied their robes, letting them slide to the floor, standing naked in front of the crowd. Flames reflected off their lotion-moistened skin, licking at their bodies like devil tongues. Except for one. Again the girl with the battered face stood defiant, holding her robe tight to her body. Majka appeared and yanked the robe from the girl's body and slapped her across the face. She took the robe and left the girl standing naked on the stage. Moses felt the heat of a moment before turn to something more precise, more focused, a colder, more aware anger in his heart and mind as he stared at Majka and then at the girl.

As a group, the subordinates descended on the girls. Vahid stepped forward, the imposing chaperone with his thickly muscled neck barely contained by his collared shirt. He hovered over the girls, enforcing silent restraint on those who might be too overzealous in their inspections, his smiling eyes missing nothing.

Moses doubled over, holding his ribs. The pain had returned with the exertion and anger. The big pain subsided, leaving in its place a dull, smaller pain. *I need a way into this godforsaken den of slavery.* He pulled himself away from the grotesque scene and started down the length of the house, but then thought better. He would go in the front door. They were busy inspecting the girls and he knew how to reach the room from the front.

At the front door, he tried the knob. It yielded, swinging inward without a sound. He lurched down the halls in a haze, drunk with hate, until he was at the door of the great room with the girls and the monsters. The door was open a crack, affording him a clear view. The girls were still standing naked in place. Most of the seconds were back in place behind their bosses. A few of them were in conversation, but for the most part, the bosses were sitting in their chairs, feet tapping, hands slapping, voices crackling with excitement, faces stretched in anticipation, except for Sharon. Sharon sat in her chair, her legs crossed, her mouth twisted in a tight smirk. She draped an arm over the back of her chair and nodded to Vahid. He motioned to someone out of sight, and the girls pulled their robes over their bodies and rushed toward the door. A few of them pushed the naked girl in front of them until Majka tossed a robe to her, which she quickly used to cover herself.

"Shit," he said. They were coming right at him. He turned and hurried back down the hallway. He tried a closed door to his left but his hand slipped on the metal doorknob. The metallic sound it made jangled his nerves. He tried again and it opened. He darted inside the dark room. He closed the door to a sliver of light and knelt down by the knob, watching as the girls flooded into the hallway. They formed into lines again as Majka followed the last into the hallway.

"English speakers, inform the others," Majka said. "One at a time, when your number is called. Then, when it is over, you will leave through the opposite door into your new life in America." A few of the girls spoke in hushed tones to the others. Majka stood at the door with her back to the girls, waiting for the signal. Moses felt for his cell phone in his pocket. He turned to the interior of the room and quickly typed a text message to Rakić.

At Duncan House. Found the girls. Vahid is here.

Moses didn't know how to explain it any other way. He hit send. He watched as the progress indicator spun on the screen. Cellular service was terrible this deep inside the house, situated as it was down in a deep valley. Finally, a message came up on the display: *Failure to send.*

"Fuck," he whispered. He hit send again and looked out through the gap in the doorway. He thought he could see the girl from the Jeep, Brooklyn. The girl with the bruised face. She was near the back of the line. He checked his phone again. The progress indicator was still spinning. Majka pushed the first girl through the door. Moses could hear a voice over a PA system announcing the girl.

"Girl number one on your program tonight. She's from the Ukraine, sixteen-years-old. Blonde hair, blue eyes. Five feet, seven inches and 130 pounds. You can see that the weight is in all the right places. Bidding begins at ten thousand dollars."

Moses swallowed hard. He listened as the auctioneer read off the bids. "Twelve thousand, do I hear twelve-five? Come on, people. New Year's is right around the corner. Start those parties right with this special group…" It was Duncan's voice.

Moses stood up and walked deeper into the room. The furniture was covered with sheets. Boxes were stacked everywhere. He ripped open the boxes looking for a weapon. A broom handle, anything. He ripped a sheet off a couch and tossed it against the wall. Nothing. It didn't matter. He didn't need a weapon. He went back to the door.

"Alright, now you're getting loose! Fourteen-five. Fourteen. Fourteen-five. Fourteen. Going once."

Moses threw the door open, bouncing it against the wall. He took a step out of the room. The remaining girls were huddled against the wall, pressing together in the dim corridor, looking at him with haunted eyes behind painted lids. Majka spun from her place at the door.

"You," she said.

"It's over, Majka. These girls are coming with me." Moses reached out and grabbed Brooklyn by her hand.

"You won't get out of here," Majka said as she folded her arms over her chest.

"You can't stop me."

"Maybe I can't, Cowboy. But Elvis will." Moses shook his head. Then a rough tap hammered his shoulder, sending him stumbling forward, and he lost hold of Brooklyn's hand. He whirled on his attacker.

"Elvis," Moses said. Elvis was finally standing in front of him. He was dressed all in black, contrasting with his pale face, appearing like a disembodied head floating in the corridor.

In Elvis' hand was a black pistol, a 9mm by the looks of it. He held up his other hand. In that hand, he held a smart phone. On the screen was a flashing red dot on a map of Des Moines. The top of the screen said "Moses < 1M." *How the hell was he tracking me? My phone or something in my clothes?* Moses pulled his phone out, but Elvis took it and threw it on the floor, crushing it under his boot.

"Time to go, Cowboy," he said and motioned for Moses to follow him.

Moses nodded. Brooklyn's hand was in his again and he squeezed it. Then he rushed at Elvis screaming, "Run!"

Elvis ducked under Moses' wild punch, putting Moses off balance and falling forward. He felt an explosion in the back of his head. Strong hands grabbed him and pulled him upright, and then he was watching the floor as he was being carried down a hall. He opened his eyes and saw Brooklyn's small body tucked under Vahid's arm, a steady stream of blood running from the corner of her mouth. Then Moses was sitting on his butt.

"Get up. I'm not carrying you if you can walk," Elvis said, looking away in disgust. Moses looked back while Elvis stood over him holding the 9mm. Moses got up and Elvis shoved him down the hall. He felt an immense pressure at his temples and he had a hard time following the twists and turns as they forced him through the house. He wished he hadn't been awake when they took the girl away.

Chapter 26

Rakić's phone buzzed in the cup holder of his unmarked police car. He had been watching Elvis' small suburban house for hours with no sign of the bastard. He picked up the phone and read the text message off the glowing display.

Elvis is here at the Zmaj. Went in back.

He didn't recognize the number, but it could be Biba or Šejla from a different phone. "Shit."

The Zmaj was five minutes away. He turned the car around in the driveway and accelerated down the street. He flipped on his flashing lights and cut through town, speeding through traffic lights and drawing honks and middle fingers. Sometimes cars pulled to the side letting him pass, but more often than not, he was forced to jump the car onto snowy curbs or swerve into the oncoming lane to avoid the oblivious drivers. Then he was at the Zmaj. The lot was dead. Rakić pulled into a spot in front of two bored-looking bouncers at the front door, shut the car off, and got out.

"Hello, friends," Rakić said, smiling, walking up to the men. "I'm here for Šejla." The men stepped aside and Rakić pushed into the Zmaj. The place was dark and there were a few empty tables, but the place wasn't as empty as he'd thought. He made his way to the bar and waved down a bartender.

"Šejla?"

The bartender shook his head. "She just left."

"Where?"

The bartender shrugged and gestured to the back. "Elvis took her someplace." The bartender was American, born and raised. It didn't fit with this place. Nothing was right. Everything was a façade. Rakić felt his right eyelid begin to twitch and he rubbed his temple.

"When? What happened?" Rakić said as he banged his fist on the bar.

"I don't know. He showed up. Then he went in the back and came out and took her with him."

Rakić grabbed an empty pint glass and hurled it at the feet of the man. The man skipped over it as it shattered and sent glass skittering on the tiled floor. Rakić walked around the bar and grabbed the stunned bartender by the front of his white shirt.

"Where did they go?"

The man shook his head. Rakić twisted the shirt, watching the bartender's neck tendons and flesh bulge over the top of his cotton collar, his face turning blotchy and red.

"Raif! Stop it!" Rakić looked toward the voice. Biba was running across the room as fast as she could, carrying a half-full tray of empty glasses.

"What was he driving?" Rakić said to the bartender. He relaxed his hand and the man's face turned a better color.

"I don't know. He sometimes drives a van."

"A hotel van?" The man nodded. Then Biba was grabbing at his arm.

"Let him go, Raif," she said.

Rakić released his grip and turned to see the crowd staring at him, faces mirroring the same dopey expression, something in the neighborhood of indifference and disdain at the intrusion into their lives. He thought they looked like a herd of some soon to be extinct animal, caught out in the open, too dumb to run. He slumped against the bar, brushing his hand over his hair all the way to his neck, rubbing it. He felt shame at losing control like that. The bartender didn't know anything. He couldn't blame him. He had to find that van.

"Where did he take her, Biba?"

"I don't know, Raif. I texted you as soon as I saw him and then he was just gone with her." He could see her hand at the corner of his vision, raised, poised to touch him on the shoulder or face maybe. A touch to relieve, a touch of understanding. He pulled away.

"Did you see what he was driving?" he asked, not looking at her.

"The white van from the hotel," she said.

He turned a little so he could see her face. She had taken a risk by texting him information about Elvis. He owed her. "Go home, Biba. Tonight might be a bad night."

"No, he might come back. If he does, you'll know. Besides, I need the money." She pushed her top lip out into a glossy smirk and Rakić snorted in appreciation. The best damn women in the world were born in Bosnia, he thought. He tipped his finger to his forehead and hurried out of the bar, dialing DMPD dispatch on the way.

"This is Rakić. I need an BOLO on a white van with Mayan Hotel branding. One armed and dangerous white male, early twenties, six feet, medium-build, dark hair. The passenger is my cousin. Mid-twenties, blonde hair. Name, Šejla Tahirović"

"Jesus, Raif. Who is this guy?" He recognized the voice.

"He's a murderer, Monica, and he has my Cousin Šejla. We have to find him." Rakić hung up and raced to his car. He threw the phone in the cup holder and sped off. He shouldn't have let her keep working at the Zmaj. He had to find her.

* * *

Moses had been tied to the chair in the trophy room of the Duncan house for what felt like a long time. He could faintly hear the voice of the auctioneer over the PA system, but the words were lost through the walls. He could tell when a sale was final, by the way the sound changed. It grew louder and more energetic, then stopped. A brief interlude, then the next sale began, excitement rising in the auctioneer's voice, starting the process again.

The thought of what would happen to each of those girls at the end of each transaction made Moses clamp his teeth down on his tongue and squeeze until he tasted blood. Probably be out on the street in hours. Getting trained for New Year's. Maybe turned into someone's pet project. Kept under wraps, used for their personal fuck-toy. Moses shook his wrists against the zip ties binding him to the chair, hating his impotence and feeling a sick churning in his gut.

Then he thought of the night at the cabin and the argument between Fred and Sharon. Fred had said something about Sharon loving her business more than anything. Moses had dismissed it. What had he thought? That she sold candles or jewelry to her friends? What a dope. The whole time he had known her, she had been this wretched human slime of a person. Buying and selling people, innocents, children, into lives of depravity. He had failed them. He could have stopped this.

The door opening snapped him back to the present. Elvis appeared, pushing someone to the floor in front of Moses and then was gone, slamming the door behind him. She was wearing all black except for the folded white apron that just covered her hips. Her hands and feet were tied with the same plastic zip ties that held him. She rolled to her side and scooted against the wall until she managed to push herself up. She tossed her head and the blonde hair fell away from her face. It was Šejla. She tongued a trickle of blood at the corner of her mouth and then recognized him.

"Are you okay?" she asked.

"I should be asking you that."

"Have you looked in the mirror lately?"

"I'll be alright. Did they hurt you?" he asked.

She shook her head and looked away. When she looked back her eyes were misty. "It's not me I'm worried about." Her eyes fell to her stomach. Moses couldn't be sure, but he thought that there was an ever-so-slight bump right above her apron.

"You're not…?"

She nodded and bit her lip. "It's okay. Raif will find us."

"Does he know where you are?" Moses' voice dropped to a whisper.

"I started to text him when I saw Elvis at the Zmaj. But then *he* took me," she said.

Moses nodded. Moses hadn't been sure if his text had gone through or not. They could be here on their own.

"He'll be here. I texted him," he said, trying to mean it when he said it. He held her gaze until she finally nodded back at him. He couldn't be sure if his eyes had betrayed his true thoughts, but she seemed placated for now. Then he felt his confident facade crack, so he looked down at his feet. "We can't just sit here and wait for him."

Moses started rocking the chair until it finally fell over with a crash, shattering into pieces. The pain in his side was worse, but he had managed to get a foot free from the chair. The broken chair-leg would look good smashed into Elvis' temple, he thought.

Chapter 27

Rakić had been driving the streets for over an hour. He had chased down two leads so far, but they had turned out to be the wrong vans and the wrong people. The last one had taken him to the far north side of town, near the tire plant. He was headed south on NE 14th for no reason other than it was a direction. Suddenly, he pulled off of the road into the parking lot of a fast-food restaurant. He jerked the car into park and got out, slamming the door.

He walked to the trunk of the car and popped it open. He pulled out his service shotgun and placed it in the passenger side in the special holster designed to hold the gun at the ready. He slammed the trunk and got back in the car. He picked up his cell phone and flipped back to a message Šejla had sent him a week ago.

Safe at home. Thanks for checking on me. He read it again and closed it. The message was from the day before the cabin. She had been working late on a Wednesday. Then his phone vibrated and a new message popped up on his screen. It was from Moses.

At Duncan house. Found the girls. Vahid is here.

His mind raced. Moses had found Vahid at Duncan's. Usually where there was one there was the other. He picked up his police radio and called it in. The car tires whirred on the slick surface of the parking lot as he punched the gas. He was back on the street, headed south. The snow was coming down in large flakes now. Visibility was getting worse. He had to get to Duncan's house and find Vahid and Elvis and with them, he hoped, Šejla.

* * *

Moses' feet were free, but his hands were still bound behind him to the broken chair. He was lying on his side, but had managed to scoot closer to Šejla. He heard the door open behind him.

"Cowboy. You try so hard. I admire you." It was Vahid. Moses twisted to face him. He had changed clothes since the auction. Now he was wearing a dark coat and a black European-style sweater with a large neck that hung away from his throat, like something a model on a magazine might wear, but his salt and pepper stubble gave his face a more utilitarian look. Elvis came in and quickly cut Šejla loose and dragged her from the room. She managed to lash out with a foot, but Elvis picked her up bodily, making the effort seem infantile in its futility. Moses watched, beyond helpless now, wondering why he was still alive. Was it to witness this brutal life a bit more before all memory would be erased forever?

"It's time, then?" Moses asked, wanting to get on with it. Vahid shook his head, closed the door, and pulled a chair from the wall, setting it in front of Moses.

"Not yet, Cowboy, for you." Vahid sat down and crossed his arms over his chest.

"What are you doing with Šejla?" Moses asked.

"She will be fine. Elvis is just talking to her. And I am talking to you. Now, does anyone else know you are here?"

"Just the whole Des Moines Police Department." This got Vahid chuckling.

"We would have heard about that." Moses wasn't surprised that they had cops on the payroll.

"Don't look hurt, Cowboy. We have people everywhere," Vahid continued.

"What scumbag would work for you?"

"You think only one. Good try. How does it go? I will never reveal my sources."

Moses shook his arms, straining to create slack in the unyielding ties. "Why does it matter now? You'll just kill me."

Vahid put his hands out palm up, pantomiming a scale. "Stranger things have happened. Who knows what the lady will decide."

"How'd you end up an errand boy for her? You don't seem too dumb. You could be a regular person under the right circumstances," Moses said.

Vahid slapped his leg and chuckled. "Look, Cowboy, I set my own hours. I am mostly home on holidays except when we have product or talent coming in. I make good money. I don't have to sit at a desk all day. I get outdoors a lot."

"Especially when you're killing people."

Vahid frowned. "Yes. I don't enjoy it. Also, I don't dwell on it and carry it out quickly. But it's part of the job. You like your job?"

Moses struggled against the zip ties with renewed fury.

"I see you don't want to talk about you. Well, there are parts of all jobs that you must get through. Unfortunately, sometimes in my job, it is taking care of the business that isn't working. I do that part of the job. I cash my check. Yes, a real check from a real company. Then I go home and sleep like a baby. I am providing for my family. People that I have to remove from the business are there because they wanted to be there. They know when they push things, that it is a possible outcome."

"Murder, you mean," Moses said.

"Murder is not quite the right word, but with my limited command of your language, it will do. It is a tool that should be used only when necessary, but it must still be a tool."

"What about the girls?"

Vahid shifted in his chair and crossed his leg. "I do not enjoy that part of the business, but if it isn't us, it is someone else. We are more humane."

"More humane? You shipped these girls like they were cattle. In the back of an unheated trailer, in the dead of the coldest winter on record."

"Believe me, Cowboy. I have seen much, much worse. We feed them. We take care of them. Other places shoot them up with drugs and send them on their way. We offer them training and high-end jobs. Many go on to be successful."

"Bullshit. Successful slaves. What excuses does your wife conjure to explain away your actions? It must be hard for her to see her husband in you. Maybe she's good with it. Think of that the next time you look lovingly into her eyes. Maybe she wants you to kill for her. Maybe she has less left in her soul than you do."

Vahid shook his head and leaned over Moses. "Why do you make it ugly?"

Moses couldn't believe his ears. "It was born ugly and it will die ugly. You might have a choice."

Vahid pulled Moses upright. He could feel Vahid's breath on his neck as Vahid worked on the zip ties, and it reminded him of a dog with rotten teeth. He felt the plastic tie come off and the blood rushed into his hands. Moses rubbed his wrists and turned. Vahid was holding a small switchblade and tilted it toward Moses.

"This is the best thing." Then he pointed to his hip where he had two guns tucked into his belt. "It gets worse there."

"That's my gun," Moses said.

"Yes, sorry, Cowboy. I have a weakness for collecting things like it."

"I'll need that back."

"Not in this lifetime, Cowboy. Come on. The easy way." Vahid pulled him upright and pushed him toward the door. He pushed him out into the hallway, where Elvis was holding a gun on Šejla. She looked no worse for wear. Moses managed a wink at her. Then they were getting pushed down the hallway and back into the auction room.

Moses sighed and his vision blurred. Brooklyn was there, lying on the floor, motionless. She was partially covered by a robe splattered with crimson stains. Her mouth was red with blood and her face was swollen and already starting to blacken. Next to her, Sharon was sitting in a chair with her leg crossed, holding a coffee mug to her chest.

Moses lurched forward. "What did you do to her?" Moses felt something strike his kidney and he fell forward into the room. He got to his feet and limped forward before he was struck again with enough force to spin him over. Elvis stood over him with his strange expressionless face and dead eyes, his fists ready to finish the job.

"Leave him," Sharon commanded. Moses rolled over and struggled to his feet and staggered to the girl. He fell to her side and picked up her head and held it to his ear. She was breathing. He tried to think of something to stall them. He needed to think! He needed a plan. *How many lives am I responsible for?* He felt cold panic seize him. Brooklyn from Minnesota was going to die and the other girls were going to their own hell and he had failed to stop any of it.

He let the wave of emotion run through him for a moment, and then he had a thought—one last vengeful thought.

"Don't worry. She'll live. Not good for much other than a cleaning lady, I'm afraid." Sharon pulled the coffee mug to her lips, watching him over the brim.

"You're not going to kill her?" Moses asked, getting to his feet.

"It's hard, isn't it?" Sharon asked, standing up and walking toward him.

"What do you mean?" Moses asked.

"It's hard for you to hate me."

"I don't think so."

"You think it is easy, but it twists you up inside. I think it's what drives people to do things like we do. The similarities. We want to wipe them out but we can't."

"Shut up."

"I think you see me and you see yourself. And maybe you hate that, but I think what you hate more is how we are alike. You pretend like I am a freak, but you know that you are only a few choices away from being in my position. And the choices aren't that hard, are they? Maybe you would make the same choices?"

"I would never do what you do," Moses said, pushing toward her. Elvis grabbed his arm in his steel grip.

"Okay. Think that. Breathe the fresh, free air deep into your lungs and think that you would never do what I would do. You are the problem, Moses. You, and me, and these two here," she gestured at Elvis and Vahid. "Everyone knows that there are girls for sale. Yet they go on getting sold. Why is that Moses? Is it because we are too good at hiding it? I don't think so. Go to any strip club in town. Go on the local Internet sites for a good time. Visit your porn sites. You'll find all you can handle. For a price. I think it might be that no one wants to stop it. What do you think? Do you think that all that can be done has been done to stop it?"

"If people knew, they would stop it."

"You have a lot of faith, Moses. I'll give you that. But I think that nobody wants to know the truth."

"The truth. Like you killed your husband so you could take over this damned business and sell these girls like they were animals at the stockyards? You sell them to the highest bidder and rest your head on your pretty little pillow at night, in your secure cookie-cutter house next to your doctor and accountant neighbors, like you are *them*. You're not them. You are evil and will burn in hell and I hope the Devil never forgets you."

"You think I killed my husband to take over *his* business?" Sharon walked a step closer to Moses. She was almost close enough. "I built this business. Fred had a little money in the beginning, but not the will. He had his supply business and it did fine, but when the economy tanked, we had tough decisions to make, and when the opportunity came to us, Fred got cold feet. I didn't. I stepped up. I found the muscle and consolidated operations. I took us international. Wake up, Moses. Fred worked for me. I make decisions he couldn't. I killed him because he was mine to kill. I hired you because I could tell I could control you. You are weak and malleable, Moses. I led you around like a little puppy."

"I needed an airtight alibi when Fred went missing. Jail is the perfect place to order a murder from. So I got you to take me to the cabin where Fred was shacked up with his little Bosnian whore girl. I took your gun and shot the place up. Boy, that almost happened then, too. That girl and her knife," Sharon said, chuckling.

"You showing up at Duncan's when you did and finding where they buried Fred, that was just icing on the cake. We would have had to send you out there at some point to find the body anyway. You just accelerated the timeline."

Moses jerked his arm free from Elvis' grasp and lunged at Sharon, grabbing her by the throat. He knew he had only seconds before Elvis and Vahid tackled him. Crushing her windpipe was the only purpose for his hands and he concentrated all of his being into squeezing the life out of Sharon Dunsmore's body. He saw her blue eyes widen in surprise and felt the pulse of the blood in her neck and squeezed harder, wanting to shut off the hose from her cold heart to her evil brain. *If I can send her to the other side*, he thought, *that is all I ask*. Just rip what's left of her soul from this earth. Her eyes bulged and dimmed. She was almost gone.

A weight slammed into his side. Moses fell to the floor, dragging Sharon's limp body with him. Elvis was on him, working to break his hold on her neck. Moses screamed, channeling one more rush of adrenaline into killing her. He felt failure in the iron grip of Elvis' hand, slowly bending back his index finger. One hand slipped off her neck and then both. Sharon was free, Elvis was on top of him, and he felt his head bounce off the floor as an explosion of light flashed in his brain. The first was painful, but then it diminished to a tap on the back of his head, far away.

Then Moses was back. He grabbed Elvis by the shoulders, stopping the next bounce of his head off the floor. Sharon gasped somewhere out of his field of vision. *She lives*, his woozy mind registered. Vahid and Elvis dragged him back to his feet and put him in the chair. Sharon had her back to him, her breath ragged.

"Why did you kill him?" Moses asked.

"Who?" Her voice raspy.

"Your husband, Fred."

"He was mine," she said.

"That's it. You killed him because you could?"

"He was cheating on me."

"And you didn't cheat on him?"

"Like I said. He was mine, and so is his child."

Moses looked to Šejla. Add Fred Dunsmore's unborn child to the list of his failures.

Sharon turned and walked toward Moses. Moses felt Elvis and Vahid tighten their grips on him. Sharon stopped just out of reach and folded her arms over her chest.

"What do you put in their necks?" Moses asked.

"Something that Elvis found. It's a livestock GPS tracking system. It helps when they are in the developmental stage. That way we can drop them off and not worry about them running away. Insurance on the investment."

"What about the girl that froze to death?"

"She was a hard one. She made it to a low area and the GPS lost her for a time. Long enough for her to give up."

"Can you hear yourself?"

She frowned at him and then turned and scratched her bare shoulder with a long, manicured nail. "Put him in the river. Her too."

"It's frozen," Vahid said.

"Break it open."

Vahid and Elvis pulled Moses to his feet and Vahid walked him to the door as Elvis pushed Šejla ahead of them. Vahid whistled and then there was a large, black dog walking next to him, looking up at Moses with dark, dead eyes, tongue hanging out against large, white teeth.

"Think about what I said when you give up and let the cold water enter your lungs," Sharon said.

"I'll be nice and warm thinking about the Devil pissing fire on you for eternity," Moses said.

Moses heard Sharon's laughter echo in the ballroom as Vahid pushed him through the door.

Chapter 28

Behind Duncan's house, Moses watched as Elvis pushed Šejla through the snow and down the bank. Elvis swore at her as she fell down again.

"Let me go first," Moses said.

Elvis looked back at him and said something in Bosnian to Vahid and they both laughed.

"He said it won't take much to kill you," Vahid said.

"Must have been funnier in Bosnian," Moses said. "I can do it. It's the only thing I have left to do. Don't torture her. Let me lead. I'm not going anywhere." Vahid glanced at Elvis. Elvis held a large chainsaw, letting it dangle from his hand. He shrugged.

"Okay, Cowboy. You lead." Moses pushed past Elvis and helped Šejla to her feet.

"Don't worry. We'll be fine," he said and squeezed her shoulder. Then he got out in front and broke through the snow with his boots and knees, taking extra care to make the path wide. The snow was coming down harder than ever, making it difficult to see. Moses lost his footing and slid down the last few feet to the trail below. It hadn't been cleared since the last snowfall, but there were paths from hobby skiers and snowshoers. Moses turned back and helped Šejla down to the trail. Then he followed the easiest trail and began the hike to the river.

His abdomen had been hurting since the car crash, but now everything melted away. The burning subsided to a comfortable level. Depending on which way they took, it was another half-mile to the river. It felt good to be walking. He reached into his pocket and pulled out his pack of smokes. The pack was crumpled, so he ripped it open and found one last unbroken cigarette. He fished around for a lighter in his front pocket. A black shape jumped in front of him on the path. White teeth snarled at him from the darkness and a low grumble seemed to well up from the ground. He fumbled with the cigarette, but managed to save it from getting wet in the snow.

"She doesn't like that, Cowboy," Vahid said. "What are you doing?"

"It's just a cigarette," Moses said, putting his hand with the lighter in the air. "I don't care if she doesn't like it. I'm not leaving without one last smoke."

Vahid chuckled and the dog disappeared off the trail and back into the woods to shadow them on their march to the river. Moses lit the cigarette as he continued on the path. He glanced back and saw Šejla walking easier now. Elvis was next and then Vahid a step behind them. They were far enough back that Moses could make a run for it, busted ribs or no. But he couldn't leave Šejla behind and even if he made it, there was still that fucking hellhound to deal with.

They came to a bend in the trail and Vahid told him to get off and head to the river. The progress slowed to a stumbling crawl. Moses tossed his cigarette away, breathing too hard to enjoy it. He clung to a small tree branch, then a sapling, using them as crutches in the difficult terrain. He fell down, floundering in the snow like an injured herd animal trying to keep its footing.

On the ground, he could see better now as the snowfall was blocked by the trees. He stared up at the large snow-covered tree branches like terrible skeletal claws reaching to the sky. He lay there and forgot about everything. What he had done. What he hadn't. He was going to be a cop, wasn't he? Or was he going to be a pilot in the Air Force? Why hadn't he done that? Why had he not taken a trip to see anything? To see what? He couldn't think. He wanted to see it all. *Why hadn't I?* He couldn't think of a reason. Why was he lying here in the snow? How had he ended up on a death march to the Des Moines river?

Then Vahid was standing over him, pointing an old Nazi gun at him. It was his grandfather's and now Vahid held it.

Moses reached out his arm, and Vahid tucked the gun away and offered his hand.

Make it count.

He pulled hard on Vahid's hand, forcing him to the ground. He rolled on top of him and punched him in the chin. Moses landed another blow, stunning Vahid and then grabbed at the gun at Vahid's waist. His fingers fumbled on the handle. He pulled on it, but the barrel got stuck on Vahid's belt. Then he saw Elvis charging at him. He braced himself but couldn't protect his side and the younger man barreled into him as the light in Moses' eyes flickered. He snapped back as Elvis cocked his fist to strike him. Moses felt the wooden grip of the gun in his hand, but it was pinned underneath Elvis's leg and he couldn't reach the trigger. Moses threw up his left arm to block the next blow, then he felt the weight fall off him. Šejla stood over him with a large tree branch held like a baseball bat. Elvis was gone, and Moses had his gun back.

"Come on." She held out her hand.

"Goddamn, I love you," Moses said as she helped him to his feet. Vahid, already recovered, blocked their path back to Des Moines. Vahid had his gun leveled on them and whistled a sharp note.

"Run!" Moses shouted, pushing Šejla down the path away from Vahid. That fucking demon dog. If it wasn't for that dog, they would have chance. They needed to find a place to make a stand. They were sitting ducks out in this forest. "To the river!" Moses yelled.

"What? That's what they want. They'll kill us!" Šejla shouted back.

"They're going to kill us either way. We can make a stand at the river." Moses grabbed her arm and dragged her behind a tree.

Blam.

The shot zipped by his ear. Moses peeked around the trunk of the tree. Vahid marched down the path, gun aimed, no pretense of taking cover. Elvis and the dog were gone, out of sight, the snowfall harder now and making it difficult to distinguish shapes at a distance.

"Stop this, Cowboy! Come out and die with dignity!" Vahid shouted. Then a gust of wind ripped through the trees, knocking snow from the branches and creating a thick screen of white. This was their chance. Moses pushed Šejla down a short gully and through a thick set of bushes. Hopefully the dog was having as much trouble as they were. Not likely, he knew. The damn dog probably found every trace of game trail and shortcut through a hollow bush out here, gaining on them with every stumbling step. Then they ran into a trampled-down area with a clear path open to the river. Šejla ran in front of him. Moses tried to jog, but his side felt like it had been torn open by a jagged piece of glass. He stopped and tried again. Šejla was getting farther away. He slowed and settled on a hopping fast walk, just short of a jog and he managed to keep Šejla in sight through the swirling snow. If they could just get farther away, they might lose them.

Blam.

A shot rang out, closer now, splitting the quiet. And then a shout that seemed a long way off. Šejla looked back at him, and he waved her forward. The snowfall had stopped for now and Moses chanced a look back. He thought he saw a flash of light far away, reflected off the low clouds. Could be a plane landing, or… He couldn't let himself hope. He had to keep moving. Already Šejla was just a shadow up ahead. They couldn't be far from the river now. Then he heard it. It was a low, deep rumble, barely audible over his gasps for air. A few steps more and he saw it.

Šejla was on her back, battling against the bared teeth of the great black dog. Moses froze for an instant. Jaws snapped at her as she shrieked. Moses raised the gun and fired. Snow exploded into the face of the beast, causing it jump to the side and bark in surprise. He had missed the mark and now the animal was aware of him. Moses fired again as the beast trotted back into the safety of the tree line. He couldn't tell if he had scored a hit.

"Are you okay?" Moses felt his eyes dim with the adrenaline dump. The gun felt heavy in his hand.

"Yes, I'm fine." Šejla was already on her feet and moving toward the river. "He lunged at me out of nowhere."

"Try to stay close," he said.

There was another crack of gunfire. Closer, echoing through the night. Moses saw Šejla flinch, but she pressed on. Then they were at the fallen tree. Yellow emergency tape surrounded the deep hole.

"Shit. We're right back where Fred was."

"What?" Šejla's eyes were wide.

"This is where we found him," he said.

"Poor Freddy. Those assholes." She looked at the hole and then turned back the way they had come. "What do we do now?"

"You need to get down on the river and run. There is a park on the other side and then Fleur Drive. Flag someone down. Don't stop running."

Šejla nodded and Moses held her hand as she climbed down the bank. He let go and she slid the remaining ten feet, landing on her butt. She stood up and flashed a thumbs-up. He returned the thumbs-up and smiled at her through the darkness with a genuine feeling of happiness that felt out of place, like he was playing a game and was ten-years-old again.

He turned back to the path and the feeling passed. Now he was sure he could see amber lights glowing in the snowfall some distance away near Ducan's mansion. Maybe he could hold them off and the cops would find him in time. He grinned and shook his head. Too far. No one would find him tonight. Even if they followed the gunfire it could be hours before they found him, and by then it would be too late.

That's okay. Šejla just needs a few minutes and she'll be safe.

Moses leaned against the stump as he waited for Vahid. The rough bark of the tree felt good under his hand.

Chapter 29

Rakić's Mossberg shotgun led the way through the open front door of Henry Duncan's house. He stalked down the hallway, deeper into the house. He entered a large room with a flowing staircase to the left. A set of fifteen-foot double doors dominated the wall in front of him. Rakić trained the shotgun up the staircase and then swung back to the doors at the faint sounds coming from behind them. He padded to the doors and put his ear to them. Indistinct voices. Laughter. Silence again. He had a choice to make. Go, or wait for backup.

The chatter on the police radio had been mostly traffic accidents all over the metro due to the snowstorm, draining resources away. He had been assigned a single patrol cruiser until the emergency response SWAT team could be brought in and it still hadn't shown. He'd had no choice but to come in on his own. Šejla was in here somewhere; he was sure of it. The backup cruiser was a few minutes away. Hansen had answered the call. He pulled his handheld radio out of his coat pocket.

"Rakić to Hansen. Over," Rakić said into the radio.

"This is Hansen. Go ahead, Rakić."

"I'm inside the Duncan house. Located the van parked in the driveway. I am proceeding into the interior of the residence. What's your twenty?"

"ETA in two minutes."

"Roger. Rakić out."

Rakić shrugged his coat off and tossed it on the floor. He leaned the shotgun against the wall and tucked the radio into his back pocket. He unholstered his .40 from his hip, chambered a round, and flipped the safety off. He holstered it again and took his backup piece from his ankle holster. He made it ready to shoot, and he tucked it in his belt. He took the shotgun and checked that the safety was off. He cracked the door and peered inside a huge room that looked like an old ballroom. Several doors spaced the walls at regular intervals, suggesting more that he couldn't see. Three goons dressed in black leather coats huddled to the side. Their low voices were washed out in the acoustics of the room. Not Vahid. Not Elvis. He pushed on the door and a podium and stage came into view. A woman walked past his line of sight, her back to him. She barked an order and the men jumped. She turned and he saw her face.

Sharon Dunsmore. *What the hell is she doing here?*

Moses' message had said Vahid was here, nothing about her. Rakić couldn't think. He needed to find Šejla. The van was here. Dunsmore was involved. Rakić tensed and took a deep breath. On three. Anticipation coursed through him. He used the three count to focus. He plunged into the room, shotgun ready.

"Nobody move! DCI! On the floor! Keep your hands visible!" Rakić shouted.

The three thugs had doubles on the opposite side of the room. He now faced six. Sharon Dunsmore screamed something, but everything had gone silent as his mind focused on the thugs. She snarled at him and darted behind the men and was gone through a door. The original three trained their weapons on Rakić. Rakić strode to the side, leveled the shotgun at the closest of the three, and squeezed off a round from his hip. They scattered like birds. Rakić pumped the shotgun, chambering a shell as he pivoted to the other three. They blocked the door Sharon had disappeared through a moment before. They pushed over part of the stage and used it as a makeshift barricade. Rakić unloaded into the center of it, blasting a coffee can-sized hole in the wood and metal. A round zinged by his head as he bounded forward and slid on his knees. The muzzle blast of a gun flashed in front of him at three o'clock. Rakić fired again, scampered ahead, then two more times on the way to the barricade. Then he was on them. He flipped the shotgun in his hand and smashed the stock into the face of the closest thug. The man's face caved under the blow with a wet smack, leaving a hollow where his nose should be. He pushed the maimed man into the next man and they fell to the floor. Rakić pulled out his .40 and fired it into the air. The other man threw up his hands. Rakić looked back for the original three. Gone.

"On your knees! Toss your guns away!" Rakić yelled. The two men that were able threw their guns into the middle of the ballroom. Rakić kicked the other guns away.

He tossed heavy-duty plastic zip tie cuffs at the nearest man. "Put these on. Arm to arm. Leg to leg." Rakić waved his gun at them. "Come on. Come on. Hurry up."

Rakić pulled out his stainless-steel handcuffs and placed one on the man he had smashed in the face and attached the other end to the crossbar on the leg of the stage. "Be back in a minute. Don't go anywhere."

Rakić plunged through the exit Sharon had disappeared through a short eternity ago. He found himself in a slightly smaller chamber, some sort of sitting or smoking room. He dashed to the door on the opposite wall and found another, similar room behind it. This had a door to his right and straight ahead. He kept going straight to the next door and was in a large kitchen. Stairs led down. He took them two at a time until he emerged in an underground garage. Dim light reflected off the floor. Two antique limousines, a Land Rover, and a Mercedes were parked side by side. A key box with its door half open hung from the wall. Rakić opened the box. A set of Land Rover keys was missing. He stalked down the row toward the Land Rover. Creeping to the passenger window of the vehicle, he peered inside. Empty. A buzz behind him, then bright fluorescent lights flooded the room, reflecting off the whitewashed stone walls.

Metal scraped on concrete. He spun around in time to see Sharon Dunsmore swinging a shovel at his head. He lurched forward, ducking under the blow. Sharon squealed as the shovel's weight pulled her off balance and continued on its arc, smashing into the windshield of the Mercedes. Rakić lowered his shoulder and launched into her midsection. Air was forced from her lungs with a whoosh. He grabbed her thighs and picked her up over his shoulder and slammed her down on the hood of the Mercedes, sending the shovel clattering to the concrete floor. Rakić straddled Sharon's body, pinning both her wrists over her head with one hand and training his gun on her with the other. She glared at him, her face twisted and ugly.

"Let me go. Who are you? What are you doing in my house?" She tossed her head, struggling to buck him off of her.

Made Safe

"This isn't your house," Rakić said.

She relaxed and her face softened as she giggled. "Oh. I know you. You're that cop. I thought you were..." She cut herself off and smiled, beauty returned. Her body seemed to melt into his. Her knee rode up his thigh.

"Stop it." The heat of her body coursed through his hands as he held her down against the chill metal of the car hood. Šejla leaped to his mind. He shook Sharon and pressed the gun to her temple.

"Mmmm." She bit her lip as her eyes followed the gun.

He slammed her arms on the hood and pressed the gun under her chin, his face inches from hers.

"Where's Šejla?"

"Who?" Sharon had a dreamy look on her face and he felt her body press into him again.

"Šejla. Šejla Tahirović. Your husband's mistress." Sharon transformed once again, from beauty back to ugly hate.

"That bitch is dead. Who cares?" Her face softened and she started grinding into his body.

Rakić lowered the gun from her chin and let go of her wrists. Sharon was forgotten. He felt her tug at his waist and she pulled his jacket open, but it was happening to someone else. He put the gun to his mouth and a single drop of moisture leaked from his eye and traced a path down the side of his nose to his mouth. How had he allowed her to die in this country when he had managed to keep her alive so long in Sarajevo? In this sleepy capital of the heartland, he had let his precious cousin get consumed by this evil, while he wore a badge and had a city of cops at his command. He had let her get taken. Get killed.

Sharon stopped pawing at him and leaned on a hand studying him. "She was pregnant," she said, like it was the weather she was talking about.

"What did you say?" The words traveled slowly through his scattered mind.

"She was pregnant with my husband's bastard baby."

"*What did you say?*" Something black and smoky swam through his vision. He could see parts of Sharon. Her eyes. Her mouth. Then it was just her teeth and eyes. The white in her teeth turned yellow and then a charred, gray-black. Her skin shriveled up and eroded until it was just her black teeth, white bone, and blue eyes. Then they turned green, then red, then orange. Dark thoughts pressed to the front of his mind, clamoring for action, drowning out every other thought. Pressing the gun to his cheek he tried to concentrate on the words. *She was pregnant.*

"What? What did you say?" He was speaking Bosnian, he thought. *Is it Bosnian I speak? Was that what I spoke? Am I Bosnian? No, I'm Iowan. I'm from Iowa. I am an American.* He felt laughter rumbling in his chest but couldn't hear it. He opened his eyes, looked at the gun, and thought how silly it was. He pressed himself off of Sharon and strode to the wall of the garage. Something better.

"What are you doing?"

"*Looking.*"

"What did you say?" Sharon asked.

"*I'm looking for something.*"

"Speak English, I can't understand what you're saying."

Rakić ignored her and then found it. It was hanging on the wall. It had a long wooden handle and was slightly curved at the end. The head was wedge-shaped. Perfect for splitting wood. He set his gun down, pulled the axe off the wall, and let it rest on his shoulder.

"What are you going to do with that?" She no longer had a name to him. She was the thing that he would destroy and nothing more. He walked to the key box and pulled out a set of Mercedes keys.

Sharon was still lying on the hood of the car, her red dress bunched up at her waist. Her legs pressed together now in a final reflexive show of modesty. Rakić sprang on her. Grabbing her wrist, he dragged her to the back of the car. He pushed her face down toward the trunk and popped it with the set of keys.

"Get in."

"You're going to kill me."

"Get in."

She climbed into the car and laid down, facing away from him. She pulled her knees up to her chest and he slammed the trunk down.

He took off his jacket and tossed it away. He picked up the axe and his rage boiled over.

The axe smashed into the thin metal of the car trunk, splitting it with a screech. The axe fell again. And again. And again. Sharon screamed something between blows. Again. Again. Again. He was sweating and couldn't breathe but he kept swinging. Again. Again, until the trunk was so full of holes he could see flashes of Sharon's red dress inside. He stopped and leaned against the adjacent car, feeling its light frame shift with his weight.

He heard Sharon sobbing. He checked the lock on the trunk. She was secure. He retrieved his gun and jacket and climbed up the stairs into the kitchen. He contemplated going back through the house, but it didn't matter. He heard a door open behind him.

"Des Moines PD! On the ground!" A voice shouted.

Rakić turned, his firearm trained on the intruder. Hansen.

"It's me, Hansen. Rakić. Stand down," Rakić said. Hansen relaxed and entered the kitchen.

"Sorry, Rakić."

"Don't be sorry. You always need to expect the worse."

"Anybody left in here?"

"Yeah, three are cuffed back that way." Rakić pointed into the interior of the house. "But they aren't who I'm looking for." He didn't feel like talking about Sharon just yet.

"No, who are we looking for then?" Hansen asked.

Rakić reached up and clanged together a group of pots hanging overhead and set his weapon on the stainless-steel prep area. He adjusted his backup piece in his trousers. "One of the girls they have is my cousin, but she ain't here."

"Shit. I didn't know. Sorry, Raif."

"Let's take a look out back. Maybe they ran when they heard the shots." Rakić and Hansen went out the door and searched the back patio. There was a great expanse of open space that would be green lawn in the spring. The wind had picked up and the snow swirled. The outlines of the trees were barely visible even at fifty feet.

"You see that?" Hansen asked.

"What?"

"There's a line of tracks leading out to the woods. I'm sure of it." Rakić squinted. He could barely make out the outline of partially filled in tracks in the snow.

"Holy shit." Rakić slapped him on the back. "Grab your flashlight. We are going hunting."

Chapter 30

Moses thumbed the safety on the old gun, the German words hidden and exposed with each flick of his finger. *Geladen. Gesichert.* Geladen meant loaded. Gesichert meant something like safe or protected in German. He had tried to protect people these last few days. He had tried. It hadn't been enough. He had another chance with Šejla. He would try to protect her, buy her enough time to get away.

Something in the night changed. It wasn't something he heard necessarily, but he sensed it. A smell maybe. Or something deeper in his DNA had alerted him. Whatever it was, he felt it deep inside. He was not alone. Then his ears picked it up. First, deep breathing and then a dark shape materialized in front of him, its head hung low and its teeth yellow against the white snow. Eyes glowed from yellow to green as Moses trained his gun on the spot between them. The beast jumped to the side and disappeared. Moses turned his back to the large stump and waited. He searched the ground for anything else he could use to defend himself. He found a short, thick branch and hefted it in his left hand. *Come on, you bastard.* He waited, thinking how the animal would come at him. That last had been a probe, to see how strong he was, how he reacted. Testing. The next time it would be faster, deadlier. He whirled to his left. Then back to his right. Nothing. He raised the gun and fired into the air.

"Come on, you dirty shit eater. Come dance with me!"

Moses lowered the gun. Let's get this over with, he thought. A sharp double-whistle pierced the night. Then nothing. He scanned the darkness, hoping to see a hint of the animal before it was on him. At the last second, he heard the growl and his right arm was locked in the jaws of the beast. He felt his flesh tear like slow-smoked barbecue meat in the razor-sharp teeth of the animal. No longer able to feel his hand, he realized he must have dropped his gun. He swung the branch at the head of the beast and felt the club bounce off its skull. But the dog kept coming. Moses slipped and was dragged down to the ground. He swung again and hit the dog in its side with a meaty thump. But the dog ignored the blow and now had Moses pinned beneath it. Moses couldn't move the weight off him. Primal, claustrophobic terror welled up in his chest and he couldn't breathe. He gasped for air and then he heard the laughing.

"Cowboy. You are such a bastard. Why do you fight so hard?" Moses felt the dog release its grip and move away. The pain in his arm doubled in intensity and he felt his consciousness holding on by a sliver. He sat up and pulled his damaged arm into his lap.

"I just have so much to live for." Moses choked the words out, swallowing pain in large buckets. He managed to push himself to his feet with the club and then jerked the club up to his shoulder. Vahid chuckled again.

"Okay, Cowboy. You made your point. You are dying bravely. But the night is wearing out. Let's go." Vahid pointed down to the river. Moses glanced back at it.

"Think you have time to cut a hole in the ice?" Moses said. Then he heard it. The slow steady hum of an idling chainsaw.

"Elvis will be done by the time we get there." Moses let the club fall to his side. Šejla should be gone by now. She would at least make it. Then he looked back at the dog and Vahid. *Just one more burst of energy, old man.* Moses felt his legs come back to life and the adrenaline surged through him one last time. He flew across the last few feet to Vahid and had the satisfaction of seeing the shock in Vahid's face as he struck him in the head with the club. Vahid's eyes rolled up in his head, but he was still standing. Moses swung again. The dog hadn't moved from its position, but that bit of good fortune wouldn't last long. The second blow seemed to wake Vahid up. He slipped Moses' next swing and chopped down with his arm, trapping Moses' forearm under his armpit. Moses strained to free himself as Vahid slowly twisted his arm, putting pressure on his shoulder and injured side. Vahid punched him in the head and his legs went rubbery and he dropped the club. He had nothing left. His feet wouldn't stay under him. Another punch landed to his side like a baseball bat into a side of beef. Vahid squeezed Moses' shredded forearm and his legs finally gave out.

"Let's go, Cowboy. The water waits." Moses felt himself dragged to his feet and then he was sliding down the bank. He felt something he figured was blood freezing on his cheek. The dog was somewhere in front now and they were getting closer to the sound of the chainsaw. Elvis appeared out of the blowing snow holding the idling chainsaw in his hand.

"How's the water?" Vahid asked.

"It is open but not for long."

"Okay, Cowboy, your hands." Moses didn't understand the words. He felt his hands pulled together behind him and then felt the click of the zip tie as it bit into his wrists. The pain from his forearm at some point had dissolved into a numb ache. Vahid pushed him to his knees, and now he could see the hole. It was a dark rectangle of water framed by the gray and white of the frozen river around it. He watched as the falling snowflakes whirled around in the air and fell into the hole and disappeared. Already, a thin layer of crystals had formed on the surface. He looked up at Vahid and Elvis next to him and then he back at the water. At least Šejla would be okay.

"Did you get Šejla?" Moses asked.

"We will get her. I have her on GPS." Moses closed his eyes. The bastard had time to implant a damn GPS device in her. *Humanity fails to disappoint practically never. All lives lost are truly wasted.* He managed to grin one more time. He looked up at the two bastards that would end him, and he had another thought.

"I didn't really get to finish that cigarette."

Vahid chuckled low. "I wish we had more time, Cowboy. You probably deserve it."

Moses nodded and looked into the cold, black water.

"Okay, let's get this over with." A pause and then he felt a pressure on his back. A foot, he thought.

"Sorry, Cowboy." Vahid said.

Moses felt the cold water of the river against his face, and he thrashed out as his entire body struggled to absorb the shock.

He felt himself being dragged under the ice by the current as he reflexively gasped for air, water flooding his mouth, choking him. He coughed and fought the urge to gag. He twisted and saw the opening at the surface and kicked his legs, propelling himself up. His head broke the surface and he coughed up water. His legs fought to keep his head above water.

Vahid looked down at him and frowned. Elvis stood behind Vahid and the dog lay on its belly between them. Moses felt his legs deaden in the ice water. Vahid stepped forward and raised his foot. Moses jerked away, but Vahid planted his foot on Moses' head, forcing him back under.

The frigid water stabbed into his eyes, numbing his brain. His legs kept kicking on their own. He felt like giving up. He thought of stopping. His legs kicked. He kicked, fighting the current. He kicked forever. Somehow, he was under the hole in the ice and Moses broke free of the water again. And he saw Šejla standing over Elvis' prone body, holding a tree branch. *What a wonderful woman.* Vahid had his gun drawn and she was backing away from him. *Run!*

Moses felt his legs give out and his head fell back under the surface of the river. The current dragged him away from the hole. He kicked with all he had left and broke free one more time. The water burned on his skin as it hit the night air. Vahid was clutching his chest, kneeling on the ice, and Elvis lay motionless next to him. Šejla had vanished. In her place stood Majka, holding a revolver trained on Vahid. Moses twisted in the water, searching for Šejla.

Nothing. Maybe she had escaped. Majka saw him and rushed forward. Just then, Moses felt his body shudder, his legs gone, his head slipped back under the black water of the Des Moines river.

He felt his mind slipping as he admired the air bubbles rushing from his mouth. He tasted the cold water. He hadn't realized how thirsty he had been and so cold, but now he was warm and his arm didn't hurt. He heard a girl's voice in his head. He couldn't understand her. She was above him. Moses kicked hard again. His head broke the surface of the water and he saw his chance. A large branch was laying over the hole. He let himself slide lower in the water, gathered himself, and then kicked again, throwing his torso over the branch. Finally, he drew a large clear breath of cold delicious night air. His senses returned and Moses heard ragged breathing. He craned his head to the side and could see Vahid sitting on the ice next to the hole, holding his chest. Majka stood over him, a gun dangling from her hand. Elvis was nowhere to be seen. "It's okay, Cowboy. I came back for you. I couldn't let them kill you."

Moses couldn't think. The cold was grinding into his body. What was she talking about?

"You let lots of people get destroyed. Why am I any different?"

She knelt down over him, her face next to his. She looked at his lips and then kissed him. His body seemed to warm a degree as her tongue pushed into his mouth. She broke the kiss and stood up.

"I can't be explaining myself to you constantly, Cowboy. You know my apartment?" He grunted. "There are some of the girls there from other times."

"What about the girls tonight?"

"They still have GPS. You should be able to get them back." She set a phone down next to him. "That has the app."

"What are you doing to me, Kata?" Vahid groaned. "You shot my dog. You shot me. Elvis will find you." Vahid fell backwards onto the ice. "You killed me."

Majka looked toward the bank in the direction of the Duncan house and dropped her arm. "Don't thank me now, Cowboy." She stepped over Vahid, then dropped the gun into the water and ran into the darkness. He could hear voices. Voices calling his name. He shifted his head in their direction and shouted. He shouted again and he heard a response. Then one last time.

"Rakić!"

"I'm here, Moses." Rakić was next to him, pulling him out of the water. He saw Vahid and drew his gun, but Moses put his hand on his arm.

"Šejla." And pointed toward the opposite bank.

"I'm here." Moses saw her face and smiled. She was okay. Rakić stood behind her, his face drawn and pale but okay.

"The girl? The girls?"

"Relax. We got them," Rakić said.

"Majka?" Rakić looked away. She had escaped. Moses relaxed. Paramedics showed up and cut his clothes off, covered him with blankets, and put him on a stretcher. He looked over and saw another team of paramedics working on Vahid. Then he was on the back of a four-wheeler and the trees whizzed by overhead, the pain less now. Exhaustion overtook his body as his energy swirled away in the warmth of a thick blanket he was wrapped in. He drifted off, thinking of a woman with black hair vanishing in the snow.

Chapter 31

Moses felt warm and didn't want to wake up. But his arm was itchy and numb and he began to remember the dog. The sun shining through the window finally won and he cracked an eye. Bright light bounced through his vision, making his eyes water. He closed it again. Then he forced both eyes open and waited for the blurriness to pass. When it did, he could see his arm wrapped in thick gauze. His fingers sticking out the end were purple. He saw beyond his hand to the beeping machines and the cruel white austerity of a hospital room. He moved his head to the side and immediately regretted it. Sharp, angry pain ripped through his side and head. But now he could see her sitting in the chair at the foot of his bed. She was dozing, with her head leaning on her hand. She had a slight crinkle in her forehead, like she was having a bad dream.

He pushed himself up and she stirred. "Claudia." The name caught in his throat and he coughed, pain wracking his body. Claudia was suddenly at his side with a cup of water.

"Thanks," he said and sipped the water.

"Are you okay?"

"Yeah. Just—" He paused and looked up at her, cracking a smile. "Just a little banged up. What time is it?"

Claudia frowned and sighed. "You've been out a while, Mos. It's New Year's Eve."

Moses blinked. "I've been out that long?"

"Yeah."

"Jesus, no wonder I got a headache. I need a smoke."

Claudia laughed and Moses could feel the pain melt away. "Where are Rakić and Šejla? Did they find all the girls?"

"They got all the girls from that night at the house you were at. That much they told me."

"And Majka?"

"They don't know where she is." Claudia leaned back and folded her arms over her chest.

Moses shook his head and frowned. He could feel Majka's lips on his, her exciting taste. Then he remembered Claudia. He smiled at her and changed the subject.

"Rakić probably has it all in hand. He's a hell of a cop," he said.

"Yeah. I like him."

"You talking about me?"

Moses turned and saw Raif Rakić stride into the room. "Yeah, we were. I was telling her you probably couldn't find your badge." Moses grinned.

"You hear this, Claudia?"

"He was actually just telling me what a good cop you are." Claudia raised her eyes as she glanced at Moses and then Rakić.

"She's been drinking," Moses said.

"Well, I'll let you boys talk. I need to go get a sandwich. You need anything while I'm out?"

"Pack of Marlboros," Moses said.

"Not with that rib of yours. Anything else?"

Moses sighed. "I guess not."

Claudia smiled and patted Rakić on the back as she slung her purse over her shoulder. "He's all yours."

Moses glanced at the door as Claudia left and then turned to Rakić. "How is Šejla?" Moses asked.

"She and her baby are doing well. I will be its uncle," Rakić said with a glint in his eyes.

"That is good. It will be a strong baby. What about the case?"

Rakić sat on the edge of the chair. "We got most of it wrapped up. We traced the girls with GPS. One was already halfway to Kansas City, but we got her."

"And the buyers?" Moses asked.

"That's been tough. We got Sharon Dunsmore. She'll go on trial. You'll be a big part of the case we are building, along with the girls we rescued. Those that are willing to testify, anyway."

Moses nodded. "Duncan, Coyote, Elvis, Majka?"

Rakić spread his hands. "In the wind. Elvis has been seen around town but we haven't heard anything on Majka. No one's seen Duncan or the Coyote either."

"Vahid?"

"He pulled through. He actually might flip and testify. We'll see."

"He's just as guilty as Elvis or Majka or Sharon."

Rakić lowered his eyes and fidgeted with his watch. "He could have inside knowledge that we could use to reach further than Des Moines. I don't like it much either, but if we can extend this, it might make a big difference."

Moses snorted. "It's not going to make a difference. No one cares. It will be a big story for a day or two and then everyone will forget and turn a blind eye. Pretend that it's not going on in their backyard. The goddamn Bible Belt."

Rakić stood up and walked to the window. "You're right."

"I know I'm right," Moses said.

"People might forget and they might not really care, but I do. That's all we can do. Take care of what we can." He turned and looked at Moses. "You and me are going to make this the biggest fucking case we can and we are going to press this as far as it will go and as deep as it will go. Then we'll keep talking about it as long as they'll listen." Rakić's chest heaved with the last word. "And when the powerful want it to go away and push us, we'll push back."

Moses scratched his forehead with his good arm and managed a grin. "Yeah, we will."

* * *

Moses stood looking at the frozen river. There was no trace of the hole that had swallowed him two weeks ago. The sun did little to warm the air or stop a shiver from shooting through his body. He turned and leaned on the stump in the spot where he had stood his ground against Vahid and the dog.

Made Safe

The snow was untouched now, undisturbed since the last snowfall a day ago, except for his trail of footsteps. He kicked around in the snow near the hole. He had stood here the last time he held his grandfather's gun.

He walked away from the stump in the direction he thought his gun might have fallen and started walking a grid, back and forth methodically, testing every inch with his booted feet. He stepped on something that felt right and bent down and dug into the snow. He found the offending object. A thick branch. He tossed it to the side and continued pacing his grid.

Again, he stepped on something that felt right. This time it was a rock. He had been at it for twenty minutes when he took a break and leaned against the stump again.

He looked back at the river. She hadn't killed him. She could have. But she hadn't helped him either. He glanced down at his feet. His chest tightened. There, next to his foot, a speck of dark, polished wood contrasted with the white snow. He fell to his knees and scratched at the snow with his fingers. The snow shifted and the Luger was half visible.

He tore his glove off and grasped the pistol in his hand. He held it close to his eyes and inspected the barrel and the mechanism. He flipped it over, completing his inspection. He flipped the safety on so now the German word *gesichert* was visible and the word *geladan* was hidden under the safety switch. He wiped the gun down with his scarf and wrapped it up, then tucked it into his coat pocket.

He put his glove back on and stared out across the river for a moment. He would remember. The trafficking case would go forward and he would help in any way he could. He would keep being an investigator, but would choose his cases so that his work was meaningful even if it left him penniless. Finally, he turned, starting the long journey back to his car.

* * *

It was almost February and Rakić was no closer to finding out the identity of the girl they had found frozen to the street. He sat at his desk in his office in the State Law Enforcement building, trying to come up with another angle to go at the problem. As of now, she was just another Jane Doe. He had conducted close to a hundred interviews of the trafficking ring all the way down to the bartenders at the Zmaj and no one knew her or where she had come from. The press had jumped on the story and made him out to be a hero of some sort. He hated it, but press was what he had now. They had done their part and aired follow-up pieces on the girl and the reward.

Ten thousand dollars hadn't gotten them any viable leads, but it was a start. The department had been gung-ho on this and he felt like he could get some attention directly from the governor. But all that didn't matter if no one knew anything. He swiveled in his chair as Wilson stepped into the office they shared.

"Rakić, you see that game?"

"No, what game?"

"Ah jeez, never mind. I forgot you don't like football."

"Just not the kind with pads," Rakić said, offering a grin.

Wilson sat at his desk and leaned over his keyboard keying in his password with a flurry of clacks. He stuck his tongue out of the corner of his mouth and Rakić watched as his eyes went back and forth reading something on the screen. Rakić turned away and crossed his foot over his knee. Wilson was a good partner. He was there and did his job. Wilson wouldn't surprise you in a good or bad way. He could hear the keys continue to clack as he tried to take his mind's focus away from the girl. He'd been trying that out a lot lately. Meditation. Removing the busyness of his mind. It would supposedly allow greater focus and almost magical insight by removing the background buzz of unorganized thought. It was good in theory but it had only given him a headache until now.

"You were gone quite a bit during that case a few months ago," Rakić said.

"What?" Wilson asked, peering over the top of his monitor at Rakić.

"I was practically by myself on that case a few months ago. You were MIA. What were you doing?"

"What case? The trafficking? It was fucking Christmas, Raif."

"Christmas? What the fuck are you talking about? We had a girl frozen to the street and another guy killed down by the river. Fuck Christmas."

"Fuck you. I guess you don't believe in it, but people like me have to get shit done. Presents and that. It all turned out anyway."

Rakić stood up and kicked his chair away. "It turned out? We still got the frozen girl that no one knows who the fuck she is. You know what they do with unclaimed bodies?"

"They cremate them and store them."

"How would you feel if someone found your daughter, but then told you, sorry we burned her and here is a shoebox? That's all that's left. How'd that feel, Wilson?"

"That would never happen, Raif. That would never happen to my kid."

Rakić stood with his mouth open and a retort on his tongue, then realized the truth in Wilson's words and closed his mouth. He felt his anger drain away and his knees felt weak. He was right. It would never happen to him or his family. It would never happen to any family. It didn't happen, did it? It never happened. He turned and pushed his chair back to his desk and picked up his coat and threw it on. They would burn her and put her in a shoebox and store her on a shelf and it never happened. She had never been frozen to the street, because no one believed that it happened and there was no proof that it happened other than the dead girl in the shoebox on a shelf.

"You're right, Wilson. I'm going out." Christmas, lazy, crooked—or all three.

"Heads up, Raif," Wilson said as he tossed something small and shiny to him. Raif caught it. It was a shell casing. It was the size of 9mm cartridge. The same ammo that Winter's Luger used.

"I got your back, Raif. You got mine?" Wilson said. Then he got up and walked out into the hall, leaving Raif holding the spent casing.

***

Moses awoke to his cellphone buzzing. He slipped from under the covers and found his pants next to the bed. He pulled his phone out and looked at the caller ID. He flipped the phone open and quietly slipped out of the bedroom and into the hallway.

"This is Winter," Moses said.

"Moses. She is downtown," the voice said simply.

"Where?"

"Molly Roger's. Downtown by the sculptures," the voice replied.

"I know it." Moses looked at his watch. It was close to midnight. "Thanks," Moses said and hung up. He went back to the bedroom and pulled his pants on. Claudia stirred and he leaned over her.

"It's okay, Claud. I just have to go out for a minute."

She was awake now and rose up onto her elbow. "It's late, Mos. Can't it wait till tomorrow?" He shook his head. "Call me when you are on your way home," she said, still half asleep.

"I will, Claud," he said. Leaning over, he kissed her on the forehead. He closed the door to their bedroom and walked down the short hall. A deep, steady breathing greeted him in the living room. The source was a sleeping pile of teenage hair, with one leg dangled onto the floor. His face cracked into a grin. She was acting like a normal kid more and more every day. The brave girl who had jumped into his Jeep a few months ago. Brooklyn. He pulled the blanket up to her chin, and she turned and tugged it tighter with her hand. Then he was out the front door.

He pulled on his jacket in the hallway, bolted the door, and went outside to the car. It was warmer now, and the car heated up quickly. By the time he was downtown, he had to shut the heater off.

He parked on the street in front of the Molly Roger and walked in the front door. It was still busy, even for a Friday night. Then he saw her at the bar, recognizing her by her posture. She turned and he saw her smiling face.

It had been two months since he had seen her. He had heard lots of rumors, all of which turned out to be unreliable. She was in the Bahamas. Someone had seen her in the Twin Cities. She was dead. Now he had reliable information. She was in the city, right in front of him. He slid onto a stool at the end of the bar and ordered a beer, watching her.

She was wearing a black dress, one long slender leg crossed over the other, leaning back and laughing with a man standing next to her, his arm on her back. She leaned forward and sipped from her martini. She glanced Moses' way. She paused with her martini glass halfway back down to the bar, but only for a moment before placing it there gently as she resumed chitchatting with her date.

Moses knew he should go and collect her from the bar and take her in, but something held him back. He should call Rakić, he thought, but there was nowhere she could go; he had her. All he had to do now was go and get her. How would she react when he did? Would she be all smiles or would she try to run? Would she want to talk to him? Explain to him why she did what she did? Who could know with Majka?

"Majka!" he said, smiling as he walked up to her. The man next to her stood taller.

"Cowboy. Long time no see," she said, returning to her drink, keeping her smile painted on her face.

"Yeah. Who is your friend?" Moses gave a token glance at the man next to her.

"James McCoy," the man said, sticking out his hand.

"Moses," he replied, shaking the hand.

"Hey, what do you say we do some shots, Majka? For old time's sake," Moses said, raising his hand and gesturing to the bartender.

"I'm really not in the mood," she said, her smile tightening.

"Yeah. Never know what will happen when the shots start," Moses said.

"Hey. She's covered on drinks, pal," McCoy said.

"I don't remember her saying that. Are you covered, Majka?" Moses asked, allowing his scorn for the man to color his tone.

"Who is this Majka he keeps talking about?" McCoy asked.

"It's nothing." She leaned off her stool and stepped closer to McCoy. They talked for a second. Then James McCoy walked past them toward the other end of the bar.

"We have five minutes," Majka said, sitting back on the stool.

Moses stood in next to her. "Listen. You have to turn yourself in," Moses started.

She snorted. "What for?"

He expected a denial but this was too much. "Those girls that you had locked up."

"*They. Chose. Cowboy.*" Majka drew out the words. She turned back to her drink. She finished it, setting the glass on the bar.

"They didn't choose that. They didn't choose that life. If they did, they didn't know what they chose," Moses said, getting angry.

"Listen. We are bound to the river of our lives. Sometimes the river is fast and strong, the water rushes us through, and we fight to keep afloat. Other times, the river is slow and shallow. We can touch the bottom and we are in control."

"Bullshit. Is that what you tell yourself?" Moses asked.

"The truth is. It is flowing in two directions and you are sometimes stuck. Then a log or a violent storm frees you and you are moving in another direction. Like right now, Cowboy. You are moving again."

"What a pile of shit." Moses voice grew louder.

Majka shrugged. "I liked you, Moses." she said, using his name for the first time. She picked up her purse, leaning in closer to him as she shimmied off the barstool. He couldn't help but feel her warmth. She whispered as their faces neared each other. "But you are boring now and my wisdom seems to be lost on you."

He caught a whiff of her perfume. He shook his head and grabbed her by her upper arm. She growled into his face and stomped on his foot. He stumbled into the bar as she grabbed her empty martini glass and flung it into the mirror behind the bar. It shattered and glass rained down on the bottles below it. A flood of people washed away from the bar between him and Majka.

He saw her running out the front door. He fought his way through the frantic crowd. Bursting out the door, he caught a glimpse of her in the crowd outside. She crossed the street, dodging a car, and sprinted into the sculpture park.

She was fast. She glided over the new grass and disappeared behind the towering statue of a little girl smiling. Moses felt slow and old but the adrenaline was helping. He rounded the statue in time to see her disappear over a mound. He hit his stride and gained sight of her as she cut through a group of twisted wooden horses that the artist had ripped from a bad nightmare. His lungs felt terrible, but he kept going. He was closing on her. He dug deep and turned on the gas. He was within feet of her as she ran off the lawn and around the corner of a low wall. They were on the sidewalk again, so close he could almost grab her. She got to a building where a crowd waited in line to get into a restaurant. She ran across the street toward an office

Made Safe

building as he closed in and grabbed her in the middle of the street. She whirled around, her green eyes filled with anger.

"Gotcha!" he wheezed.

She swore at him in Bosnian.

"I know." He held onto her arm and started to drag her back across the street. "We are going to talk to Rakić."

She relaxed and he loosened his grip. She leaned into him a bit as they stepped onto the sidewalk next to the restaurant, looking up at him with a strange expression of pity. *I caught her, why did she pity me?*

"Sorry, Cowboy. It was on my way back," she whispered.

There was a slight stick of pain under his ribs. He stiffened as he felt the blade slice through his flesh.

"It's okay, Majka," he said. His hand weakened and his head felt dizzy.

She leaned in and nuzzled his chest, her hand still holding the handle of the knife. He patted her hair, and then she pulled away and he couldn't stop her. She pulled the blade out of him and he grunted in pain. She smiled at him and he felt tightness in his throat. She turned, walked quickly away from him, and rounded the corner, gone. He leaned against the brick building, the crowd staring at him, and put his hand over the small pain. He removed his hand and looked at the spot. It was dark and felt wet.

"I didn't want to keep going, anyway." But she couldn't hear him. She was already gone. He smiled a bit, and then he couldn't stay on his feet. He slumped into a heap, wedged into the corner of the building and the sidewalk. A mass of human Jell-O. He felt himself being moved, but it felt like it was far away and happening to someone else. He felt a heavy weight on the middle of his chest, and then he felt warm, and then he felt nothing.

"Hey there, cowboy." The bartender grabbed his empty beer bottle. "Want another?" he asked, tipping the neck of the bottle toward him.

"What?" Moses looked around the room then checked his watch. He looked in the long mirror behind the bartender. She was still there and he wasn't dead. Still there, sitting on her stool, flirting with her date. Moses stood up and put a few dollars on the bar. "I'm good."

The End

Acknowledgements

This book couldn't have been written without years of support from a large group of very important people in my life that are too numerous to list in this space. A special thanks to my wife. I couldn't have written this book without her sacrifice and love. Thanks to my Dad for never giving up on me. Thanks to my sisters, Staci and Stefanie, who taught me practically everything I know. Thanks to my good friend, Terry Crane, who pushed me to be a better writer. Finally, thanks to my publisher, Zara Kramer, who took a chance on me.

About the Author

Francis Sparks grew up on a farm in northwest Iowa where he spent his days avoiding bulls and other livestock as he created castles in the pasture made of fallen trees, twine pilfered from his father's hay baler, and his imagination. Since graduating from college, he has lived in the "big" city where he continues to build castles and fight dragons in the IT industry. Francis Sparks is a writer living in Des Moines, IA, with his amazing wife where he is always working on his next novel or short story and teaching his children about dragons.

Thank you for purchasing this copy of **_Made Safe_** by Francis Sparks. If you enjoyed this book by Francis, please let him know by posting a review.

Growing good ideas into great reads…one book at a time.

Visit www.pandamoonpub.com to learn more about our other works by our talented authors and use the author links to their sales page.

Mystery/Thriller/Suspense

- *122 Series Book 1: 122 Rules* by Deek Rhew
- *A Flash of Red* by Sarah K. Stephens
- *A Tree Born Crooked* by Steph Post
- *Fate's Past* by Jason Huebinger
- *Juggling Kittens* by Matt Coleman
- *Knights of the Shield* by Jeff Messick
- *Looking into the Sun* by Todd Tavolazzi
- *The Moses Winter Mysteries Book 1: Made Safe* by Francis Sparks
- *On the Bricks* by Penni Jones
- *Southbound* by Jason Beem
- *The Juliet* by Laura Ellen Scott
- *Rogue Alliance* by Michelle Bellon
- *The Last Detective* by Brian Cohn
- *The New Royal Mysteries Book 1: The Mean Bone in Her Body* by Laura Ellen Scott

Science Fiction/Fantasy
- *Becoming Thuperman* by Elgon Williams
- *Everly Series Book 1: Everly* by Meg Bonney
- *.exe Series Book 1: Hello World* by Alexandra Tauber and Tiffany Rose
- *Fried Windows in a Light White Sauce* by Elgon Williams
- *The Phaethon Series Book 1: Phaethon* by Rachel Sharp
- *The Sitnalta Series Book 1: Sitnalta* by Alisse Lee Goldenberg
- *The Sitnalta Series Book 2: The Kingdom Thief* by Alisse Lee Goldenberg
- *The Sitnalta Series Book 3: The City of Arches* by Alisse Lee Goldenberg
- *The Crimson Chronicles Book 1: Crimson Forest* by Christine Gabriel
- *The Crimson Chronicles Book 2: Crimson Moon* by Christine Gabriel

Women's Fiction
- *Beautiful Secret* by Dana Faletti
- *The Mason Siblings Series Book 1: Love's Misadventure* by Cheri Champagne
- *The Mason Siblings Series Book 2: The Trouble with Love* by Cheri Champagne
- *The Long Way Home* by Regina West
- *The Shape of the Atmosphere* by Jessica Dainty

Made in the USA
Charleston, SC
30 January 2017